SAIGON RED

PETER HANLON

ISBN: 9798669265267

About the author:

Peter Hanlon is from Manchester, England.

To contact the author, email saigonred@protonmail.com

Table of Contents:

Chapter 1

Tequila Sunset

Brent was standing outside his hut when he noticed a young woman walking down the dirt path towards him. She had checked in at the guest house and was now cautiously making her way to her room, treading carefully on the slabs of rock that made up the steps on the winding track.

They were in Kanchanaburi, a small town in Thailand halfway between Bangkok and the Burmese border, and the guest house they were staying at led down to the River Kwai, to the bamboo-crafted huts for rent on floating pontoons by the riverbank.

Brent walked down the ramp that connected the pontoon to the bank, holding out his hand as she approached.

"Hi, there," he said. "Let me help you. That backpack looks pretty heavy. Are you travelling alone?"

"Thanks. Yes, it is too heavy. It's my fault, though. I never know what to throw away and what to keep."

"Me too. I'm exactly the same."

"Yes."

"Be careful walking up here. It's a bit wobbly. We don't want you falling in the river, now, do we?" he said, slinging the backpack over his shoulder and taking hold of her arm.

"This looks like my room here," she said, standing in front of the hut adjoining his.

"Yes. I'm Brent, by the way."

"Hi, Brent, thanks for being such a gentleman. These days they seem to be few and far between, sadly."

"Yes, they are, aren't they..."

"Faye," she replied, smiling.

1

The river was fairly wide at this point, and they spent their first evening together sitting on the veranda of their stationary raft, exchanging travel stories, sipping tequila, smoking herb, and watching the long-tail boats speeding past, causing their pontoon to rock as it was hit by the wash.

The long-tails varied in length and carried differing numbers of people, but some of them were short, slim, very fast one-man boats, used for racing. The Thais liked to decorate them, painting huge goddess-like eyes on their pointed bows, similar to the ancient Greek fighting ships. They got their name from the long shaft at the stern that connected the engine to the propeller.

Neither Brent nor Faye was a smoker, whether it was cigarettes or drugs. He had bought the grass merely for the fact that he was on holiday, and Thai stick, like Nepalese temple balls, was part of the trip.

Brent had rolled a neat one without tobacco and took a blast on it before passing it back to Faye, who timidly drew another mouthful. She coughed and blew the smoke out quickly without inhaling it.

Brent rambled on endlessly, laughing to himself, telling Faye his travel anecdotes, his intentions, plans, wishes, and dreams for the future.

Eventually, he paused, noticing that she wasn't listening. She was gazing into the distance in some sort of trance.

"Faye. Faye! What's up? You've gone all quiet all of a sudden," he said.

She said something incoherently, whimpering to herself like a young girl.

"What?"

"I'm going to die. I can't feel my legs."

"You're not going to die, Faye. I promise you. Trust me on that one."

"What's that thing in the river?" she shouted.

"What thing?"

"There! Over there! Oh my God, it's coming straight for us!"

"Faye, there's nothing in the river except small harmless fish."

"Look! It's making waves as it swims towards us!"

"Faye, you have to relax," he said, laughing. "Just relax and keep a grip. There's nothing to worry about. You're spinning out, seeing things."

"No! No. I can see it. A river monster!" she screamed.

2

Faye stood up, panic-stricken, trying to make a getaway just as a wave from a passing long-tail boat rocked their pontoon. She lost her footing and tripped, falling head first into the river. Before Brent could react, she was being carried away by the slow but steady current. He considered diving in to rescue her, but he was too intoxicated. At the end of a pontoon further down the river, he spotted an inflated inner tube from a truck tyre. Running down the ramp from his pontoon onto the dirt track that ran along the edge of the bank, he boarded the other pontoon and grabbed the tube.

Faye was almost parallel to where Brent was as he threw the tube at her. She swam a few feet and clambered onto it, sitting inside it with her legs hanging over the sides. Brent jumped into the river and grabbed the side of the tube, steering it to the riverbank and safety. She stumbled onto the bank, collapsing onto her hands and knees, throwing up. Helping her to stand up, Brent put her arm around his shoulder, gripping her waist tightly as he led her back to the cabin.

The sun sank slowly and faded away behind the mountains, which lay beyond the dense vivid green jungle in the distance, leaving in its stead a saffron sky.

For most people, upstream was merely water under the bridge, that insignificant little bridge that stood as a proud testament for a few others. For Brent, it meant something personal. His grandfather had been forced to work on that bridge in 1942 after Singapore had fallen, and the Japanese had relocated him there as a prisoner of war. Brent had come to visit his grave. He would find out later where his final resting place lay, with the hundreds of others, in the cemetery that the sun was now about to set on.

The following day, Brent hired a powerful off-road motorbike and took Faye to see Hellfire Pass, part of the so-called Death Railway that was built by the Japanese army during the Second World War using slave labour.

Starting at Ban Pong and crossing the bridge on the River Kwai in Kanchanaburi, the line had once snaked its way through two hundred and fifty miles of dense jungle to Thanbyuzayat in Burma.

Brent pulled the motorbike off the highway and drove down a dirt road. He parked the bike and they walked down a winding jungle path that eventually came onto a clearing where the railway track had been during the war. They followed it until they came to the railway cutting.

Hewn out of a sloping rocky hill and wide enough to allow access for a single track, the cutting was four hundred feet long, the walls sixty feet high. It had been cut using manual labour and was named Hellfire Pass by the men who had been forced to work by the light of fires at night, some sixty-nine of them beaten to death by the Japanese before it was hastily finished.

Brent and Faye were alone as they walked through it, conscious of the deathly silence. Not even a bird made a sound.

Looking at the marks made by the labourer's tools still visible on the walls, Brent noticed a long steel chisel stuck in the rock face and stared at it, wondering if his grandfather had been the last person to use it.

A strange feeling came over him, and he could sense the presence of somebody standing close to him. He turned around and called Faye over. They walked to the end of the cutting and stood in front of the thick forest and tangled vegetation which had completely overgrown where the track used to be. Turning around, they returned to the bike and headed off back into town.

Along with the humdrum of the small sleepy town, Faye grew tired of Brent's obsession with his grandfather and the war and wanted to go back to Bangkok for some fun. They booked two tickets for the next day.

Chapter 2

Bangkok

Arriving in Bangkok around midday, they headed for the backpacker area where they had to endure the Kao San catwalk. That meant walking down Kao San Road while being checked over by the travellers sitting outside the bars and restaurants on either side. Exhibitionists loved it.

Brent and Faye found a happening place to stay in the heart of the action and took an air-conditioned room with two single beds. While she spent the day writing letters, he indulged at one of the local bars.

That evening they went to a lively night spot with loud music playing. The place was packed, and they joined a table with a couple of American guys. Brent had been in the bar all day and was already heavily drunk.

"So waddaya do, buddy?" said Rick.

"I'm a fireman," replied Brent.

"A firefighter?"

"Yeah."

"No shit. Me too! I'm from New York. I was at 9/11, man."

"Noo Yawrk?" said Brent, trying to imitate his accent.

"Yeah, buddy."

"So you were at some convenience store then, were you?"

"Say what?"

"They call them 7-Eleven over here. I've noticed they're everywhere."

"Dude!" said the American. "You gotta be pretty canned, right?"

"Yeah, I'm fucking smashed, actually. Been drinking all day," said Brent, slurring his words.

"This bozer here is my buddy from Texas," said Rick, pointing at the guy next to him.

"You looking for me to bat your ass right outta the fucking ball park, shmucker?" said the Texan, grinning.

One of the Thai bar girls walked over to Rick and started chatting to him.

"I want to fuck with Mr Pete," she said.

"We don't got no Mr Pete, honey. He ain't here. He gone done a ghost on us," replied Rick.

"Where Mr Pete?"

"If I knew that I wouldn't tell you."

"Ok, baby," she said, putting her hand on Rick's shoulder. "You want to fuck me?"

"Sure I do, honey, but not right now. I'm real busy," he said, swigging his beer. "Why don't you run along and go play somewhere?"

He turned to his Texan friend and continued the conversation.

"So anyways, like I was telling you about how I met some of the mob down at Dixie's, one time. You know who came—*a lotta people came*—you know who came? Big Joey Di Maceti! Can you fucking get that? *Jo-Ey-Di-Ma-Ceti* fucking shows up!" he said ecstatically, emphasizing the name as he slapped his buddy on the back.

Another American came over. He was a friend of Rick's, equally loud, drunk, and obnoxious.

"Hey, you guys wanna go see Ding Dong do some Ping Pong down Patpong?" he blurted.

"Who's Ding Dong?" said Brent, laughing.

"Ding Dong is one of the babes who works in the clubs down Patpong Road. You ain't seen the shows?"

"We just got here today. Haven't really done much at all yet. Have we, Faye?" replied Brent.

"Dude, you gotta see this shit. Come on, let's go do it."

They jumped in the back of a tuk-tuk and sped off, weaving in and out of the traffic, the warm air of the evening blowing into their faces through the open sides of the vehicle.

Patpong Road, one of the world's most famous red-light areas, was chockablock. Tourists, mostly male westerners, thronged the street and the multitude of joints where you could easily get stripped,

6

one way or another, in the bright lights of the neon signs.

They were ushered inside The Kinq's Arms, a large club with tables, soft seats, and sofas dotted around a stage. Waitresses, dressed in nothing but skimpy underwear, took orders and served customers.

Ding Dong approached the American and sat on his lap, welcoming him with big kisses. He groped her like a beast and then bought her a drink.

Sensing that Faye felt uncomfortable in such a male-dominated environment, Ding Dong struck up a conversation and asked her where she was from.

"I'm from London, England," she replied. "How about you?"

"I from Golden Triangle. You know Golden Triangle?"

Before Faye could reply, the American butted in.

"Only golden triangle I'm thinking about is that one right there between your pretty little legs, Dingaling. I'm gonna be down there like a hog grubbing for truffles just as soon as you're ready, honeypie," he shouted.

A young girl who looked about fifteen, wearing nothing but a pair of skimpy lace knickers, came and sat on Brent's lap. Brent wasn't sure what to do and looked sheepishly at Faye. She turned her reddened face and acted as though she was having a great time.

Ding Dong disappeared, but after a while she came onto the stage with a group of Thai girls. They were all naked. For their first act, they squatted and laid ping pong balls, like chickens laying eggs. Other girls squatted and pulled out razor blades, one after another, tied together by a piece of string.

Lying on their backs with their legs raised and spread apart, they inserted a straw into their beaver and fired tiny projectiles at the balloons that were being tossed around above them. Most of the girls were bursting the balloons easily, but Ding Dong's shots were running out of steam and falling way too short.

The Madame walked onto the stage and took her to one side, making it perfectly clear that she had better start performing, otherwise she would be out of a job.

For the final piece in the repertoire, a naked Thai couple came on stage, and with background music playing, shamelessly had sexual intercourse in every conceivable position possible.

Later, the American took Ding Dong to one of the private rooms upstairs and pumped her up. During her next routine on stage, she lay there firing like an anti-aircraft gun, bursting balloons with gusto and pinpoint accuracy.

"How about that then, Faye?" said Brent as they left The Kinq's Arms. "Was that entertaining enough?"

"What do you think, Brent?" she said with a disgusted look on her face. "I can honestly say that I have never felt so embarrassed in all my life. Can we go home now, please?"

"I take it you weren't very impressed, then?"

Sitting on the edge of his bed early the next morning, Brent looked over at Faye. She was awake, wrapped up in the blanket and hugging the extra pillow, with her back turned towards him.

"Did you sleep alright, Faye?"

"Mmm," she replied softly.

"What should we do today?"

"Don't know," she mumbled.

"I've been reading this guide book on Bangkok. There's a couple of things we could do today that you might not have done yet. I'll tell you about them while we have breakfast."

"Mmm."

"Are you going to get up some time? It's nearly ten o'clock."

She let go of the pillow and swung her arm over, half turning towards him to reply.

"I'll see you down there in a few minutes, Brent. After I've had a shower."

Brent was sitting at a table reading the guide book as Faye came down for breakfast.

"You smell absolutely divine, Faye. What perfume are you wearing?"

"It's just shower gel. I don't like perfume. Have you ordered anything yet?"

"No, of course not. I've been waiting for you. Perfect gentleman, Faye. Haven't you noticed that by now?"

"Brent, really," she said, smiling.

"You know, you've got the loveliest smile, Faye. You really have. And such perfect white teeth. Your parents really took good care of you, didn't they? I can tell. I bet it was your dad, right? He always made sure that you'd cleaned your teeth before he tucked you up in bed at night. Didn't he?"

They gazed into each other's eyes, smiling at one another warmly.

"Has my little teddy bear cleaned her toothy pegs for daddy?" said Brent in a childish voice. "Show daddy your little toothy pegs."

Faye blushed.

"Brent! Stop it," she said, picking up the menu and turning the pages.

"Hey, check this out, listen to this," said Brent, reading from the guide book. "How do you fancy going to the Bangkok Forensic Museum at the Siriraj Hospital? It's right opposite the Grand Palace, so we could go there as well if you like."

"Forensic Museum? What does it say about it?"

"Babies affected by genetic disorders preserved in jars of formaldehyde; a room with the bodies of accident victims and murderers, including the preserved corpse of the cannibal, Si Ouey, who murdered seven children and ate their organs. Hey, check this out: He's stood upright in a glass cabinet case, totally naked, and you can even see the bullet holes in his body where he was shot by a firing squad. *And* a thirty-five-kilogram human testicle affected by elephantiasis pickled in a jar. Jeez, that man had some balls!"

"Well, thanks a bunch for that, Brent," she huffed.

"What's wrong now?"

"Nothing, *really*. I was just about to order dumplings, that's all."

"Oh. So what do you reckon about the museum, Faye? Are you the morbid type?"

"Not really, but we can go if you like. It's up to you. We've done just about everything else. What are you having for breakfast?"

"I fancy a full English, to be honest. Hanging out for one. What about you?"

"I think I'll just order a coffee now," she said, with a disappointed expression on her face, looking over her shoulder to attract the waitress's attention.

Faye turned her face and stared into the distance. Brent looked the other way, but through the corner of his eye, he admired her, the way that she puffed her cheeks slightly, her bottom lip extending a little, glistening. How he desired just one passionate kiss as she was lost in thought.

"Do you still want to go to Chiang Mai with me, Brent?" she said, turning to look at him.

9

"Of course I do. Why?"

"I was just thinking we could go tonight on the train."

In the evening they took the river taxi down the maze of canals that spread like arteries throughout Bangkok and arrived at the station, boarding the train and making themselves comfortable in an upper and lower berth that ran the length of the carriage.

Drawing the curtain, Faye switched on the small light and rummaged through her bag, taking out her phone and a few of the snacks that she had bought.

Above her, Brent took out his pen and pad and continued writing his notes.

In the early hours, the train rocked steadily on through the night, backwards and forwards to a rhythmic clickerty-click beat as one of the cleaners slowly moved along the carriage, mopping the floor from side to side.

The morning came quickly, and Brent woke to the sound of stewards pushing breakfast trolleys and converting the lower berths back into seats for those who required them. Sliding his curtain to one side, he looked down at Faye. They gazed at each other with sleepy eyes, not knowing whether to get up or not.

He dressed and waited for a while before climbing down and sitting opposite her.

"That was a great kip that I had last night. How about you, Faye?"

"Yes, it was like being a baby again," she replied.

"I wrote a pretty mind-blowing poem for you too. The sound of the tracks must have inspired me. Read this," he said, taking out his notebook. "It's about King Arthur and Cameltoe, and—"

"Camelot," she interrupted.

"What?"

"Camelot. King Arthur's castle is Camelot, not Cameltoe."

"Really?"

"Yes."

"Whatever. Anyway, get a load of this. You'll love it," said Brent, opening the pad and passing it to her. "It's not finished yet, just the opening verses."

She took the pad and read the poem.

Out of a grey mist a horse did appear
Flanked by a half score, legions more at the rear
Warriors ready, hearts steady, ten knights to a side
Stride forth, *nay* gallop, spare not their hide
Hasten your steed, the hour draws near
Wend forth as Merlin and subdue your fear

At the drop of a sword
And they were off, odds on, all aboard
Arthur's horse on the outside
Hits the first bend in the track, what a ride
Favourite to win, crosses the line by a nose
It's your station in life, the one you never chose

Faye put her hand across her mouth, laughing loudly and looking at him for some kind of response to indicate that he was just playing games with her. He stared at her with a blank look on his face.

"Brent, what is this? Is it a joke?" she said, giggling.

"A joke?" he said with a stern expression on his face.

"Yes. Surely it's a joke, right?"

He looked at her with a disbelieving look.

"Let me see if I've got this straight. You're calling my poem a joke! Right?"

"Well…"

"I stay awake half the night to write a piece of magic for you, and you dismiss it so flippantly with ridicule, like that?" he said, staring at his feet.

"Oh, Brent, I'm sorry! It's lovely. It really is. I didn't mean to…"

As she leaned forward to put her arms around his shoulders to console him, he reached out and grabbed her, pulling her onto his lap and tickling her.

"Brent! Stop it. What are you doing?" she yelled, pushing herself away from him.

"I got you. You're my April fool!"

"What are you talking about, Brent? April the first was about two weeks ago, you idiot."

"I know, but we didn't meet each other until the third of April. But I got you anyway."

"Well, I'm not speaking to you now. You can go away. You're a horrible pig."

Chapter 3

Songkran

As Brent stepped off the train, a teenage Thai girl tipped a bucket of water over his head, and then her friend smeared white paste across his cheeks. Brent couldn't believe what was happening and stood there with an incredulous look on his face, unsure whether to react aggressively or not. The girls laughed and waited for Faye to step off, squirting her with a toy water gun and plastering her with the same gooey mess.

Brent and Faye looked around and saw that most of the people on the platforms were wet and in the same condition and figured that there must be some kind of celebration going on.

Walking out of the station, the scene on the streets was even more party-like. Pickup trucks with people sitting on the rear drove around, showering onlookers and then refilling their buckets from the barrels of water they carried. It was the second week in April, and Brent and Faye soon realised that it was the start of Songkran, the traditional new year celebration in Thailand. The act of throwing water represented purification and the washing away of sins and bad luck.

After they had checked into some digs, they found a quaint coffee shop by the Ping River and sat on the grass under the shade of a tree.

"I think we've chosen a bad time to come here, Faye."

"You would have got wet wherever you went."

"No, I don't mean that. I've just realised why we're coughing so much. Some guy in the shop just told me this is the time of year when the farmers burn the brush and the undergrowth, big time. Look at the air. It's full of ash."

"Well, we don't have to stay here long. Just a day or two."

"What do you want to do while you're here, anyway?" said Brent.

"I'd really like to visit the hill tribes and see the Karen people. The women are the ones who wear the brass rings around their necks."

"Yeah, the Long-Necks. I've heard about them. Imagine stretching your neck like that. Must be pretty painful."

"They're not actually stretching their necks. They're pushing their shoulders and rib cage down. That makes their necks appear longer."

"Just to look beautiful," said Brent.

"And tradition. I also read that it was to protect against tigers. That's why they wear rings on their arms, in case they get attacked. But I think the tiger would kill you anyway if it was hungry enough."

"It doesn't turn me on. It looks abnormal. Like the Chinese women who bind their feet to make them really tiny. It's pretty gross if you ask me."

"How about you, Brent?"

"Me?"

"What do you want to see in Chiang Mai?"

"Don't know, really. I've been thinking about hanging out in a temple for a while with the monks and doing some meditation," he said, crossing his legs and sitting in the lotus position. "Hey, have you heard about that sticky waterfall?"

"Sticky waterfall?"

"Yeah, some guy in Bangkok was telling me about it. Said there's a waterfall around here that you can run up. It's not really a gushing waterfall, more like a flow of spring water down a rocky slope, but he said your feet stick to the rocks as you run up it. Everyone's going there, apparently."

"Is this another one of your April fool jokes?"

"No, honestly, I'm just telling you what I heard, that's all. Hey, look over there, they've got one of those pools with the fish."

"What pool?"

"Over there where that girl is, sitting on the edge of that small pool with her feet in the water."

"What is she doing?"

"There are tiny fish in there. She's letting them eat the dead skin off her feet. Go and try it. It tickles at first, but after that, it's quite stimulating."

As she walked over to the pool, Brent admired her long slender legs and the little hot pants that she was wearing. She bent over and removed her trainers and little white socks to sit on the side of the pool and dangle her feet in the shallow water. Turning to look at him,

13

she giggled, palming her long brown hair behind her ears as the fish nibbled away at her toes.

Faye insisted they spend the afternoon down at the local jail getting a massage from some of the female prisoners who were coming to the end of their sentences and would be released soon.

Supervised by guards, the inmates were learning skills that would give them a better chance of earning a living once they were on the outside.

Browsing through the night bazaar and watching the artisans crafting their wares was followed by a barbecue dinner and drinks before heading back to their room.

"Hey, get a load of this, Faye," said Brent the following morning. "I've just been talking to some guy who went on a trip out in the rainforest a couple of days ago. Said it was called *Fly With The Gibbons* or something. We could go out there, get away from this foul air for a bit if you like."

"Gibbons are like monkeys, aren't they?"

"Yeah, exactly. They hang out in the trees."

"So what is that all about?"

"They've got this zip line strung up in the trees and you scoot down it real fast. He said it was just the best blast he's ever had. Fancy having a go on that then, Faye?"

"What do you mean, a zip line? What's a zip line?"

"It's a long, thick, steel cable. They've got it fixed high in the air from tree to tree. You hook on and slide down it quicksmart through the jungle canopy. He reckons the zip line goes for about four miles."

"Four miles!"

"That's the full length of it, from start to finish. I think the longest single run is something like a thousand feet. That's from one tree to the next without stopping."

"But how do you stop when you reach the tree? You're just going to crash into it and break all of your bones, aren't you?"

"No, listen, let me tell you how it works. You'll love this. Ok, so they fix you up with a harness that you wear: safety gear, hard hat, everything, and then you climb up some steps to the first platform. There are two Rangers with every group, and one of them goes ahead of you, down the zip line to the next platform and waits there to

14

guide you all in. The other attaches your harness and your safety line to the cable and off you go, smashing your way through the jungle, giving hi-fives to the gibbons on the way."

"Are the gibbons really that friendly?" said Faye naively.

"I'm joking. But hey, he said you can do it like Superman, diving head first with your arms stretched out in front of you. What do you reckon? Are you up for it?"

"I don't know. It sounds a bit dangerous, really. How high off the ground is it?"

"It's not more than two hundred feet. Trust me."

"Brent! Stop it. Don't say things like that," she said, slapping him on the arm.

"What's happened to your sense of humour just lately? Anyway, I thought you told me you'd done a bungee jump in Queensland."

"Well, I did, so…"

"You don't sound too sure about it, Faye."

"I have a photo to prove it if you don't believe me, Brent," she said with the facial expression of a little girl who was trying to convince her mom that it was their dog that ate the chocolate.

"You jumped?"

"Yes… well, I was just about to and then somebody pushed me."

"And you screamed all the way down. Faye, you're so lovely! Give me a big hug. So, how about it?"

"How about what? Are you being suggestive again, Brent?"

"I wouldn't dream of it, Faye," he replied, trying to sound serious. "No, he said the gibbon ride was better than sex. I just thought that you might like to see for yourself, that's all."

They spent the rest of the morning making a plan for a trip to the rainforest, debating whether to change their accommodation and move to another place nearer to where they would be doing the zip line.

The worsening air quality decided it for them, and so they packed their bags and headed out.

Chapter 4

Altering Shadows

Arriving at The Jungle House on the edge of the forest, Brent and Faye were met by a very sombre-looking woman who led them down a track and showed them the small wooden huts that were vacant. They chose one that was elevated on stilts, partly concealed by the overhanging branches of the surrounding trees.

It was late in the afternoon, and the mosquitoes were already starting to buzz around. Brent made sure that the mosquito nets were draped over the two beds and then lit a couple of candles, placing one of them outside the room on the table that stood between the two bamboo chairs on the balcony.

In the evening, Brent and Faye climbed down the spiral wooden staircase outside their hut and walked up the track to the restaurant.

It was deserted and dimly lit by a single kerosene lamp hanging in the middle of the room with bugs flitting around it, mesmerised by the glow. They slid the chairs out from under the table, hoping that the noise would attract somebody's attention. But nobody came.

The restaurant was open-sided and very basic, with a concrete floor and wooden poles supporting a thatched roof. They sat in the corner, staring out at the dark silence of the forest all around them.

"Everywhere is so quiet," said Faye.

"Yeah, where is everyone? That woman who showed us the rooms is the only person that I've seen so far. I don't think I've seen any lights on in any of the other huts, either."

"It looks like we're going to sit here all night. Should I go and find the cook? I'm starving."

"You stay here. I'll go and get somebody. And don't talk to any strangers while I'm gone," said Brent, smiling.

"I'll try my best not to," she replied, returning the smile.

"Hello?" shouted Brent as he walked over to the dark reception area. "Hello? Are you there?"

Eventually, the woman came and took their order. Brent and Faye tried to make conversation with her, but she seemed to be preoccupied with something. They could sense that she had something on her mind. She had a strange look in her eyes, and the smile that she wore in the dim glow of the lamp didn't seem genuine.

After they had finished their meal, Brent ordered a bottle of Mekong Whiskey and a bucket of ice, placing them on a tray with a couple of glasses. They went back to their room and sat on the balcony, drinking and talking, the candle gently flickering in the warm breeze of the night casting altering shadows onto the foliage that hung in front of them.

Past midnight, they locked the door, got undressed in the dark, and slipped under the mosquito nets on their beds. It was hot and the fan did little but circulate the warm air. Brent had drunk most of the whiskey and slept easily, but Faye was restless and lay there listening to the sound of the rainforest and the geckos clicking in the trees.

She felt the hut vibrate and heard the wood creak outside, giving her the impression that somebody was coming up the steps. She called out to Brent in a low voice, slipping her hand underneath the net to try and shake him awake. But his bed was too far out of reach.

"Brent! Brent!" she whispered, but he continued snoring.

Pulling the net over her head, she got off the bed and shook his shoulder until he woke up.

"Brent, there's someone outside, coming up the steps," she whispered.

"What?" he said, half asleep.

"I think there's somebody outside our room."

Brent lay there for a while looking through the net at Faye, standing next to him and leaning forward, the moonlight shining through the cracks in the bamboo walls highlighting her little white top and knickers. He got off the bed and opened the door.

"What the hell do you think you're doing?" said Brent.

"Oh, shit, man, I got the wrong room," sobbed the drunken guy

17

staggering up the last few steps.

"Are you alright?" said Brent.

"No, he's dead, man. He's fucking dead!" he said, crying and falling to his knees.

"What's going on?" said Faye.

"It's ok. He's totally drunk off his head, out of his tree. Got the wrong room, that's all."

"Why is he crying so much?"

"I don't know. Here, let me help you down the steps," said Brent, picking him up and carefully walking him down the staircase. "Stay there, Faye. I'll help him find his room."

The next day, they went down to the restaurant to eat breakfast and then book the gibbon tour.

"I don't know about you, Faye, but I'm beginning to regret coming here. It's pretty dull, isn't it?" said Brent as they waited for their coffee.

"At least the air is fresh. We can move on after we've done the gibbon ride."

"Hey, here comes that guy that was outside our room last night."

"My God, he looks awful," said Faye. "He must be hungover or something."

"You look like I feel," said Brent as the guy walked into the restaurant.

"You guys didn't hear the news?" he replied solemnly.

"What news?"

"My friend, Karl, the other Dutch guy that was staying here. He's dead."

"Dead! We never got the chance to meet him. What happened?"

"There was an accident. He fell from the zip line yesterday. I don't know exactly what happened. I Just heard something about his harness came loose, and he fell. The ride now is shut down. I feel so terrible today. You know, he was a really nice guy."

"Shit! That's frigging awful news."

"Oh my God, no! I'm so sorry to hear it. And we were just about to go on it, too," said Faye, visibly shocked.

The Dutch guy wandered off into the rainforest.

Brent and Faye spent the early morning sitting around the restaurant in the guest house, glumly watching the rain as it dripped off the thin layers of palm fronds that covered the wooden poles of the roof, contemplating life and death and what to do with themselves next.

"We can do some trekking instead, Faye," said Brent, sounding very disappointed and bored.

"Trekking?"

"Yeah. Three days and two nights walking through the villages, visiting the hill tribes and riding on elephants. What do think about that?"

"Yes, it sounds like fun," she said, trying to be cheerful.

"Let's do it tomorrow. Hey, I think I just spotted another human. At least, I think it was a human. Not sure, though. Might have been the last Neanderthal or some other cave-dwelling thing."

"Who are you talking about, Brent?" said Faye, busy sending emails on her phone.

"That guy over there. Oh, my mistake, it's a hippy. He's probably off to have a conversation with a tree or something."

"Don't be so rude, Brent. Just because you're bored doesn't mean that you have to insult everyone," she said without bothering to turn around and look.

"Yeah, but look at the state of him."

"Who?"

"That eco-warrior with half a ton of matted dreadlocks curled around on top of his head. I'll bet he's got spiders and the lot living up there."

"Stop being so nasty, Brent. He's probably a very caring person."

"Well, he doesn't care very much about what he looks like, does he?"

"Just because you have a nice neat haircut doesn't mean that everybody has to have one."

"No, come on, Faye. Look at him. I'll bet he's walking around with a bird's nest and everything up there in that ragged mop."

"Why don't you go and talk to him? I'm sure he won't bite you."

Brent stared at the rainforest, thinking about the Dutch guy who had just walked off, looking suicidal.

"You know what I think?" he said.

"What."

"I think we should pack up and get out of here."

"You mean right now?"

"Yeah. I don't want to hang around here any longer. It's too depressing. What do you say?"

"Where will we go?"

"We might as well get on with the trekking. When we were driving down here, I saw a place just up the road that takes you out there. Do you want me to go and check it out while you stay here?"

"Yes, alright. What about breakfast?"

"You get some if you want. I don't feel hungry any more. Can you settle the bill? I'll give you the money when I get back."

Brent jogged up the jungle track and onto the road as the rain slowly eased off and the sun broke through the grey clouds.

He came to a row of small establishments advertising local tours and called in at the one selling treks. They informed him that the tour guide would be setting off shortly and that if he wanted to join the group then he would have to book soon. He phoned Faye and told her to pack the bags and get ready to leave.

Brent returned to The Jungle House. There was nobody around to say goodbye to so they placed the room key on the counter in reception and left, walking briskly up to the tour place.

"They said we could leave our main backpacks here until we return, Faye. So just bung a few things that you might need into a small bag and take that."

"I've already done that, Brent. So what's on the itinerary, then?"

"We've got a bit of a drive out to the elephant camp first, and then we get to watch the grand old nellies doing some tricks."

"They aren't going to be cruel to the elephants, are they? I don't want to go there if it's going to be like that."

"No, don't be silly, Faye. The elephants will be kicking footballs and painting pictures for us, things like that. They can give you a massage as well, according to this flyer. Here, do you want to read it?" he said, passing her the brochure.

They jumped in the minibus and greeted all of the other travellers, heading off for the starting point at the village near the national park.

The show was entertaining, and everyone was amused by the sight of a guy lying on his back being gently massaged by an elephant's foot, laughing as the snout on its trunk repeatedly grabbed his crotch.

Brent bought Faye a portrait of herself done by one of the elephants, trying to cheer her up a bit after she initially complained

20

about the way the poor animals were also being used as slave labour in the logging industry. The painting made her laugh, and Brent claimed jokingly that it was a true likeness that did proud justice to her natural beauty.

"It's time for the elephant ride to the next village, Faye."

"I'm not sure I want to do that, Brent."

"Why not?"

"It's not fair to make those poor animals carry all that weight around. How would you like it? That big wooden seat on its back looks really heavy."

"Oh, for God's sake, Faye. It's an animal. That's what animals are for."

"Don't you like animals?"

"I like eating them. Yes."

She stared at him with a disappointed look on her face.

"Ok, listen," he said, putting his hand in his pocket. "Here's some money. Go over there and buy some bananas to feed the elephant. Stroke his trunk, have a bit of a word with him, and then see how you both feel. Ok? Look, it's wagging its tail and licking its lips now that I've mentioned bananas."

"It's not a dog, Brent."

"Can dogs paint pictures and give you a massage? This is a super intelligent beast, Faye. Trust me, it knows what bananas are. Look, it's wagging its tail again."

After Faye had fed the elephant and been reassured that it really didn't mind carrying people around, she climbed up and sat next to Brent. They set off, slowly winding their way along the jungle track, climbing higher up the hills as they went, gently rocking from side to side with the gait of the elephant.

Ambling along, the elephant threw its trunk from side to side and over the top of its head, blowing snot over them before it decided to stop suddenly as the trail rounded the side of a hill. Turning to face uphill, it hung its rear-end over the side and lowered its haunches, squatting down. Brent grabbed Faye's legs as she fell backwards, screaming.

"What the hell is it doing?" she shouted.

"It looks like it's having a double dump. Hang on!"

"Hang on to what—its tail?" she yelled, her arms flailing wildly.

"Kap! Kap!" shouted the Thai mahout, whacking the elephant

with his thin wooden stick.

"No! Don't hit the elephant! Don't hit the elephant. Stop it," screamed Faye.

"Fuck the fucking elephant. You're about to get a steaming hot deluxe dung facial before you go rolling off down the hill," said Brent with one arm holding on to the seat and the other wrapped around her legs.

The elephant finished its business and they carried on with the ride, stopping at a waterfall for a short break before reaching the end of the trail. The last leg of the journey up a steep trail was done on foot, and they arrived at the first village just before sunset.

Their lodgings for the night consisted of a long bamboo hut with a thatched roof, nestled among a number of smaller dwellings occupied by the villagers.

Brent, Faye, and the other eight tourists were shown the raised wicker platform that ran along the inside of the hut where they would sleep and then taken to the shower block outside for anybody wishing to refresh themselves with a cold wash.

They unpacked their bags and sat in a circle on floor mats, enjoying the traditional cuisine cooked by the old woman and her two daughters who lived there.

A fifteen-year-old boy came into the lodge and sat down against the wall near the group. Brent noticed that he didn't have the same features as the local people, that he looked more like he was from the city. He smiled whenever he was spoken to but said nothing.

Brent saw something amusing and turned towards Faye, speaking to her in a low voice.

"That boy is hard," he said.

"He probably does that kickboxing thing that they all do," she replied.

"Yeah," said Brent, laughing as he ate his food. "Her daughters are a bit cheeky as well, aren't they?"

"The old woman's?"

"Yes."

"Why? What have they said?"

"Apart from me, it looks like everybody else in the group is a vegetarian, so those two girls have taken all the meat off the chicken leg and given me the bones," he said, looking over at them as they smiled at him. "How old do you think they are?"

"I don't know. It's hard to tell with Asian women. The one that keeps smiling at you is probably about seventeen, though."

After the meal, the group got to know each other a bit better, sharing their travel tips and anecdotes.

"I was just talking to the tour guide, Faye. He said there's a hut at the end of a track over there where you can smoke opium. You fancy coming with me? I've always wanted to try it, so now's my chance," said Brent.

"No, I'm more interested in talking to some of these villagers. They're ethnic minority hill tribes. We've been invited to their homes to try some of their herbal drinks. Why don't you come along?"

"The lure of the louche den beckons, Faye," said Brent in a theatrical tone, holding an imaginary skull in the palm of his outstretched hand.

"Brent, really," she said, giggling. "By the way, you chose the wrong tour. These people are not Karen. But it doesn't matter. Maybe we can pass through their village tomorrow."

"They're probably the same mob anyway. They've got the brass neck. No, this sounds like an opportunity that's too good to miss, and I heard that you have trippy dreams when you're high on opium, so that settles it. I'll bugger off up the hill and you can go for tea with the savages."

"Stop being so rude, Brent. They're not savages."

"I'm joking. So if I don't see you later, I'll take it that you're in their cooking pot or something."

Brent followed the trail over the hill and came to a set of wooden lodges, entering the small hut that was set off to the rear that had been described to him by the guide. Inside, an old man welcomed him, offering him a space on the floor where he could lie on a thin mattress.

The old man loaded a small ceramic bowl with a ball of sticky brown opium and placed it on top of the metal stem at the end of a long thin pipe. Passing the pipe to Brent, the old man held the bowl over a purpose-made oil lamp as Brent lay on his side inhaling the intoxicating vapour.

An intense feeling of euphoria came over his body, and he laid his head backwards on the cushion, closing his eyes as the old man reloaded the bowl and smoked one himself.

Brent drifted out of the hut, not remembering how long he had been in there, how much opium he had smoked, or even where he was.

Wandering around in the dark, he eventually found the place that he was staying at and cautiously went inside.

"Brent, where on earth have you been? I was just about to send out a search party," said Faye in a low voice.

"I've been walking around that fucking jungle all night trying to find this lodge."

"Stop shouting. People are trying to sleep," she whispered.

"There's another group of huts over there. I nearly got beaten up trying to get in somebody's house by mistake."

"Well, just go asleep. We have to get up early."

Brent lay next to Faye and tried to make himself comfortable.

"God, I'm freezing! Can I get in your sleeping bag with you?"

"Don't be ridiculous, Brent. It's hardly big enough for me."

"Why didn't they tell us it would be this cold at night? Haven't they got any blankets?"

"I don't know, but they're all asleep anyway. I don't think they would be very happy if you woke them up. I did mention that the nights might be cold up here in the mountains, but you obviously weren't listening."

"If you wake up tomorrow and find me lying next to you, frozen stiff, just promise me you won't feel guilty about it," he said, sniffling.

"Can you stop making that chattering sound with your teeth, Brent? It's beginning to irritate me. Move closer and snuggle up to me if you're really that cold, but watch where you put your hands."

The next morning, they awoke early and had a light breakfast before continuing with the trek.

As they set off, the darkened sky broke, and it started to rain.

"So how were the mind-bending dreams last night, Brent?"

"Shut up, Faye," said Brent, trudging along, looking miserable.

"What for?"

"You're having a laugh."

"Why?"

"Dreams? I lay awake all night freezing my bollocks off, listening

24

to you snoring and grunting like a wild animal."

"No you didn't. Stop being so nasty. I don't snore, and I certainly don't make animal noises either."

"How do you know that you don't snore? Do you lie awake listening to yourself? Maybe you make tape recordings or something, do you?"

"Brent, could you carry this bag for me, please? It's getting a bit heavy now that it's wet," she said, passing the bag to him and charging off ahead, vexed.

Trekking through the jungle, the group followed a stream until it came to a river. They boarded a long bamboo raft and drifted steadily back to the village where they had started from.

"What are you sulking about now?" said Brent, looking at Faye's miserable face.

"Is that it? You said it was going to be a three-day trek. I was so looking forward to seeing the Karen women, and now it's all over."

"Hey! Can you do me a favour?" snapped Brent.

"What."

"Can you let me know if I *do* something right, *get* something right, or *say* something right?" he said, throwing her small backpack on the ground and walking off in a huff.

"Brent!"

"I'll book another trip for you tomorrow," he said, walking towards the waiting minibus. "Come on, let's go."

They climbed in the back of the van and headed off, neither of them feeling in the mood to make conversation with each other or anyone else.

Pulling up outside the tour shop, the group piled out and went their separate ways.

Brent and Faye stood silently under the corrugated tin roof of the shack next door, watching the rain.

"Do you want to book another tour to go and see the Karen tomorrow?" said Brent.

"Yes, I think we should while we're here. Don't you?" replied Faye.

"I don't want to go. You can just do a day trip to their village if you want. You don't have to stay overnight, but it's up to you."

"What will you do?"

"I'll just hang out in Chiang Mai. Maybe do a temple or something."

"I will go inside and book it then," she said.

"What is the name of that village that we stayed at last night?" said Brent to the tour guide.

"Mae Tang Hnung village," replied the tour leader.

Having booked Faye's tour for the following day, they stood outside under the shelter again and waited for a songthaew to pass by.

Hailing the shared taxi, they climbed on board the back of the pickup with their backpacks. The Thais moved forward along the bench seats to make room for them under the low canvas top as they headed for town, the rain lashing in from the open sides and the rear.

The rain had cleared when they woke up the next day, and the sun shone brightly again through the white clouds, making a perfect day for trekking.

"Are you sure that you don't want to come with me to see the Karen tribespeople, Brent?" said Faye.

"I don't want to think about villages. Not after yesterday's cock up."

"What are you going to do then?"

"I'm not sure, Faye. I might just go to the bar and have a drink, spend the day doing nothing. Do you want me to go to the tour shop with you?"

"No, they said they would pick me up at the hotel. They should be here soon."

After Faye had gone, Brent walked across the street and sat outside a bar, wondering whether he should make better use of his time and do something positive. He thought about going to a temple to do some meditation, and then his mind wandered onto the village that he had been in the day before.

He waved over a local motorbike driver who was sitting around smoking a cigarette and asked him if he knew Mae Tang Hnung village. The driver shook his head, indicating that he didn't understand. Realising that his mastery of the Thai language was below par, Brent wrote it down on a piece of paper. The driver looked at it and smiled, pointing in the general direction of the village.

Brent finished his beer, got on the back of the bike, and headed off to Mae Tang Hnung village for the day.

Faye returned from the day trip quite late in the day, and as she got out of the minibus, Brent called her over to join him outside the bar opposite their hotel. She looked at him briefly, without speaking, and then walked up the steps into the lobby. He surmised from her body language that she was in a bad mood, so he ordered another beer and spent the rest of the evening by himself, watching people waltz by, forming ever-worsening opinions of them as the night wore on and the drink took effect.

Having drunk his fill, Brent bought some takeaway Indian food and went up to their room. The light was on, and Faye was on the bed, lying on her back with her right arm covering her eyes as he walked through the door. He tried to talk to her but she ignored him. She wasn't interested in the food, so he sat on his bed and ate half of it, leaving a couple of onion bhajis for her in case she changed her mind later on.

Faye was still brooding the next day as they sat opposite each other at the breakfast table.

"How did the trip go?" said Brent.

"I don't want to talk about it."

"Did you get to see the Karen people?"

"I just told you. I don't want to talk about it," replied Faye sternly.

"If you're done with Chiang Mai, we could move on. I fancy hitting the beach. I saw an ad for cheap flights down to Phuket. We could go from there over to Koh Phi Phi and then—"

"Brent, could you stop talking, please?" she said, holding her head in her hands, her elbows resting on the table.

"I'm going to book myself a ticket before the flight gets sold out," he said, standing up and walking off.

"Brent!"

"What."

"Yes," said Faye.

"Yes, what?"

"Yes, I want to go to the beach."

"I'll get you a ticket," he said.

Walking out of the hotel, Brent saw an Australian guy that he had been talking to at the bar the day before.

"Hey, Wayne. How's it going, mate?" said Brent.

"Pretty good. Yourself?" he replied.

"Yeah. What are you up to?"

"Nothing much, just having a wander. Fancy a beer?"

"I'm just off to book a couple of tickets down to Phuket while they're still on offer."

"In that travel agency over there?"

"Yeah."

"I think the tickets have all gone, mate. My girlfriend's bestie was going to book one yesterday, but she was out of luck."

"I'll go and check, just to make sure."

They walked into the shop to see if there were any tickets left, but the flights were all fully booked.

"Back to the drawing board, then," said Brent, sounding disappointed. "Hey, come and meet Faye. We've been travelling together for about three weeks now. She's having coffee back at the hotel."

"Yeah, no worries," said Wayne.

"You've been in Thailand for quite a while then?" said Brent as they walked back to his hotel.

"Ah, yeah, mate. We've done just about everything there is to do, eh?"

"This is a mate of mine that I met in the bar last night, Faye," said Brent, sitting down at the breakfast table.

"G'day," said Wayne, smiling at Faye. "How's it going?"

"Hello," replied Faye in a dull tone, glancing up at him and then continuing to use her phone.

"Is it worth going down to Phuket?" said Brent.

"Phuket's alright," said Wayne as he sat down. "We stayed on Koh Phi Phi, instead. Went out to see Viking Cave. That's pretty awesome, mate. You get off the boat and walk through this limestone cave entrance, and it just opens up inside, and it's massive, like a hollowed-out volcano or something. And you look up, hundreds of feet above you, and it's like totally dark with birds flying around going crazy. The Thais have strapped bamboo poles to the sides of the rock so they can climb up to get the birds' nests. We watched them climbing up with torches strapped to their heads. Mate! Those guys have got some balls, eh? The bamboo poles right at the top looked just like little matchsticks."

"Sounds pretty scary. Have you tried bird's nest soup?"

"Ah, yeah. It's alright. Bit expensive for what it is though, I reckon."

"Have you ever tried it, Faye?" said Brent.

Faye didn't comment. She sat at the table looking depressed, ignoring the conversation and doing something or other with her phone.

"Then we went over to the east coast and did the islands on that side," said Wayne. "It was pretty funny taking the boat over to Samui. We passed by this Thai fishing vessel, and there was this guy with his pants down, hanging on to the back of the boat as it bobbed up and down, like a monkey hanging on to its mom. There was like heaps of tourists watching him take a dump. He wasn't embarrassed at all, eh? He just smiled at everyone."

"Yeah, nothing seems to embarrass the Thais, does it?" said Brent, smiling. "I heard that the full moon parties are pretty wicked too."

"Yeah, Phangan is the best place for that, eh?" said Wayne.

Wayne stayed for a while talking to Brent about India, and Nepal, and all of the places that he was going to visit on his way to Europe, and then he went off to meet his girlfriend.

"The cheap tickets to Phuket have all been sold, Faye. I forgot to tell you," said Brent.

"I don't want to go to Phuket," she replied, still sulking.

"Where do you want to go?"

"I don't want to go anywhere."

"You want to stay here, then?"

"No."

"What's bugging you, Faye?"

"Brent! What is wrong with you? Can't you see that I'm busy?" she snapped, looking up from her phone.

"What is it that you're doing, exactly?"

"It doesn't matter what I'm doing, does it? The point is I'm busy."

Brent turned his face, staring at the street scene and giving thought to whether it was worth continuing the conversation with Faye, considering the mood that she was in.

"He's an interesting guy to listen to, though. Some people really do have the art of the gab when it comes to yakking. Wayne's good, isn't he?"

"Good at what—giving people a headache?" she replied.

"He had some pretty amazing stories, don't you think?"

"I don't know, Brent. I wasn't listening."

"How about the snorkeling off Koh Tao that he was talking about? And the beach with sand like talcum powder that squeaks when you walk on it?"

"Was he telling you or was he asking you a series of questions about it? The way he kept saying *'eh'* after every sentence was just about driving me insane. Maybe somebody should teach him how to use intonation properly."

"How about going down to Koh Phangan for one of the full moon raves? Magic mushroom omelettes, wild sex on the beach, the works."

"And just who do you plan on having sex with, Brent?" she said, rather caustically.

"That's a very good question, Faye," he replied awkwardly, trying to think of an answer. "But I didn't actually say that it was me who was going to be having—"

"Listen to this traveller's description of an island," she said, smiling and looking at her phone.

"Listen to *what*?"

"Brent, read this for me."

"What does it say?" he said, taking the phone.

"Don't do that, Brent. Just read it."

"*We sat next to each—*"

"Brent, it's supposed to be romantic. Start again, please."

"Ok. 'We sat next to each other on a secluded beach, a gentle breeze breaking the warmth of the evening, watching the tranquil sea as it gently lapped against the shore. There was no need for words or other souls that night. The perfect sphere of the blood moon hung barely above the horizon, as a red lantern casting a glow on the darkness of the body that sat before it.' How was that?"

"Mmm, yes. Perfect."

"Yes, that's beautiful, Faye. Did you write it?"

"Of course not," she replied, her face blushing slightly.

Brent looked deeply into Faye's brown eyes and hoped for a moment that her mindset was back to normal. But it soon became apparent that their planetary motions were temporarily out of sync with each other. Maybe it was just that time of the month, he thought, as he looked at her flicking through her phone again.

"Myanmar looks interesting," said Faye.

"Burma? Yes, I've heard it's great. Do you want to go there?"

"No."

"Where do you want to go next, then?"

"Vietnam."

"Go from here to Vietnam?"

"No, I want to see Cambodia first. How can we get there?"

"You have a think about it, Faye," said Brent, feeling a bit despondent. "Let me know whether you want to fly there or go overland. I'm going to the bar across the street. Do you want to come with me?"

"No," she murmured, staring at her phone and sounding disappointed.

Brent had a good drinking session over at the bar while Faye spent the day pottering around town, making sure that she had seen all of the sights while she was still in Chiang Mai.

They went for dinner in the evening and discussed their ideas for travelling to Cambodia.

"I checked a few things out, Faye. We can go back to Bangkok then over to Trat, near the border. It will be a full moon in three days, so we could spend some time at the beach on Koh Chang. I've worked it all out. If we stay at a guest house on the far side of the island, we should get a ripping view of the full moon as it comes up over the sea."

"Is it going to be another one of your trek-style plans?"

"What do you mean?"

"Are we going to be staring at the stars all night while the moon comes up behind our backs?"

"Ok, so do you want to make the plan yourself then? You're quite adept at making great trekking plans. Aren't you?"

"And just what do you mean by that, Brent?"

"Are you asking me what *adept* means?"

"Don't be ridiculous. What are you talking about—*my trekking plans*?"

"Nothing, honestly. I just couldn't help noticing that you seemed pretty pissed off after you came back from visiting the Karen villagers when we were up in Chiang Mai. That's all."

"I haven't got the faintest idea what you're talking about, Brent."

"Maybe you were pissed about the Indian take away that I brought back for you. Hey, Faye? Is that why you looked so down?"

"Well, you know I don't like onion bhajis, Brent. Maybe that's why you bought them, is it? So that you could eat them all yourself?"

"Really? You don't like onion bhajis?" he said, smiling. "Then how come you pigged out on them when we were in—"

"Brent, could you be quiet, please? I'm trying to concentrate," she said, picking up her phone.

Travelling through the night, Brent and Faye arrived at Trat the following day and took the boat out to the main island, Koh Chang, where they rented a hut among the palm trees on the beach, spending the remainder of the day relaxing in hammocks strung between the trees.

The long sleepless journey from the north had sapped their energy, and so they had an early night, waking the following morning to the sound of the sea crashing against the sand. Brent lay in his bed watching a beam of sunlight that had pierced through a crack move slowly across Faye's bare waist, between her top and her panties.

After breakfast, they took a stroll along a winding sandy track that led through the coconut trees and into thick jungle vegetation beyond, coming across a small rocky lagoon surrounded by overhanging trees, the vivid bluish-green water shimmering in the sunlight.

Long vines hung from the branches of a large tree by the edge of the pool, and taking hold of a stick, Brent was able to reach out and hook one of them towards him, passing it to Faye for her to hold while he removed his trainers and top. After pulling down on the vine to test how strong it was, he swung out over the pool and jumped into the water. He called out for Faye to join him for a refreshing swim, but she was quite happy sitting on a rock, watching him as he frolicked around.

They joined all of the other travellers that evening and started the full moon party a day early, enjoying the crab and lobster barbecue and drinking and dancing on the beach and in the sea.

32

Brent knew that you couldn't have an exotic beach party without a dude banging the bongos, so sitting with a small group in a circle, he grabbed a guitar and impressed Faye with his instrumental skills while the girls sang along, clapping their hands.

Faye fulfilled her romantic vision of a couple sitting alone on a beach in the light of a full moon the following night. And later, as they strolled along the sand, Brent gently took hold of her wrist, caressing her fingers and then firmly holding her hand.

They left the island early the next morning, crossing the border and entering Cambodia along the coast, heading for Phnom Penh. They had decided to visit Angkor Wat at a later date, choosing instead to get a proper feel for the country by travelling through the smaller towns and villages along the way.

Chapter 5

Cambodia And The Boy

The poverty in Cambodia was clear right from the start, and even the capital, Phnom Penh, seemed so remarkably behind that of neighbouring Thailand. But Brent and Faye soon adjusted and found the Cambodians to be just as welcoming and friendly, if not more so. In fact, they knew that behind the charming smiles on the faces of Thai people lay the undeniable truth that Thais secretly disliked foreigners, regardless of where they came from.

They checked into an old building from the French colonial period on a tree-lined boulevard in central Phnom Penh and went for a stroll around, excited about being in a strange new land.

Faye spent the following morning scrubbing the grime out of her kit and her clothes, while Brent did a recce of the best places to drink at.

He returned around lunchtime to see if Faye wanted to go somewhere, but their room was empty, and she was nowhere to be found. He sat around and waited for a while, but when she failed to show up, he decided to go back to the bar.

He was drinking at a bar nearby and returned twice to see what Faye was up to. But each time he went back to the guest house, she wasn't there.

He walked the streets looking for her, but it wasn't until later in the afternoon that she returned to the room.

Faye was all out of sorts again, and Brent wasn't in the mood for playing mind games with her, so he left the room and went to the street that he had spotted before, the one with lively bars and a mall.

The mall was an open-fronted complex on Street 51, with a large floor space in the middle covered by a high ceiling. On all three sides of the floor there were numerous bars and restaurants with tables and chairs in front. Two corridors ran off from the centre of the mall in opposite directions, one on each side, with smaller bars, clothes shops, hair salons, and amusement arcades full of local Cambodians.

Brent walked into the mall and chose a quiet bar that had just opened for the evening. Most of the other bars were busily serving food and drink to their customers, predominantly middle-aged western men and their Cambodian girls for the night. Brent looked at them and felt slightly envious, trying to work out what was wrong with Faye.

Having quarrelled with Faye earlier, Brent was not in the best of moods and sat at the counter chatting to the barmaid, trying to make himself feel better. He drank quickly and ordered another jug of beer.

A Cambodian girl came and stood next to him. She was holding a small bag of fried food and offered him some.

"Why you sad?" she said, looking at Brent.

"Why are you ugly?" he replied.

"You want lady?"

"Yeah, do you know where I can find one?"

"Why you don't have girl?"

"I *do* have a girl. Her name is Faye."

"I drink with you, ok?"

"What's that you're eating?" he said.

She sat down on the stool next to him and said something to the girl behind the bar, who put some ice into a glass and obligingly passed it to her. Without asking, she picked up the jug and poured herself a beer, taking a sip and putting the bag of food on the counter in front of him.

"What the hell is *that*?" he said, taking one from the bag with a grimaced look on his face.

"You try. Very good."

"Is that a bug!"

"Eat," she said, taking another mouthful of beer and replenishing her glass from the jug.

"Eat that? Are you serious? That's an effing fried cockroach, isn't it?" he said, examining it closely.

"He not cockroach. You try. He very delicious."

"Thanks, but I'm not hungry now. What's next—sewer rat soup?"

Brent finished off the jug of beer and ordered another one. He felt better having some company, and the beer was cheap, so he topped up the girl's glass and asked her name.

"My name Kun Thea," she said.

"Cunt what?" said Brent.

"Kun Thea," she replied, raising her voice.

"Cunt here?"

"KUN THEA," she shouted.

"Alright, calm down. There's no need to shout. Here, have some more piss."

A stranger walked up to Brent.

"You don't mind if I sit here, do you?" he asked.

Brent turned his head to see a man standing next to him.

"No, course not. Have a seat," he replied.

The man sat down and ordered a bottle of lager. He was about sixty, six feet tall with short silver hair, and apart from a plump waist, he was fairly well built. He dressed casually but smartly and spoke with a crisp, educated accent.

"I see you've got yourself fixed up for the night," he said.

"What? Oh, her? No, she's not my girl. She's all yours if you want her," replied Brent.

"No. Thank you for the offer, but bar girls are not my bag."

"Married then, are you?"

"No, that neither," he laughed, taking another sip from the bottle.

"Been here long?"

"Cambodia? Yes, I live here. I left the UK a long time ago. By the way, my name's Jack."

"Brent. Nice to meet you."

"Is it really?"

"What?" said Brent.

"Nothing. I just hate hackneyed clichés, that's all. I take it you're on vacation. Travelling alone?"

"No, I'm with my girlfriend, Faye."

"Boys night out then, is it?"

"We had a bit of a spat. You know what women are like."

"I don't have anything to do with them. Never have," said Jack.

"What are you doing in Cambodia? Are you retired?"

"He no good," said Kun Thea, pointing at Jack as she got up to leave.

"I do a bit of charity work," he said, ignoring her.

36

"Oh, sounds interesting. What kind of work is it?" said Brent.

"Helping orphans, boys, that sort of thing."

"Did you say your name's Jack?" said Brent drunkenly.

"Yes, my name's John, but I prefer Jack."

"Just like Richard prefers Dick," said Brent, laughing as he ordered another jug.

"Yes, that's right. Well done. You've got it now," replied Jack, his lips forming a tight little smile. "If there's anything you need while you're in town, just let me know. I'm here most nights. How long are you staying for?"

"Haven't really thought about it, but we'll probably stick around for a few more days, at least. Faye wants to have a look at that place where the Khmer Rouge tortured their victims. S21, or whatever it's called."

"Let me give you my number," said Jack, handing Brent a contact card. "I'll be here tomorrow, around the same time. Why don't we meet up? I have a feeling I might be of some use to you."

"Yeah, whatever. If I'm here. Catch you later then."

"Be careful with that girl. Keep your eye on her," said Jack as he left the bar.

It was five in the morning, and Brent had been drinking all through the night. Outside, the dark sky was taking a lighter shade and thin wisps of orange appeared on the horizon, bringing a new day. Most of the other bars had closed, and only a handful of people remained. He listened to a row going on between two drunken men over a game of pool in the centre of the mall and watched Cambodian girls as they cruised around the tables in search of a punter to escort home.

He ordered another jug of beer and thought about Faye and the petty tiff they'd had over something he'd said. He concluded that she was just way too prudish and that his behaviour was definitely not the cause of it.

Picking up his beer, he sat at one of the tables in front of the bar, unsure whether the table belonged to the bar he was drinking at or the one next to it, as they were all mixed together around the sides of the mall. But that was the least of his concerns.

Kun Thea returned and sat down next to him. She had changed her clothes and smelt of pleasant fragrance.

"You look like you've just been fucked," said Brent, slurring his words.

"What you say?"

"I said you look like you just took a man to a hotel."

"You want go with me hotel?" she said.

"No, babe, I don't. I told you. I already have a girlfriend."

"Today, I no lucky. You help me? My baby, he hungry."

"You have a baby? How old are you?"

"I twenty. You help me?"

"Why did you say that man was no good?" said Brent, changing the subject.

"What?"

"That man at the bar, before," said Brent, describing Jack. "You say he's no good."

"Yes, he no good. He bad man."

"Why is he no good?"

"He not take girl. He take boy. He like boy too much."

"Ladyboy?"

"Not ladyboy. Boy. Young boy," she replied.

The sun was up, and it was already hot, despite being just after daybreak. Kun Thea had left, and so Brent, deciding that he had drunk enough, paid his bar tab and started to walk back to the guest house that he and Faye were staying at.

Entering the guest house, he went up the stairs to the second floor and tried to turn the handle on his door. The room was locked. He shouted Faye's name, but there was no reply. He knocked, shouting her name again, but there was still no answer. He went back down the stairs and enquired at the reception desk. He was told that Faye had gone out, so he sat by a table in the front garden and ordered breakfast.

By the time Faye returned, the coffee had sobered him up somewhat. She took a seat opposite his, and they sat for a while in stony silence, staring at each other.

"What have you just been doing?" he said.

"I went for a jog to clear my mind."

"Hey… about last night. I really didn't mean to piss you off like that."

"Well, you did. And then you stayed out all night fraternising with bar girls, probably."

"I swear, I never went with any of those dogs. Honestly, Faye, I just sat at the bar drinking beer and thinking about you."

"Why do you have to be so foul-mouthed all the time, Brent?"

"Well, I don't really think I've got anything to apologise for, but how about if I take you to see S21 today? And then we can go to the Killing Fields afterwards. What do you say?"

After an awkward silence, she turned her face to him again.

"Yes, alright," she replied.

"Have you had breakfast yet?"

"No, I always eat after I've been jogging. Not before. Have you?"

"I ordered some, but then I cancelled it and just had coffee. I thought I'd wait for you so that we could eat together."

Having eaten breakfast, Brent decided to get a couple of hours sleep while Faye practiced her yoga.

Later that morning they showered and prepared themselves for the trip to Tuol Sleng, the genocide museum.

They left the guest house and climbed in a tuk-tuk, waiting outside.

Cambodian tuk-tuks were different from the ones in Thailand and consisted of a single-axle carriage which hooked onto the back of a motorbike.

They lowered their heads as they stepped on it, ducking under the canvas canopy and sitting next to each other on the narrow bench seat at the rear.

The driver weaved his way through the streets of Phnom Penh and pulled over in front of a large three-storeyed building complex in a busy suburb. Five blocks of rooms stood among the palm trees and lawns of the former high school that had been converted by the Khmer Rouge in 1976 into a prison and interrogation centre.

It had been one of many torture and execution centres, and during the occupation, the buildings had been enclosed in electrified barbed wire, the classrooms converted into tiny prison cells and torture chambers, and the windows covered with iron bars to prevent any attempts of escape or suicide.

Inside the former classrooms, rusting iron bed frames with chains and shackles rested on the heavily stained tiled floors that once held desks and chairs; displays of iron bars and other implements for extracting confessions stood next to waterboarding devices. On the walls hung photographs of the victims: the doctors, dentists, teachers, monks, and ordinary people emptied from the streets of Phnom Penh and murdered; their skulls, retrieved from the mass graves, now held in glass cabinets nearby.

They left the museum and headed for the Killing Fields at Choeung Ek on the outskirts of the city, just one of the twenty thousand sites where an estimated two million Cambodians had been brutally killed. Pits, from which the bodies had been exhumed, scarred the ground surrounding a tall Buddhist stupa, a memorial containing five thousand skulls and bones.

"I'm starving, Faye. Let's go and eat something," said Brent, arriving back at their guest house.

"I want to have a rest first. I feel a bit tired," she said, lying on the bed.

"How about if we meet later at that little restaurant then?"

"Which one?"

"That one opposite the nightclub, The Art of Darkness."

"Yes, ok."

"Are you alright, Faye? You seem a bit down."

"Yes, I'm fine," she said in a dull tone.

"Don't be thinking too much about what you saw today. It's not good for you. Ok?"

"Ok," she replied faintly.

"What time should we meet?"

"I don't know. Maybe in a couple of hours or so, I guess."

Brent sat down on the edge of the bed next to Faye. He put his hand on her shoulder and then ran his fingers through her long fawn hair, massaging the back of her head and neck.

"Do you want me to give you a massage, Faye?"

"Not now. Maybe some other time."

"Are you sure? You're all stressed up. It will make you feel a bit better."

"I'm fine," she said softly.

"Ok, so I'll see you at the restaurant later then," he said, rubbing his hand gently up and down her back.

Brent quietly locked the door and headed for the mall.

His favourite bar hadn't opened yet, so he took a table at the one next to it and ordered a beer. He spotted Kun Thea sitting with a middle-aged western guy, who didn't appear to be showing any interest in her. She turned around and smiled at him, but he looked the other way, pretending that he hadn't seen her.

"Hello, Brent. Mind if I join you for a beer?" said Jack, who appeared suddenly.

"Sure, have a seat."

"Don't tell me you've had another argument with Faye?"

"No, we're fine. Having a great time. She's just a bit tired, that's all. We had a big day out, so she's having a bit of a kip. I'll be seeing her later for dinner."

"You had a big day out, you say?"

"Yeah, we went to that former high school where they tortured and murdered half of the population, and then we had a look at the Killing Fields where they murdered the other half."

"Yes," said Jack, laughing. "Pol Pot. He had the right idea, didn't he?"

"So what have you been up to then?" said Brent.

"Oh, nothing much. Bit of a lazy day, really. I helped a couple of boys with their English speaking, took them back to my place, had something to eat. By the way, there's a place that I'd like to show you. I think you might be interested. Are you free later on?"

"No, I'm going to meet Faye when I've finished this beer. What's this place that you want to show me, anyway?"

"It's part of Phnom Penh's culture. Something that you should experience on your visit. How about tomorrow evening? Let's make a definite plan."

"I don't know. Maybe. I don't know what I'm doing tomorrow."

"Perfect. So I will meet you here tomorrow evening around ten," said Jack as he got up from his chair.

"Goodbye," said Brent.

"Ciao."

Brent drank his beer and walked around to the restaurant to see Faye, who was already there, sitting at a table holding a huge green coconut with a straw in the top of it.

The restaurant was small and very cozy, the inside having barely enough room for a counter and kitchen area, with just four tables outside. At the front, two rows of large plants marked the boundaries on either side, separating it from the bar on its right and the kebab stall on its left.

"Hello, honey," he said, smiling. "Been here long?"

"No, not long at all," she replied.

"Are you feeling better now? You look a bit more cheerful, anyway."

"Yes. Absolutely famished, though. How about you?"

"You bet! Let's order. What do you fancy?"

"Some more Khmer food. There are so many dishes to try," she said, looking at the photographs in the menu.

"How about Tarantula?" he said, imitating a waiter. "Deep fried with chili, crunchy on the outside, deliciously warm intestinal juices on the inside. Or maybe you would prefer to try the Scorpion, skewered and deep fried? Perhaps Madame is feeling a little naughty tonight and would like our speciality: Balut, the fertilised embryo of a duck, still inside its shell, feathers and all."

"You sound like that Spanish waiter, Manuel," she said, laughing.

"These people eat just about anything," said Brent, sounding serious. "Dogs, rats... I'll get a jug of beer while you decide what to have."

"Yes, I know. But I heard that the rats come from the fields. They're not sewer rats."

"You still wouldn't want to eat it though, would you?"

"Do you want to try this, Brent," she said, pointing at the Fish Amok.

"Yeah, looks delicious. Are you going to share it with me?"

"No. I'm a vegetarian. You know that already," she said.

"Yeah, just thought you might fancy a day off, that's all."

"Well, I don't, but thank you anyway. I will be fine with the Spicy Mango Salad. Could you chop this for me, please?" said Faye, holding up the coconut for Ary, the girl who ran the restaurant.

"Yes, I can. Wait moment, please."

Ary brought the steamed fish in creamy coconut milk sauce, made with egg and spices and topped with lemongrass, served in banana leaf shaped into a bowl. She asked them if they would like any rice, before returning with the other dish and a plate of soft white coconut meat.

"I think today was a bit too much for you. Wasn't it, Faye?"

"How do you mean?"

"I mean, the thought of paranoid illiterate peasants and child

42

soldiers taking control of society and smashing your head in with the butt of a rifle for some stupid reason or other—like, you were seen as an intellectual just because you wore glasses."

"Brent, are you trying to put me off eating my dinner so that you can have it?" she said, smiling.

"Damn! You've gone and sussed me out again. You're just too smart, Faye. No, but seriously, it did get to you. Didn't it?"

"Kind of," she conceded. "I just can't come to terms with the way human beings can be so needlessly cruel to their own kind. The way they can become like automatons, blindly following some ridiculous ideology."

"I thought you said you had a degree in psychology."

"Yes, I do."

"Power, Faye. That's what corrupts people. Some of those guards at S21 were only fourteen or fifteen years old. Think about it. Armed with a rifle, having the power to control people, beat people, kill people."

"Yes, but even if I had all the power in the world, I still couldn't bring myself to do those kinds of things. It's evil personified. I can't even kill a cockroach, and if I tread on one accidentally then I feel terrible about it for the rest of the day."

"The human race is insane," he said. "What kind of nutjob thinks that it would be a good idea to get rid of all the educated people, including doctors and teachers, and then turn everybody into a rice farmer?"

"Brother number one," she said. "Pol Pot."

"*Crack* Pot, more like. The mind boggles, Faye."

They whiled away the evening, drinking and entertaining each other until it was late.

Leaving the restaurant, Faye linked her arm under Brent's, and they walked back to their digs.

The following morning they had breakfast and then returned to their room.

"I want to have a quiet day today, Brent. I think I'll just lounge around the guest house and write a few letters, read my book," said Faye.

"Yeah, good idea," he replied.

"What are you going to do?"

"I'm going to stay here with you."

"Why don't you go and get drunk for a change?" she said, giggling.

"Are you trying to get rid of me?"

"No, of course not. Just close the door on your way out, would you?"

Brent put his arms around Faye, lifting her off the ground and shaking her from side to side in a playful manner. She started laughing and squeezed his neck, pretending to throttle him. He carried her to his bed and gently collapsed on top of her, biting her neck and tickling her armpits. She laughed uncontrollably.

"No! Brent, stop it."

"Stop what?"

"Stop it! Leave me alone."

"Come on, Faye," he said, holding her shoulders and kissing her neck.

"Brent! Stop it! Leave me alone, you horrible pig."

"Faye, how long have we known each other now?"

"What are you talking about, Brent?"

"I mean, how long have we been together, now?"

"No, get off me, leave me alone."

"Have you got somebody waiting for you back home?"

"No, nobody."

"So what's the problem, then?"

"Brent! Stop talking like that. I don't like it."

"Suit yourself then, you smelly pig," he said, getting off the bed and walking to the door feeling slightly miffed.

Brent had been drinking with Jack at a bar all day, and it was quite late in the evening when he returned to the small restaurant where Faye was. She was sitting outside chatting to one of the local girls who earned their living entertaining the foreign men. Brent told Faye that he had to go somewhere, but he wouldn't say where. She noticed that he was slightly nervous and apprehensive.

A motorbike pulled up opposite the bar they were at, stopping on the other side of the street. The rider wore a full-face helmet and sunglasses, a black leather jacket, and grey slacks. He stayed on the bike, looked at Brent, and nodded his head, indicating that he was ready to leave.

Faye picked up the uneasy feeling about Brent and stared at him.

She could see that he was hesitant.

"I'm just going somewhere," said Brent.

"Going where?"

"Just somewhere. You stay here. I'll be back soon."

"Who's that man?"

"Just some guy that I met at the bar. Don't worry about it."

"I hope you're not going to do anything stupid," she said.

"No," he murmured, but he wasn't really focusing on what she was saying.

Faye wanted to tell him about all the horrible stories that she had heard about people who had been set up in drug smuggling deals and the numerous scams that prevailed, but the man on the motorbike was slowly driving off, looking at Brent.

"I gotta go. He's waiting."

"What time are you coming back?"

"I don't know. I'll send you a message."

"Brent, look at me! What are you doing?"

"Nothing, we're… just going to check some place out."

"What kind of place?"

"Faye! I have to go."

He left and hurriedly crossed the street. Faye sensed that there was something not quite right and felt uneasy about the way the man on the bike seemed to have control and dominance over Brent.

The bike was powerful and growled as it sped off down the street, past the brightly lit restaurants and bars and into the darkness beyond.

Outside the tourist area, Phnom Penh was asleep and closed, and the streets were deserted. They made their way down an unlit highway, past the old dwellings on either side that were set back from the road and almost unseen.

The bike slowed. Up ahead, some of the houses were faintly lit by small red lanterns hanging over the door, and some had a girl or two sitting outside in the gentle warm air that occasionally blew through the stillness of the night.

Turning off the highway and crossing a small patch of rough ground, they stopped outside a large wooden residence, switched off the engine, and sat motionless in the dark and the quiet.

Without speaking, Jack turned his head, lifted his visor, and motioned for Brent to get off the bike. They approached the house, knocked once, and waited.

An old woman opened the door and let them enter, smiling at Brent as she led them down a long, narrow, dim corridor and past rows of small, flimsy, wooden box rooms. One of the doors opened, and a client walked out, leaving a girl, wrapped in a towel, sitting on the edge of a bed.

The old woman showed Brent and Jack to a larger room, dark and dingy, where she sat them down on a long, worn, shabby leather couch opposite a group of girls and offered them a glass of Chinese tea.

Jack remained silent as Brent sheepishly tried to look calm and relaxed, smiling and making nervous small talk with the girls.

Jack drank the tea, stood up, and walked out of the room, glancing at the old Cambodian woman as he left. She stared at Brent and pointed at the girls.

"You like?"

"Yes, they're very nice," he said.

"You want? You take her," she said, pointing at the youngest girl. "She very beautiful."

"How old is she?"

"She eighteen. No husband, no baby."

"Where is she from? Is she from Cambodia?"

"Kampuchea, Kampuchea, Kampuchea, Viet Nam," said the old woman, pointing at each of the four girls.

"These three are from Cambodia, and she's from Vietnam?" said Brent.

"Uhh," she grunted, confirming the question. "You like? You take which girl?"

"No, really, thank you, but… yes, they're very beautiful, but… I have a girlfriend already. Her name is Faye."

"You like young girl?" said the old woman, lowering her voice.

"What do you mean?"

"You want young girl?"

"No! Of course not! I mean… no… that's not why I came here."

Feeling embarrassed and uncomfortable, Brent tried to change the conversation, claiming how hot it was by fanning his face with his hand and wiping the sweat from his brow. The old woman smiled at him and filled his glass with some more cold, dark green tea.

She was small, aged about seventy, with rotten red-stained teeth as a result of chewing betel nut her entire life. She seemed nice and friendly, but her hard eyes and granite face lent her demeanour an unfeeling, heartless, almost brutal quality.

"My name's Brent. What's your name?" he said to the old woman.

"My name Sawatdee."

"Sawatdee? I heard that a lot when I was in Thailand."

"Yes. Sawatdee same same 'hello'. My father, he from Thailand, my mother, she Khmer."

"Oh, yes, Khmer. They're the original people of Cambodia, right?"

"You from where?" she said.

"I'm from England."

"In ger land?" said Sawatdee.

"Yes, Britain."

Brent felt more relaxed and tried to think of some interesting conversation to make without intruding too much on her privacy, now that he had hopefully sidestepped the offer of buying a girl.

The wooden floor boards creaked as Jack came back into the room and sat next to Sawatdee. He said a few words to her quietly in Khmer. She nodded her head and slowly stood up, walking delicately towards the door, her back slightly arched, beckoning the girls to follow her.

"Hey, Jack, one of those girls is Vietnamese," said Brent.

"Yes," he replied.

Brent tried to ease the tension that he felt between them by forcing the conversation.

"Have you had her?"

"I've told you already. Girls are not my thing."

Sawatdee returned, her hand placed gently on the arm of a boy as she walked into the room. She sat the boy next to Jack and spoke assertively to him in Khmer, as she had done with the girls.

"Who is he?" said Brent curiously.

"He lives here," replied Jack, putting his hand on the boys leg.

"He doesn't look Khmer. Where is he from?"

"Why don't you ask him? He speaks English well enough."

"Go and talk to Brent," said Jack, stroking the back of the boy's head and putting his hand on his bottom as he helped him stand up.

Sawatdee motioned for the boy to sit next to Brent and poured them both some tea before sitting on the couch.

"Hi," said Brent. "What's your name?"

"My name Sov."

"Where are you from?"

Sov didn't reply. He sat calmly on the couch and sipped his tea, staring at Jack smoking his cigarette. Sawatdee stood up and walked over to the small Buddhist shrine, lighting some incense sticks and placing them in front of the tiny figure on the altar.

"He very shy," said Sawatdee, returning to the couch.

"Yes. How old is he?"

"He fifteen."

"He looks Spanish or something. Are you his relative?"

"What? I not understand."

"Was his mother or father from another country?"

"He no father, no mother. You like?" she said.

"Do I like him? Yes, he seems very nice," replied Brent, looking at Sov, noticing that one of his blue eyes was a lighter shade than the other.

"Sad a day," said Sov, gazing at Brent.

"Sad a day? I don't understand. Are you sad? Feeling sad today?"

"My name sad a day."

"I thought you said your name was Sov?"

"Today, what day?" said Sov, smiling.

"Today? I think it's Friday today. Let me check," said Brent, taking his phone out of his pocket. "Yes, it's Friday. Friday the…"

Brent looked concerned, unable to say the date.

"To morrow," said Sov falteringly. "Sad a day. My name, sad a day."

"Oh! Right. Saturday. Your name means Saturday. Ok, yeah, that's pretty cool. I don't know what my name means. Probably something stupid, though," said Brent, feeling more relaxed.

Sawatdee spoke to Sov. He turned to look at Brent, put his arm around his shoulder, and whispered in his ear.

"What did you say, Sov? I can't hear you."

"You take me," whispered Sov, putting his mouth closer to Brent's ear.

"Yes, I mean… I'm not sure what you want… I don't… no, yes, I suppose we could… what did you say you said?" mumbled Brent in a totally confused, embarrassed way.

Sov took hold of Brent's arm and helped him to his feet, leading him to the doorway and down the dimly lit corridor into one of the rooms, sliding shut the rickety wooden opening and securing the catch.

Inside the box room, there was barely enough space to move. There were no windows, just a thin narrow mattress on a frame, with a small table next to it.

Jack stood up from the couch, quietly walked down the corridor, and entered the unlit room next to Sov's.

It wasn't long before Brent slid open the door and hurriedly walked out, rejoining Sawatdee on the couch. She smiled but said nothing as he sat down. As she offered him more tea, he tried to think of something to say, but his mind was elsewhere.

The girls could be heard arguing with each other in one of the rooms as Jack returned, looking solemn. He stood in the doorway and lit a cigarette. Sawatdee moved him aside as she went to see what all the fuss was about with the girls.

"It's time to go," he said, looking at Brent.

"Yeah, I know," replied Brent as he quickly made his way to the front entrance.

"You got lucky tonight," said Jack, smiling.

After she had sorted out the argument, Sawatdee followed Jack to the door and unbolted it, allowing them to leave. Nobody spoke as they walked out into the deserted stillness of the night, started the bike, and rode back into town via a different route.

Jack dropped Brent at the mall without speaking or looking at him and then quickly sped off down the road. Brent went back to the bar and ordered another beer. He felt strange and rebuffed all the local girls who tried to approach him, preferring to sit alone with his thoughts, drinking heavily.

Chapter 6

Checked Out

The sound of chairs being stacked together and tables being dragged across the floor woke Brent up. He had been at the bar since the night before, after Jack had dropped him off. He looked at the clock on the wall. It was seven thirty in the morning. His head was banging, and his mouth was dry.

He stood up to leave, wondering whether he had already paid the bill. Looking at the girl as she swept the floor, Brent tried to read her face, not wanting to ask in case it gave her the opportunity to charge him twice. He waved goodbye to her and slowly started to walk away. She called him over and gave him the bill. It looked excessive, but there was no point arguing about it as he could barely even remember where he was.

He zigzagged his way down the street, walking around in squares trying to locate his guest house.

Eventually, he found it, and as he walked in, the receptionist handed him the key to his room. He climbed the stairs, unlocked the door, and went inside.

The excuses that he had concocted for Faye were now redundant, as she wasn't there, and neither was her backpack. She had gone. He sat on the edge of her bed, holding his head in his hands, feeling devastated.

Wanting to find out exactly what had happened, he went downstairs and spoke to the girl behind the desk.

"She check out already," said the receptionist.

"What time did she leave?"

"Maybe one hour before."

"Did she say where she was going?"

"No, she don't say."

"Did she leave a message?"

"Message on phone?"

"No, on paper. Write a message, a note, on a piece of paper, like this," he said, demonstrating.

"No. No message."

He took his phone out of his pocket and called her number. It seemed to ring forever before she finally answered it.

"Faye! Where are you?" he said.

"I'm at the bus station."

"What are you doing there?"

"I'm going to Vietnam."

"Vietnam! Faye! What the hell is going on? You can't just go like that! Why are you leaving?"

"I'm done with Cambodia. I need to move on."

"Why didn't you talk it over with me so that we could have gone together?"

"Why don't you stay there, Brent? You seem to be having a great time. You don't need me."

"That's not true, Faye. I'm not having a great time, and I do need you."

"Where did you go last night?"

"That guy on the motorbike, his name is Jack. He insisted on taking me to a place, said he wanted to introduce me to someone. I felt like I couldn't say no."

"And who was the person that you met?"

"A boy. Well, not really, there were some girls there, and the mama-san tried to sell them to me, but I told them I was with you."

"A boy! You went to see a boy? Brent, what on God's earth were you thinking of?"

"I was curious, that's all. I just wanted to see what Jack was talking about."

"You left me sitting outside a restaurant so that you could go and visit a brothel! Is that what you're trying to tell me?"

"Faye! Please. I swear, I never did anything. That's the honest truth. And I didn't plan on staying out all night either. I fell asleep."

An embarrassing silence fell between them.

"I have to go now," she said.

"No! Faye, wait. Stay there, I'm coming with you. I'll grab my bags."

"The bus is about to leave. I have to go now."

"I'll catch up with you in Vietnam. You're going to Saigon, right?"

She hung up. He went back to his room, slowly walking up the stairs like a condemned man walking up to the gallows.

The thought of packing his belongings and charging off to the bus station didn't appeal to him anymore, so he lay down on Faye's bed.

Losing her made him angry and depressed, feeling hopeless. Why had he told her about the boy? It would have been just as easy not to. He searched for the answer but couldn't find it. He must act quickly and go to Vietnam, he reasoned.

He closed his eyes and started to dream, seeing Sov staring at him with those round puppy eyes, so soft, yet alluring. They seemed to be calling him.

He was tired of thinking, tired of everything, including himself. He buried his face in the pillow, wrapping his arm around it and squeezing it tightly, drawing in the scent of Faye's hair.

It was mid-afternoon when he awoke, so the decision on whether to stay in Cambodia another day had somewhat been decided for him already, as checkout time was twelve noon, which meant that he would have to pay for the room regardless of whether he stayed or not.

He considered the idea of contacting Jack to see what he would be doing later that evening but quickly dismissed it. Instead, he bought a ticket to Saigon for the following day and began to pack his bags. He would have dinner later on, maybe drink a beer or two, and then watch a movie before having an early night.

It was three o'clock in the morning, and he was still wide awake, turning over from side to side, unable to sleep. There was too much on his mind, and he hadn't drunk enough alcohol to knock himself out for the night, something that had become a routine of late. He put the light on and tried to read a book, but he couldn't concentrate, couldn't focus. He was reading the words without listening to what they were saying.

He needed a drink to calm himself and thought about going to the mall. Maybe a few beers and a chat with Kun Thea would help.

He decided against it, as he would leave in a few hours, and to miss the bus was a risk he didn't take. Faye had left him just hours before, but already he missed her badly.

Getting off the bed, he stretched out on the floor and did a set of exercises instead. His job required him to be physically fit at all times, but he was on extended leave and had allowed himself to lapse. He knew about the cognitive benefits of a strenuous workout, and as he pushed harder, he began to focus clearly on his relationship with Faye and how he had made one drunken mistake after another. He resolved to change his ways and curb his drinking.

It was time to go. He took a shower, got dressed, and double-checked the room, making sure he had his passport, money, and bus ticket, looking under the beds to make sure that nothing would be left behind.

Slinging his backpack over his shoulder, he turned around in the doorway, said farewell to the room, and left.

Handing in the key and declining the offer of a taxi, he made his way to the bus station.

Boarding the coach, Brent showed his ticket and took his seat next to a window at the rear. All of the curtains had been drawn to block out the strong sunlight that shone through, so he untied his and opened it slightly for a more interesting view along the way.

The driver started the engine as the attendant walked along the aisle and collected everyone's passport, checking to make sure they had a visa or the correct documents to enter Vietnam.

The air-conditioning blasted into life, and the small television set at the front crackled as it came on, screening a typical Khmer love story.

As the coach slowly made its way out of Phnom Penh and onto the highway, the landscape on either side changed into endless fields, mostly waterlogged, dotted with trees and scrub, and the occasional grazing water buffalo; land that seemed to have no purpose or use at all.

They arrived at the border, driving past the rows of large glitzy casinos mostly frequented by Vietnamese and Chinese gamblers who were allowed to enter Cambodia for the day on payment of a small fee.

The passengers grabbed their baggage and followed the attendant inside the building, where he placed their passports next to another stack on one of the immigration counters.

It was midday, and as another coachload of people entered the building, the other three officials left their positions unattended and went off to eat lunch together, slowing down further an already tedious process.

A Vietnamese couple walked up to the solitary counter, holding their passports under the glass barrier, expecting to be processed more quickly. The stern-faced official ignored them, but they stood there persistently, knowing that it wouldn't be long before he followed convention and assisted his fellow citizens.

Brent cleared customs and got back on the coach, excited about being in Vietnam and catching up with Faye.

The coach ended its journey in Saigon's backpacker area, and Brent soon found somewhere to stay, taking a dormitory bed in the nearest hostel, knowing that it would be a good place to meet people and gain information.

He tried to contact Faye several times, making calls and sending text messages, but she wasn't responding.

Brent walked around the streets hoping to find Faye, but luck wasn't on his side, so he sat outside a large restaurant on the corner of an intersection and ordered a beer.

The bar was more or less in the heart of the backpacker area and was a perfect place for him to chance on seeing her. The guy sitting at the table next to him tried to make conversation about a recent drug deal that had gone wrong and the westerner killed with a machete, but Brent didn't want to be distracted in case she walked down one of the busy streets unnoticed, so he made small talk, giving him a brief description of Faye and asking whether he knew her.

As the hours passed, Brent's optimism began to wane. He waited until the last rays of daylight had faded and then he left, slowly making his way back to the hostel past the spas and massage parlours, glancing from side to side to see if Faye was inside one of them.

Chapter 7

Saigon And The Grey Man

A burly Australian man sat in the dark on the small balcony of his dingy room on the first floor, above a noodle soup shop in Saigon that had purportedly been used as an operations centre by the Viet Cong during the war.

It was close to midnight as he opened another cold bottle of beer, watching people pass by on the street below, the bright neon signs on the buildings alternating and flickering in the steam rising up from the street stall. His phone rang.

"Hello?"

"Jay, it's Bee."

"Yes, what's happening? Are you still in Phnom Penh?"

"Yes. There's a possible lead on a guy that has just left. He should be in Saigon by now, so I thought I'd give you a heads-up on it."

"What do we know about him?"

"Not a lot, really. I got word that he was interested in a boy."

"Any description?"

"He's about twenty-eight, five feet ten, stocky build, short black hair."

"Name?"

"Didn't get his name. I think he's English. That's all we've got."

"Ok, we'll put a tail on him. Are we any closer to finding out who the mole is?"

"No."

"Alright, Bee, keep me up-to-date on anything you've got. And I mean anything. Anything at all. Especially about the mole."

"Will do."

Jay hung up the phone and resumed drinking his beer, taking in the aroma that was wafting up from the soup stall just below him. He called the girl and told her to bring up a bowl of Pho and leave it on a tray outside his door.

At the hostel the next morning, Brent wrote a description of Faye and posted it on the message board, requesting other travellers to contact him if they saw anybody or knew anybody who looked like her.

He spent the rest of the day wandering the streets and eventually ended up sitting in a park watching groups of Vietnamese people dancing to music in the pavilions, all of them practicing a different style with their partners, some doing disco, others doing the tango or salsa.

A young student approached and asked if she could sit next to him on the bench and practice her English speaking. Brent wasn't really in the mood for chatting to anyone, his enthusiasm for everything had gone, but he agreed anyhow. She asked him a series of questions about where he was from, what he thought about her country, its food, the weather, the people, until the boredom of it forced him to change the topic. He wanted to learn more about Buddhism. She was more than happy to take the opportunity of practicing her speaking and imparted her understanding of it, inviting him to visit a temple with her the following day.

They agreed to meet at the same spot the next day around eleven in the morning and went their separate ways as the sun set and the park began to fill with people eager to do their daily workout.

Brent strolled around aimlessly, like a lost dog searching for its owner, until he grew tired and headed for a bar.

He found a quiet place to drink down a dark back alley and sat by himself. It wasn't a bar, more of a small run-down grocery shop with a couple of small wooden tables outside, but the beer was cold, and they had a television.

He sat alone in the dim light, next to a stack of crates, and watched some Vietnamese opera of a man and a woman dressed in traditional garb singing to each other, accompanied by weird-sounding instruments. He found it strange and wondered what they were saying, as they appeared to be telling the story by arguing.

Raising his voice to overcome the sound of the television, he eventually caught the old woman's attention. She stood up slowly from her reclining chair and brought him another beer. He tried asking her a question, but she just smiled, raising her hand and shaking it.

It was past midnight, and the old woman started to lock up her shop. Moving aside the wares that hung in the way of the sliding concertina doors, she partially closed the entrance. A vagrant Vietnamese came and bought a cigarette, an egg, and a packet of noodles. She wore tattered clothes and carried a bag filled with discarded plastic bottles. She turned and smiled at Brent, holding out her hand, but he was too preoccupied with his sullen mood to respond in time. He put his hand in his pocket, but before he could take out some money, she walked away, spilling some of the noodles as she ripped open the packet.

The next day, Brent tried to get in touch with Faye again, but she still wasn't answering the phone. He felt depressed and was losing his appetite, not just for food but for everything. He needed her and cursed himself for being so stupid.

His phone buzzed, indicating that he had received a message, which instantly boosted his morale. But when he read it, his heart sank along with his hope. The message wasn't from Faye. It was from Tao, the girl that he had met in the park the day before, wanting to know where he was. He had forgotten all about it and couldn't even remember giving her his number. He sent a reply anyway, telling her that he would be there shortly.

It was another hot sticky morning, and as Brent walked through the park a young boy ran across his path, licking an ice cream and laughing. Brent continued, looking around to see if he could spot Faye or Tao anywhere. The boy ran past him again and sat on a bench further ahead. Brent smiled at him as he walked past, asking him if he could have one, putting his finger in his mouth and sucking it to simulate an ice cream. The boy laughed and ate his cone without responding.

Brent strolled along, admiring the flower beds and tropical plants that ran through the centre of the park, until he came to the end. Turning, he started to walk back along the other side and noticed a man sitting by himself on one of the benches next to a pavilion. Brent recognised him from the day before as he was wearing the same cumbersome clothing: a beige lightweight jacket, dark blue combat trousers, and heavy black boots, which Brent considered very unusual for a tropical climate.

As Brent approached, the man picked up his small brown backpack and started to look inside it for something, his face hidden by a flat-brimmed slouch hat. Sensing that the man didn't want to make conversation, Brent carried on walking through the park, looking for Faye.

Brent's phone buzzed. He had received a message from Tao, telling him that she had arrived and where she was.

They met and sat opposite the park, drinking coffee and chatting for a while before heading off to the temple on her motorbike, stopping off en route to buy a large bag of rice at the market.

Arriving at the temple, they removed their shoes and went inside, where Tao donated the bag of rice to one of the female monks, dressed in grey pyjamas. Brent was surprised that instead of being a quiet and tranquil place, like most of the other temples he had visited, this one housed babies and toddlers whose parents, for whatever reason, were no longer able to take care of them.

He sat next to Tao on the wooden floor and fed rice porridge to one of the kids, who immediately approached them craving attention.

After a while, Brent couldn't stand the stench of shit any longer and decided to go outside for some fresh air, leaving Tao to console them on her own. As he got up to leave, the young child that he was sitting with started sobbing and holding out its arms, hoping to go with him.

The rain had stopped, and the air was cool and refreshing as he stepped outside. He felt worse for visiting the temple and seeing the children, and all he wanted to do was leave. He shouted Tao's name, and she came over, smiling and gently rocking a baby in her arms as she walked through the large burgundy-coloured polished columns of the heavy wooden doorway. They crossed the courtyard together and stood beside a pool, watching the fish swim gracefully among the rockery and the plants that draped onto the water.

"I think I've had enough of this, Tao. Can we leave?"

"You can go. It's ok. Up to you."

"I don't know where we are. How do I get back to the park?"

"You take a motorbike."

"Which motorbike? Yours?"

"No, you go here," she said, pointing to the street at the end of the lane. "Take a motorbike taxi. Ask the driver. He will take you go to the park."

"How much will it cost?"

"I think not expensive."

"Well, how about you? Are you staying here much longer?"

"Maybe one hour more."

"Ok. Do you think I should put some money in the donations box, or what?"

"Yes, up to you. I think lucky for you."

"What's the name of that park then?"

"You go to Pham Ngu Lao Street. I think better for you."

"Can you write that down? My Vietnamese is terrible. I will probably end up lost somewhere. Do you have a pen?"

Tao went back inside the temple to get a pen and a piece of paper. She wrote the address down for Brent, and he left, walking up to the street and hailing a motorbike. He showed the driver where he wanted to go, agreed on a price, and then jumped on the back of the bike.

Brent soon realised that there was no specific rush hour in Saigon; it was chaotic all of the time until nightfall. They came to a halt at a busy intersection: a spider-like roundabout, choked with hundreds of motorbikes on all six roads, waiting for the green light.

Brent looked around at the local people wearing masks over their mouths while he felt nauseous breathing in the exhaust fumes.

Motorbikes that had ridden up onto the pavements to weave their way nearer to the front now jammed the pavements, barring pedestrians from moving until the traffic started flowing again.

As the lights changed and the motorbikes revved up, an ambulance approached quickly from the rear, its siren blazing loudly. Nobody moved to let it pass, and it was hampered even further as drivers cut in front of it in the race to be first off the block.

After narrowly avoiding numerous collisions, Brent finally made it back to where he had started from.

The park was long and narrow, and during the French colonial period, it had been Saigon's main railway station.

It was mid-afternoon, and the sun was still high in the sky, so Brent decided to get some sun on his face.

Sitting in the heat of the rays, he closed his eyes and let his mind wander off to those glorious days of empire that he so often dreamed of.

He imagined himself on the platform, dressed in his white suit and matching pith hat, a young servant fanning his face, his porters standing next to his leather suitcases, waiting for the whistle to sound his departure.

Putting his ivory cigarette holder in his mouth, he would board the *Oriental Empress* and take his first-class compartment, bidding greetings and pleasantries to one and all as the grand old lady huffed and puffed and chugged her way out of the station.

He would wine and dine, with conversation aplenty, to smooth the passage to Singapore where he would alight and sit under the parasol of a rickshaw while the coolie ran ahead, barefoot, his thin frame weaving in and out of the bustling crowds.

Sipping pink gin and dancing with bored officers' wives at the Raffles Hotel after dinner would precede a late night of smoking opium with his favourite Madame in some seedy backstreet den.

A ticket to Hongkers, my good man, Brent would say, to the clerk at the White Star Line office the following morning. Oh, and make it posh, there's a good chap.

The clerk, with his white gloves and his red tunic nicely buttoned up, brass buttons shining, his bell-boy's hat slightly cocked to one side, would reply: One return ticket to Hong Kong, sir? Port out, starboard home? Certainly, sir. Here you are, sir. Have a pleasant journey, sir.

The sun shifted behind the long, drooping leaves of a tall palm tree, and Brent snapped out of his reverie. He looked around to see if he had missed Faye, but there was still no sign of her. Walking to the main road, he crossed over and strolled through the other half of the park to a bar near his guest house.

Brent soon fell into a routine of walking the streets looking for Faye, ending up in the park, seeing the same people hanging around in the same places.

The next day he saw the boy sitting with a Vietnamese woman; and sitting over by the pavilion, the guy with the slouch hat, wearing the same kit as before.

As Brent was passing by the boy, the Vietnamese woman waved at him, calling him to join them. As he went over to see what she wanted, the boy ran off and hid behind a bench. She spoke reasonably good English and told him that the boy was hungry, asking for money. Brent gave her enough to buy some food and then left the park.

With the passing days, Brent found himself becoming more and more reclusive, isolating himself at the small shop that was tucked away down the alley, avoiding contact with people and drinking alone through the depression that had taken hold of him by losing Faye.

"Kay, what's the latest?" said Jay on the phone.

"I'm not sure if I've got the right bloke or not. There's a couple of guys in the park that fit the same description."

"Have you not made contact with him?"

"No, I've not spoken to any of them."

"Right, listen up. Don't be hiding in the shadows. You'll make yourself look too obvious. I want you to be friendly, get to know them. That's how you get information. Just don't be too pushy with your questioning. Understand?"

"Yeah, sure."

"I'm sending Chup to the park tomorrow."

"Who's Chup?"

"She's working for me. She's fifteen. I'm putting her out in the field. I want to get some feedback on those guys."

Chapter 8

In Your Mind

Realising that he was sinking rapidly into a bottomless pit that he didn't want to be in, Brent dug deeper and found the strength to pull himself out of it.

Dressing himself and quietly leaving the dorm room early in the morning, he went downstairs and into the courtyard. The old man who acted as security groaned obligingly, throwing off his blanket and getting up from his cot on the floor to unlock the gate.

Cracks of daylight were breaking through the darkness as Brent walked down the alleyways, past the women lighting small fires to brew their coffee and earn their pay. Thick acrid grey smoke filled the air as they fanned the smoldering charcoal.

Vietnamese people of all ages took to the park each day around five in the morning to exercise, and Brent found himself jogging behind a young woman, circling the lake and watching the older folk performing slow martial arts movements, the younger ones doing aerobic dancing.

As it came light, he pushed himself to the limit with sets of hard physical drills.

Back at his digs, he had a shower and then joined one of his room mates for breakfast.

"Hey Brent, have you ever done any English teaching?" said James, a young guy who was also from Manchester.

"No, not really. Why?"

"My school wants me to work this evening, but I can't be arsed going in. Do you want to stand in for me? I'll pay you for doing it, don't worry about that one."

"I wouldn't have a clue what to do."

"It's a piece of piss. Eight or ten adults in an intermediate class practicing their speaking skills. Just make something up for an hour. I was going to teach them how to remember words by linking them to a picture in your mind. Know what I mean?"

"Yeah, kind of."

"So what do you reckon then? Fancy giving it a go?"

"I could do with something to take my mind off things, that's for sure. I'm starting to go frigging crazy here."

"Ace. I'll phone in and let them know what's happening then. The lesson starts at seven-thirty. Here's the address."

Brent made a bit of a lesson plan based on what James had told him and set off for the language centre an hour early.

Anticipating that he would be nervous on his first teaching gig and being totally green when it came to standing in front of people and talking, Brent made sure that he had taken plenty of drinking water with him.

Arriving at the centre, Brent made himself known at the front desk and was informed that the room for his class was on the fifth floor.

Looking through the cracked glass pane on the classroom door, his legs started to shake at the sight of twenty or more people sitting in the room, waiting for him. He asked some of the students in the corridor where the toilet was situated and then made his way back to the ground floor, to use the only one that was still functioning.

There was no need to lift the toilet seat to urinate as it had been broken off already and was now leaning against the wall. The sink was resting on top of a large bucket, with a hose pipe connected to the tap, and nearly fell onto the floor as he tried to wash his hands.

Walking up the stairs and taking a deep breath, he opened the classroom door and went in, almost tripping over a loose floor tile. His mouth was dry and his hands were trembling as he tried to write his name on the board and introduce himself. He thought that he had memorised all of the advice that James had given him, but his mind went completely blank, and he stood there staring at everyone with a dumb expression on his face.

Being helpful by nature, the Vietnamese students smiled at him warmly and practiced their speaking skills, asking him questions about where he was from and what his country was like. Brent soon thawed out and found his stride.

The lesson was nearly over, and as Brent finished explaining his pièce de résistance that he had drawn on the whiteboard, the lights suddenly went out. Students began taking out their phones and holding them up, using them as torches to illuminate the room.

Noticing that the whole area was in darkness outside, Brent tried to open one of the windows to see what was happening on the streets, but the security bars that covered them prevented any from being opened. Students were calling time-out and standing up, moving closer to the door, so Brent decided to end the lesson and follow them out of the room.

He found himself pinned up against the low handrail, almost being pushed over the side by the jostling crowd as they quickly descended the stairs in the dark, the smell of burning rubber permeating the air.

Outside, hundreds of electric cables, tightly bound together and strung from pole to pole along the street, had overheated and caught fire, causing the blackout.

Brent made his way home, joining James at the bar to buy him a beer and tell him how well he thought he had done at the school.

"Do I still have a job to go back to, or have you completely fucked it for me?" said James, laughing.

"I did what you said, about teaching them how to remember something by associating it with a mental image. You should have been there, man. They were completely gobsmacked, totally blown away by what I showed them. I reckon they'll never ever forget it in a million years," said Brent, drinking his beer excitedly, totally elated and declaring the whole episode a complete success.

"Sounds wicked. So what did you do, then?"

"I chatted them up for a while and then I drew a picture of an eye on the whiteboard. And then next to that I drew a picture of two round circles—"

"Two *round* circles?"

"Yeah, one above the other, touching. And then inside each circle I drew another smaller circle so that it looked like a bold figure eight. Do you know what I mean?"

"Yeah, cool."

"And underneath the drawing of the eye and the figure eight I wrote: I ate two fried eggs. I was thinking of getting the red marker and putting a bit of tomato sauce on the eggs, but I figured that would have ruined it, so I didn't bother."

"You *what*?" said James, taken aback.

"Well, the picture of the eye helps them to remember the pronoun, 'I', and the figure eight looks like two fried eggs, one next to the other. Doesn't it? And of course, you eat fried eggs, so: *I ate two fried eggs*. I thought it was quite brilliant, to be honest."

James stared at Brent, waiting for him to laugh and show that he was just joking.

"You're serious, aren't you?" said James. "How come the figure eight is not two Mexicans that we look down on, wearing big sombreros?"

"I get your point, but that might be a bit confusing for them," said Brent.

"Fuck me! I just hope that I've still got a job to go back to. That's all I can say, mate."

Chapter 9

Chup

Friday night, the park was almost deserted. The amber glow from the light above a toilet block softly illuminated Chup's olive skin with an exotic hue as she lay on a bench, set against the backdrop of tall bushes and overhanging trees in the semi-darkness.

Resting her head on a small bag, she covered her shoulders with an old denim jacket. Her clothes were dirty, her bare feet filthy. A plastic shopping bag with some stale bread and rice inside it sat next to a bottle of water on the ground in front of her.

Jay sat in the dark on his balcony, engaged in his usual pastime of drinking cold beer and watching people as they cruised along the street. His phone rang.

"Yes?"

"Yeah, it's Kay. There's a guy been circling the park for the last hour or so. I think he might be about to make a move on Chup. What do you want me to do?"

"Which guy is it?"

"I don't know him. He's only been around for a few days. You remember what I told you? There have been two blokes coming into the park over the last few days that look pretty similar to each other. They look like twins, although they never come in together. They're both young blokes, pretty fit looking, might have been in the forces or something. One of them has got a bit of a pot belly. That's about the only difference there is, but," said the Australian.

"Right, so which one is it that we're looking at then?"

"Not sure, it's hard to tell at this time of night."

"Bloody hell! If you had done your job properly and made contact with them earlier then maybe we wouldn't be guessing right now, would we?"

"Ah, look, mate, I haven't really had the chance, eh?"

"Jeez, you're bloody hopeless, mate!" said Jay, losing his temper.

"So you want me to fuck off then, or what?"

"What? No. Listen, I want you to just stay where you are and keep an eye on Chup. Don't get too close. Not now. Just carry on with surveillance. Understand?"

"Yeah, no worries."

After midnight, Chup left the park, turned down a narrow alley, and walked into the side entrance of the soup shop below Jay's apartment. She nodded to the woman squatting on the ground washing the utensils and then climbed the bare concrete steps up to the unlit first floor. She stood outside the room, in the shadows, looking at the faded yellow paint peeling from the walls. The floor above was vacant and used solely for storage.

Jay unlocked the cracked wooden door, and she silently walked in and sat down on a chair, swinging her legs to and fro on the narrow balcony. He sat next to her in the darkness and asked her what had happened in the park. She told him that a man had approached her, asking how old she was. When she told the man that she was fifteen, he then asked her for the date of her birthday, giving her a pen and a piece of paper for her to write it down. Her description of the man was the same as the one Kay had given earlier in his phone call.

Answering a knock on the door, Chup opened it and picked up a tray from the floor with a bowl of soup and a baguette on it. She sat at the table and ate the food while Jay cracked open another beer on the balcony, drawing on a cigarette with a rather satisfied look on his face.

After Chup had finished her supper, Jay took her to the bathroom and sat her on a stool, rolling up the ends of her jeans so that he could scrub the dirt off her feet.

"Ow! Not do like that. You tick me," she said, giggling like a little schoolgirl, pulling her foot away from his hands.

"Did that tickle you, Chup? Sorry about that. How's this?" he said, gently washing between her toes.

"Yes, that good."

"That man in the park, Chup. Did he want to take you to a hotel?"

"Maybe, yes, but I don't sure. He not say."

After he had finished cleaning her feet, he turned on the hot shower, telling her to get undressed and then closing the bathroom door.

The next day, Saturday afternoon, Jay was busy poring over photographs of western men who were of particular interest to him when he received another phone call from Kay.

"Jay, I've just been talking to that woman who hangs around with the boy in the park. Know the one I'm talking about?"

"Yes. Has she got anything for us?"

"Apparently, a man was talking to the boy this morning asking him whether or not he was sixteen. It sounds like it was one of those blokes that I was telling you about. This could be the break that we've been waiting for. The age of sexual consent in Vietnam is eighteen, isn't it?"

"That's what we're going to sort out. Hanoi and Saigon are having another war. Hanoi wants the age set at eighteen, Saigon sixteen."

"Well, Hanoi is the capital, so even if this bloke takes the boy to a hotel on his sixteenth birthday, we're going to nail the bastard, right?"

"Right, listen up," said Jay, pausing for a moment to think. "We need to speed things up a tad, so I'm changing the game plan. Chup and the boy are coming off the pitch. I've got a couple of replacements. They're both sixteen. I'll send them to the park tomorrow."

Chapter 10

The Darkening Sky

Brent had not seen or heard from Faye for more than two weeks and concluded that she had probably left Saigon and headed north. With nothing better to do, he walked the streets and inevitably ended up around the park, near the far end that had a small artificial lake. He decided to stroll along the main road that ran along one side, turn both corners and go back down the other main road, a continuation of walking around in circles that he now found himself locked into daily.

Nearing the end of the road, he saw a girl with long fawn hair sitting on a park bench with her back to him. She was wearing a pale yellow dress, talking to a western man who appeared to be about the same age.

His heart racing, Brent jumped over the low bed of flowers and walked through the trees towards her. He had never seen Faye dressed like that, but she had the same slim figure and the same elegant way of sitting with her legs closed and to one side, her body leaning away slightly from the person next to her.

Approaching from the side, Brent sat on a bench nearby and waited until she noticed him. They made eye contact and smiled at each other rather sheepishly. She said something to the man next to her, and they both stood up and walked off, stopping briefly at the edge of the lake before parting company and going their separate ways. She stopped and turned to look at Brent as he approached.

"Faye, what are you doing, man? I've been looking all over town for you!"

"Hi Brent."

"Who was that guy? Is he your new boyfriend?"

"We just met. He was asking me about Cambodia. He's going

69

there tomorrow, and he's looking for someone to travel with."

"I can't tell you how much I've missed you, Faye. Can we go for a drink? I really need to explain things to you."

"Sure, why not."

Brent felt awkward, following slightly behind Faye as she strolled ahead, casting her face away from him without speaking. There was so much that he wanted to say to her, but he didn't want to ruin everything by saying something stupid. He found himself acting as dumb as a teenager on his first date.

"So… what have you been doing, Faye?"

"What? Doing?" she said, as though she was preoccupied with something. "Oh, I've been doing a lot of writing."

"Writing? What, like your diary or emails?"

"No. I'm thinking of doing a master's degree. I've been taking down some observations in case I need to write a thesis."

"That sounds really interesting," he said, pleased that the ice was showing signs of cracking. "Anything in particular?"

"Yes. Shyness. Since coming to Vietnam I've been intrigued by how shy the majority of people are."

"It's funny that you should say that, Faye. I was having an argument—well, not an argument—a debate about that with one of the guys in my room. He said exactly the same thing, but I said that the girls are not shy. They're just snobs. Of course, there are different types of girls, like the bar girls, the taxi girls, you know, the ones that work in the sex business. They don't seem to be shy or snobbish at all, really. Come to think of it."

"Well, you would know all about brothels and the sex industry. Wouldn't you, Brent?"

Brent stopped and lowered his head, staring at the ground for a moment before turning around and slowly walking away.

"Hey! Where are you going?" shouted Faye.

"It sounds like you don't want to know me anymore," he said, turning to face her.

"What are you talking about? I thought we were going for a drink together?"

"Are you sure you want to?"

"Of course I am. Why are you asking silly questions? Come on, let's go to the Sky Bar down by the harbour."

The sun set magnificently in the distance as they sat high up on the terrace and looked out across the Saigon River, winding its way through the heart of the city. There was a feeling of romance in the air, and they sat next to each other perfectly relaxed and content. Brent chatted about his newly found interest in Buddhism, while Faye expounded on her fascination with the apparent shyness that she had witnessed in Vietnamese culture.

"You know, it really is the dumbest way to be, isn't it?" said Brent.

"What. Being shy?"

"Yes. I mean, it just stops you from doing what you want and getting what you want. Doesn't it? It's just a completely useless... er, what's the word..."

"Emotion?" she said.

"Yes, emotion. I was just about to say that."

"Yes."

"So if it's an emotion, does that mean they aren't snobs then?"

"No, on the contrary. Given the fact that it's a cultural trait probably suggests that the aspect of shyness you are referring to has its roots in some higher social order that has been passed down. But it's a much more complex topic than just that."

"That's just what I thought," said Brent. "That's why all of the girls act like they're the Empress of Asia. So that's what it is. I knew I was right."

"I take it you haven't had too much luck with the girls then, while you've been here?"

"I was just trying to get to know them, Faye. But I don't think I would be able to handle a serious relationship with a Vietnamese girl, to be honest. I was talking to an English guy who's married here. He said she's costing him a fortune, expects him to look after the whole family, feed the chickens, take care of the water buffalo and everything."

"I should imagine that she's younger than he is. And exotic beauty comes with a price. He should have been prepared for that."

The sun finally slipped out of sight for a while, leaving a tangerine sky for them to admire as they sat silently with their thoughts, feeling comfortable with each other. She didn't want to ask him any awkward questions, and he certainly didn't want to answer any. So they let their minds do the talking.

"Hey, guess what?" said Brent.

"What."

"I'm thinking of hiring a jeep and driving up north."

"Oh, that sounds like fun. Who are you going with?"

"I'm going by myself. Just me."

"Oh," she replied, the enthusiasm in her voice waning.

"Actually, I'm thinking of taking a girl with me."

"Ok, well, I hope you have a nice time then."

"I just need to find the right girl first."

"And who would the right girl be?" she said, sounding disappointed.

"Well, you know how particular and fussy I am, so it's going to have to be someone really attractive. Educated, of course, for good conversation. That's a must."

"I see. Well, good luck. I hope you meet someone," she said, flicking her hair back over her shoulder and turning her face away from him.

"I've got my eye on a girl already, but I don't know whether she would be interested or not."

She turned to look at him, a wry smile forming on her pouting lips.

"What does she look like?" said Faye.

"She has the most gorgeously attractive brown eyes, a finely chiseled jaw, a somewhat Roman nose, a figure to die for. I mean, why she isn't on the cover of a magazine must be one of the greatest mysteries ever."

"And would you get down on your knees to ask her?"

"I wouldn't hesitate," he said, pushing his chair back and kneeling on the ground beside her.

They laughed, freely and happily, and as he put his hands on her knees, Faye leaned towards him, their noses almost touching, and Brent dreamed for a moment that she was about to kiss him as she held his solid arms, running her hands up to his shoulders.

"So what do you say we pack up and head out first thing tomorrow morning then?"

"Why not? It sounds great."

Pulling up on the street near the guest house, Brent sounded the horn, jumping out of the dark green jeep and walking down the alley to collect all of the backpacks and boxes of stuff they had decided to take with them.

It wasn't even seven o'clock in the morning, and yet his shirt was already stuck to his broad chest with sweat from the exertion.

They put their sunglasses on and hit the road under a blue sky and a beautiful sunny day, a gentle breeze caressing their face as they headed north in the open-top vehicle.

Brent drove slowly at the request of Faye, who knew how dangerous driving could be on Vietnam's highways. She had also forbidden him from drinking any alcohol until they had finished driving for the day.

Stopping for lunch, they parked under the shade of the trees next to a group of roadside shacks, where a woman, lying in a hammock, slowly fanned her face as her husband repaired the tyre on a customer's motorbike.

As they set off, refreshingly cold air suddenly quelled the suffocating humidity that drained their energy, and the darkening sky heralded the onset of the wet season.

The rainy season had started early, and the monsoon rain lashed down heavily, forcing Brent to pull over to the side of the road and stop. Horns blasted loudly from the passing trucks as they jumped out of the vehicle, trying to raise the canvas top as it thrashed about in the strong wind that accompanied the torrential downpour. Within seconds they were drenched, their clothes completely sodden, and by the time they had figured out how the roof worked, the jeep had collected almost six inches of water on its floor.

Shivering, they sat inside and moved closer to each other under the canopy, the rain still blowing in from the open sides where the flimsy clear plastic that hung down and acted as windows flapped around uselessly. Faye kicked off her sandals, leaving them to float in the well, and squatted on the leather seat, wrapping her arms around her legs. Brent put his hand on her shoulder and smiled, but she turned her face and sighed, sulking like a young child.

Brent decided to press on and started the engine. Realising that the windscreen wipers didn't work forced him to drive even slower, but before long the storm abated, and the sky returned to blue.

"How do you feel, Faye?" said Brent.

"Wet."

"Do you want me to pull over so that you can change your clothes?"

"How much further is it to where we're going?"

73

"Mui Ne? We should be there soon."

"I'll wait until we get there," she said, sounding miserable.

"Cheer up, Faye! This is all part of the adventure. A hot shower and some hot food, you'll be as right as rain."

"*Really.*"

They arrived in town and spent the evening drying their baggage before having a late-night stroll along the seafront. Mui Ne was little more than a beach resort stretched along the coast, but the surrounding area was delightful.

Chapter 11

Trapped

The next day they took a saunter through the warm waters of the Fairy Stream in a colourful limestone gorge lined with vivid green palm trees, which reminded Brent of his trip to Morocco, making him wish he had brought some ganja to smoke.

They had walked along the huge white sand dunes earlier and now enjoyed the sight of them turning red as the sun set, and they made their way back.

Early the next morning they set off for Nha Trang and spent a couple of days snorkeling off the coral islands.

Their next stop was the quaint little town and ancient trading port of Hoi An, where Dutch and Portuguese sailing vessels once called.

They walked the cobbled streets and admired the traditional single-storey houses, some made of hard polished wood, others made of carved stone, that sat alongside the tiny harbour; and the round lanterns that hung above the doorways, glowing red into the night, creating a serene, vibrantly coloured picture.

Driving further north they entered the city of Hue, the former capital of a Vietnamese kingdom.

Brent had noticed the scores of bullet dents in the steel spans on the bridge when they crossed the wide Perfume River, and owing to his obsession with the Vietnam War, he spent the afternoon walking its length imagining American helicopters overhead, firing at the advancing communist soldiers as they charged across.

Jumping down onto the stanchions, he searched for souvenirs, hoping to find a shell casing or a spent bullet.

Faye was more interested in the ancient Citadel, which enclosed the Imperial City, with palaces and shrines, and the Forbidden Purple City, once the Emperor's home.

They left Hue in the darkness of the early morning and drove north for the Ben Hai River, which separated the north from the south during the war.

Turning onto Highway 9, they headed for Khe Sanh. Brent had not mentioned it to Faye, but the main reason that he had rented the jeep was so that he could visit all of the former bases and battlegrounds. He had read about a hill that held a particular interest for him and wanted to check it out.

The hill was about eight hundred feet high, with gently rolling slopes on all sides. The summit had been used by the Americans as an observation and mortar fire-base during the war. It commanded stunning views of the surrounding forests and river valleys and the dense jungle canopy that covered the hills, often shrouded in mist, as they rolled away to the horizon.

They walked around the base of the hill on the trails made by local villagers. The top looked inaccessible, but it would have been easy for the original occupants who had used helicopters to access and resupply it.

Leaving the track, they waded cautiously through the waist-high elephant grass. Occasionally, the thin beige-coloured sticks of grass swayed gently in unison, backward and forward as they blew in the breeze.

A solitary tree stood on the plain near the hill. Sitting under the shade of the tree for rest, Brent lit three incense sticks, placing them upright in the ground, contemplating which route to choose.

He laid his head against the trunk and watched the blue-grey smoke spiral upwards.

Turning to look at Faye, he softly called her name.

"Faye."

"Mmm?" she replied.

"Look how the smoke dances around as it rises through the air... like it was a carefree spirit."

"Where?"

"In the shafts of sunlight where they penetrate through the branches. Can you see?"

"Is it the tree's spirit, Brent?"

"Maybe. Or maybe it's the spirit of a soldier who was killed here during the war. And now it's destined forever to view, as a spectator, its final role in the play on a stage that it can never leave."

"That's very sad," she said.

"Yes."

"But that idea appeals to you quite a lot, doesn't it?"

"What idea?"

"Being a spirit on a battlefield, especially one in Vietnam. You would be in your element. Wouldn't you?"

"You've got me figured out down to a tee. Haven't you, Faye?"

"I had you all worked out from the day we met, Brent."

"Are you super clever, or am I just so predictable?"

"Neither."

"Neither," said Brent, looking up at the smoke.

"Brent."

"What, Faye."

"Promise me that you won't die," she said, smiling.

"I could promise you the earth, Faye, but I can never promise you that. And anyway, why would I want to die when I have everything that I've ever wanted sitting right here next to me? But if I do, then the trees or the breeze will let you know about it. How does that sound?" he said, smiling and putting his arm around her.

"Promise me anyway. And remember to never break your promise."

"Should we go?" he said, standing up with his hand outstretched towards her.

The morning was still young, and the sun had not been up long, yet the heat was fierce. Brent could feel tiny beads of sweat trickling down his back.

Everywhere was quiet and peaceful, and since arriving, they had seen only two people. But they were farmers, in the distance, too preoccupied with scraping a hard living out of a hard land.

The arduous task ahead of them in the heat was a daunting prospect, but Brent was determined to get to the top, confident that a glittering prize awaited him. He reminded himself of the mission, which was to procure for his display a weapon or other worthwhile trophy, and ambled up the hill with Faye in tow. He was drooling at the mouth at the thought of what could be waiting for him once he made it to the top, telling himself that he could be the first person to step foot on it since it was abandoned.

Faye had been reluctant to go along with him at first, and so, as a little sweetener while they were in Hue, Brent had bought her the brown canvas boots that she now wore.

With little white socks, a pink cap, primrose yellow shirt, and tiny dark blue shorts, she looked as hot as she felt. Ironically, Brent had chosen to wear a light brown shirt, dark green shorts, and a pair of matching brown boots, hoping to blend into the background, away from any prying eyes that might question their motive for being there.

They climbed steadily through the patches of scrub and over small rocks and boulders, keeping a close eye on the ground for safety reasons and in the hope that something might be spotted glistening in the sunlight. Brent estimated they would make the peak just after midday.

Approaching the top, they stopped at a point where the gradient of the hill changed. Further up the slope, terraced outcrops started to rise at a steeper angle, like a huge set of crooked steps, and to reach them, Brent and Faye had to scale a short vertical rock-face.

Surmounting the face, they paused for breath. The intense morning sun had taken its toll already, and their saturated shirts clung to them awkwardly.

The flat ground in front of them led towards another short vertical rock-face about nine feet ahead of them. Brent had motioned for Faye to take the lead so that he could help her to scale it, as it looked harder to climb, but she had taken only a few steps forward when he heard a distinct metallic sound as she lowered her foot.

"Faye! Don't move. I just heard a click. Don't make any rash movements. It could be a mine," he yelled.

The sweat welled up on his forehead and began to sting his eyes. He had been well aware of the possibility of leftover ordnance from the war and thought that he had chosen a safe route. The easiest way to the top had looked too obvious, so he had taken a different, less pronounced approach. Given two choices he would choose the wrong one every time, he thought, berating himself about his misfortune.

It was not a good time to be feeling sorry for himself. That much he did know. But he knew nothing about mines except for the fact that they blew people up.

A question repeated itself in his head, and he was desperate to find the answer.

"Faye, does a mine explode as you step on it, or does it detonate as you step off?"

"I don't know!" she yelled angrily. "What the hell do you think I am—a bomb disposal expert?"

"Stay calm, honey," said Brent.

"I am being calm. And the answer is blatantly obvious, isn't it?" she shouted.

He could see how upset she was and felt like he had made a complete fool of himself. But of course, she was right. If the mine was designed to explode on contact then they would be hamburger on a hill already.

"Brent, go back down the hill and get help," she pleaded.

"No. I don't want to leave you here all by yourself."

As the rain began to fall, the gravity of their situation became apparent. Soon, they would be wet, cold, and stranded on the side of a hill, with the possibility of being blown to pieces by a potentially live mine.

He recalled an incident from a war movie that he had seen years before about a soldier who was trapped in a similar position in a field. His mates, who had deemed any rescue attempts as too dangerous, had left him for dead. Why had they not tried to peel his boot like a banana and pin it to the ground with their bayonets before they legged it, giving him a chance to get away.

"I've got an idea, Faye," he said, taking out a small pocket knife and digging away the earth around her foot.

"What the hell are you doing, Brent?"

"I'm going to expose whatever it is so that we can decide what to do."

The rain, although it was heavy, was a blessing in disguise as it made removing the soil much easier, and it didn't take long before he could see what it was that she had stepped on. It was a round object roughly six to seven inches in diameter.

"It's definitely a mine, Faye."

"Oh my God!" she murmured, her legs shaking.

"Ok, here's what we're going to do," he said, trying not to sound nervous. "I'm going to peel open your boot and wrap the tongues around the sides of the mine. I'll use your boot to hold down the detonator while you remove your foot. Got it?"

"And then what?" she sobbed.

79

"Don't know. Don't worry about that. We have to get you safe, first of all."

Clearing the remaining mud from under each side of the mine, Brent peeled open her boot. Laying each flap over, tucking them around and under the base, he took a firm grip with both hands. The canvas was wet and so were his trembling hands, but he knew that this whole mess was entirely his fault, and it was down to him to fix it. Cometh the hour, cometh the man, he repeated to himself. He would save her, whatever price he had to pay.

Taking a firm grip of the mine, he looked up at her, possibly for the last time. She looked like a drowned rat, but at least the rain hid her tears.

"Listen to me, Faye. Lift your leg out, gently. Ok?" he said, breathing heavily.

She placed her hand on his shoulder, crossed herself, and slowly slid her foot out of the boot.

Nothing happened. She stood there, speechless.

"Faye, get the hell out of here!"

She jumped down off the ledge and took shelter behind a large rock, nearby.

"What on earth are you going to do now, Brent?"

"It's ok, don't worry. I've got it. I've got it. It's going nowhere," he shouted.

Brent had been crouching there for what seemed like hours thinking about the next critical move. The torrential rain was turning the overhang above him into a waterfall, and the surge of water pounded the back of his head so hard that it forced his face downwards. It felt as though a thousand ancient warriors were simultaneously banging their war drums, waiting for him to freeze to death, pass out with the numbing pain, or blow himself to pieces.

Images of the most disciplined and pious Buddhist monks who meditated for hours under harsh self-imposed conditions flashed through his vision. He had made his own karma, for sure. Now, what must he pay?

"Maybe we should take it to the nearest police station," shouted Faye.

Brent felt as though his head was about to explode, even if the mine wasn't.

The monsoon rain came crashing down even harder, and he knew that he had to make a decision soon. He was barely able to think as sudden branches of purple and yellow lightning momentarily lit up the darkened sky, and a blast of thunder, like an exploding bomb, sharpened his senses.

He shouted to Faye, telling her to go and get help, but she was reluctant, as she didn't want to leave him trapped and alone.

There was only one course of action, he told himself. His plan was to keep a firm grip on the mine and take it to the edge of the ridge that he was on. There, lying flat on his stomach, holding the mine over the edge, he would release it, quickly drawing in his hands as he dropped it. He reckoned that the angle of the ridge would protect him from the blast, and any worst-case scenario would be merely a couple of lost fingers anyway.

Brent told Faye about his intentions and made sure that she was at a safe distance and behind a rock.

Grasping tightly, he gingerly raised the mine and slithered on his stomach towards the edge of the ridge. Lying flat, with his arms extended in front of him, he inched his way forward until his wrists allowed his hands to droop over the edge, holding the mine below the level of the ground that he was lay on. Quicker than anything he had ever done in his entire life, he released the mine and withdrew his hands.

Silence. Nothing. He stayed motionless for some time, too unnerved to act. He had not heard an explosion, but maybe the sound of the hammering rain had somehow muffled it. He wasn't sure.

Eventually, the storm abated, and the sky returned to crystal blue with fluffy white clouds.

Brent chanced a glimpse over the edge. He saw the mine lying face up. The detonator had released, but obviously it had not exploded. He climbed down the ridge and went to check on Faye. She was exhausted and looked extremely dejected. Brent put his arm around her and explained what he had seen.

They sat and talked for a while, hugging each other for warmth and comfort, and after they had dried off sufficiently, they returned close to where the mine lay.

"It must be a dud. That's excellent," said Brent.

"What's excellent about that?"

"Remember why we came here? We came because I wanted to find a souvenir from the war."

"So?" said Faye, looking perplexed.

"So there it is," he replied, pointing at the mine.

She stared at him, looking for a sign that he was joking, but the gleam in his eyes said it all.

"You might have one or two problems getting it through customs, Brent. Not to mention taking it on board an aircraft," she said sarcastically. "And in any case, I've had enough. I just want to get out of here."

Brent walked over to the mine and picked up the quartered boot that was lying next to it. Taking hold of Faye's arm and leading her to a small rock, he sat her down while he strapped it to her foot in a makeshift fashion.

"You could always keep the boot as the souvenir, Brent."

"That's actually not as stupid as it sounds, considering the amount of time and effort that it took to find them."

"What do you mean?" she said.

"You told me that you don't wear anything made out of leather. Didn't you?"

"Did I? I can't remember. Well, anyway, yes, that's right, thank you."

He helped her stand up, and she almost cried as he embraced her tightly, kissing her softly on the side of the head.

Holding hands, they began the descent, walking steadily back down the hill.

Brent abandoned his quest to find a souvenir from the war, and they continued driving up the coast, stopping off at a few places before they arrived at Halong Bay.

They spent the night in a private cabin onboard a large Chinese junk, cruising the emerald waters that surrounded the hundreds of craggy limestone islands, topped with rainforests, that towered high above them.

A short drive the following day saw them arrive in Hanoi. They dropped the jeep off at the company's northern office and spent a few days in the Old Quarter before flying back to the south.

Chapter 12
Air The Ghost

Back in Saigon, Brent and Faye checked into a hostel. The floors had dormitory style accommodation, but instead of the traditional bunk beds, the owner had installed modern capsules, a lower berth of four and an upper berth of four, running the length of each wall, on either side. Each capsule was seven feet long, three feet wide, four feet high, and enclosed at both ends. A curtain covered the side facing into the room. At the foot of each bed was a small flatscreen tv and a fan. At the head, next to the pillow, was a shelf, an electrical socket, a dim light, and a jack for headphones, enabling the guest to watch their tv without disturbing others. Each floor had one room, accommodating sixteen people, with a shared toilet and shower block outside. It was cramped, but they would be moving out soon anyway.

Sitting outside a small coffee shop down an alleyway nearby, Brent spotted an old friend.

Wells, an elderly obese African American man, wavered, leaning heavily on his walking stick as he slowly limped towards him. He was a veteran of the Vietnam War and had been advised by his psychiatrist to return to Vietnam to air the ghosts that haunted his mind. Like many of his fellow servicemen, he had become addicted to heroin during his tour of duty and was still a heavy user. He tended to mind his own business and was about to pass by without noticing him.

"Hey, Wells, how's it going?" shouted Brent.

"Hey, Brendan, how you doin? I ain't seen you for weeks, man. How you been?" he said, speaking in a slow, typically Black American drawl.

"Yeah, good to see you. We just got back. Took a bit of a trip up north. Fancy a drink?"

"Uh-uh. I gotta go fix myself up. You know what am sayin?"

"Yeah. Where are you staying at now?"

"I got me a little place down that alley over there, sharing a house. They got a spare room if you guys is lookin for some place to stay."

"I'll talk to Faye about it when she comes back."

"Hey, man, I gotta go," said Wells, limping off.

"Yeah, no sweat. I'll come and check it out later."

Brent waited until Wells walked down the hem and turned off into a narrower alley, barely wide enough to drive a car down, before catching up with him.

They entered the house and went up the stairs to the first floor, Wells painfully taking one slow stride after another and stopping on each step to regain his breath.

Breathless, he opened his door, sat at his bedside table, and prepared a fix, taking a small spoon, heating the heroin that he had just bought, and drawing it up into a syringe. Pulling his shorts up, he injected himself in the upper thigh.

Feeling better, Wells talked about the foreigners who shared the house and the vacant room on the top floor, telling Brent that the owner lived next door if he was interested in taking it.

Brent had a look at the room and discussed it with Faye later on that evening, over dinner.

"I think we should take it, Faye. Two of the guys that are staying there are working as teachers, and they can help us to get some work if we need it. And if we pay monthly it will work out cheaper. What do you think?"

"It's one room with its own bathroom, and we get to use the kitchen upstairs?"

"Yeah. It's got a monster-size double bed as well. You'll love it. It's as comfy as."

"Oh, no, Brent. How is that going to work?"

"What's wrong with that? Are you saying that you don't want to sleep with me?"

"Brent, don't say that. I don't like it."

"I'm just teasing. How about if I promise not to cross the line? How does that sound?"

"Well, I hope you don't break your promise, Brent. Because if you do, then I won't speak to you ever again. I mean it."

"Ok. Would you like my signature on it?"

"No. But you can cross your heart and promise."

"Oh, for God's sake. Well, I'm moving in tomorrow. Let me know if you want to join me."

Brent took the room and sat in the courtyard at the front of the house, relaxing in the shade provided by the vines and creepers that hung down from the wooden trelliswork overhead, talking to Wells and Mike, another American guy who had just called in to see the owner.

"Scariest thing I've ever seen was a ghost," said Brent. "I'm in a guest house. I've just gone asleep. Must be about one, two o'clock in the morning. I get woken up by this thin, dark, shadowy figure standing over me with its arms stretched out in front of it, like it wants to strangle me or something. I think somebody is in my room, so I start kicking out at them, but obviously, no physical contact is made. Anyway, so I jump out of bed, and as I jump out, this thing moves backwards and along the side of the bed. I switch the light on, and that's it. It's gone, disappeared."

"You had probably been drinking heavily or smoking drugs during the evening," said Mike.

"No, I distinctly remember the evening before it happened. No drugs, just a couple of beers. In fact I wasn't even drunk, which makes a change."

"Your mind can play strange tricks on you, all the same. It was probably just your imagination."

"Maybe, but there's a couple of things that I still find weird. First, what was it that made me wake up? I don't normally wake up in the middle of the night. And second, when I jumped out of bed I knew exactly what I was going to do: switch the light on. That means I was wide awake, in control of my thoughts and actions, and yet I could still see this ghostly figure. I mean, dreams or tricks of the mind are usually over by the time you wake up, right? And guess what? I found out later that my father had passed away the previous day, about seven or eight o'clock in the evening."

"That's almost a coincidence."

"That's more than a coincidence. He passed away in England. My time zone in Vietnam was seven hours ahead which would correspond with the exact same time that I'd had that experience."

"Sounds like the first thing he wanted to do was come strangle yo ass!" said Wells, laughing.

"I prefer to think that it was Miss Twee's husband. She owned the guest house, and she told me that he was killed in a motorbike accident a few years before and that she used to see his ghost quite often," said Brent.

"I don't believe in paranormal activity, but one of the scariest things I've ever seen was actually a documentary film about this dude who climbs a three thousand feet vertical rock face without any ropes, just his bare hands and a bag of chalk. He was literally clinging on to the side with his fingertips and toes. Man, I could barely watch it. The palms of my hands were sweating so badly I needed to dry them on a towel," said Mike.

"I got me pretty spooked at that tiger temple in Thailand, the one at Kanchanaburi. You guys ever see that place? Man, those monks was rappin with those cats like they was the same goddamn species. Maybe it's coz they wearin them orange robes. You know what am sayin? They got them cats all hooked up real fine," said Wells.

"No, they feed them regularly and take good care of them. Poachers and deforestation are forcing them out of their natural habitat."

"Well, this one motherfucker was lookin at me n lickin his lips. Came n sat down right in front of me. Had me all set on dinner. Ain't no two ways about that."

"Maybe it's never seen a black man before."

"I thought tigers were colour blind. All animals are colour blind, aren't they?" said Brent.

The old woman who rented the rooms placed a metal container on the ground by the gate and lit a fire, burning toy dollar bills, a paper shirt, a pair of paper trousers, paper shoes, and other items that her deceased husband might need in his afterlife. She lit a cigarette and stuck it upright on the stub of a used incense stick in front of the altar and offered her blessings on the anniversary of his death.

"I told her she gotta do that for me one day," said Wells, laughing and gesturing towards the woman, who looked at him and smiled politely.

"You think you'll die here then, do you?" said Brent.

"I should of died here a long time ago. *Long* time ago. Boy, I sure as hell seen enough shit go down. Ain't no two ways on that one, neither."

"Is the war something you like to talk about? Most vets seem to bottle it up."

"It ain't somethin that I wanna talk about too much, but I was advised to by my doctor. You know what am sayin?"

Wells put a cigarette in his mouth, lighting it off the previous one and coughing as hard as Brent, whose eyes stung from the thick acrid smoke that drifted towards him from the dying fire. Wafting the smoke aside, Brent noticed through the iron railings and tall thin bamboo plants that Faye was slowly walking down the alley, checking the numbers on the houses. She spotted him and stood at the gate, checking out the surroundings.

"Hi, Faye. Here, let me help you with your bags," said Brent, jumping up and slipping her backpack off. "The room is on the top floor. Come on, I'll show you where it is. You don't have to take your shoes off, don't worry about it."

She followed him up the stairs and walked into the room. Frowning, she inspected everything, running the shower to check that it was sufficiently hot and pressing the mattress to test how firm it was.

"Which edge of the bed are you going to be sleeping on, Brent?"

"I'm not bothered, Faye. You can choose which side you want to sleep on."

"I wonder if the landlady has a spare bed that she could let you have. There's plenty of room in here. You could put one over there, next to that wall."

"I'm going downstairs, Faye. Don't forget to bring the key with you if you're coming down," he said, slamming the door as he left the room.

Their room on the fourth floor was large, the end of their balcony barely a few feet away from the one on the private residence opposite, in the narrow passage. And there was a shared kitchen on the terrace above.

Most of the residential buildings that lined the web of alleys were slim, having just one room on each floor, with no side or rear windows.

Despite being terraced, joined together, sharing common dividing walls on all sides, each property was unique and individual, having its own style and decor.

Huge plants and delicate flowers adorned the entrances, complimenting the pink, or primrose yellow, or sky blue facades, and it was a common sight to see small palm trees in large clay pots among hanging gardens on the rooftop terraces and balconies.

Faye made herself a coffee and joined Brent downstairs while he engaged in his favourite pastime of talking about the war.

"We was just gettin back on the trucks and them Vietnamese started shelling us," said Wells, continuing the story. "Those white boys wouldn't let me get on the truck, so I pulled a pin on a grenade and rolled that on for em to take instead."

"Hi, I'm Faye," she said, joining them at the table.

"Hey, how you doing?"

"You must be Wells. Brent told me you fought in the war."

"Yes, ma'am. I'm a United States Marine," he said proudly, as though he were addressing a senior officer.

"So there was a lot of racism towards black soldiers?" said Brent, eager to hear the rest of the story.

"Hell, yeah! They gave us a hard time all the way. Blacks only made up somethin like ten or twelve percent of the population back home, yet twenty-five to thirty percent of combat troops in Vietnam was black guys. They made me carry all the heavy shit when we was out on patrol, too. Like the early night-vision gear with its bigass motherfuckin battery. We all fell for that communist bullshit, man, but the Vietnam War weren't about nothin but gettin rid of niggers off of street corners so as them fatass motherfuckin businessmen could sell their shit what they had left over from Korea. You know what am sayin? Hell, we was even eatin rations what was left over from the goddamn Second World War," he said angrily.

"Shit. Eating cans of food that were twenty years old! Imagine that."

"One time me n the other marines was all just doin nothin but guardin the perimeter wire n we see this kid walkin towards us with some kind of pack on his back. We was all yellin n shoutin at him to turn around n go back, but he just kept right on comin. He was smilin at me too."

"How old was the kid?"

"He just turned twelve."

"You knew him!"

"Yeah, he used to come by all the time, him n the other kids. I liked to give em some chewin gum n joke around with em. You know, play with em a little bit. Coz we could do that kind of shit.

You know what am sayin?"

"So what happened? Did he turn around and go back?"

"Uh-uh, he just kept right on walkin towards us with that dumbass smile on his face. The marines was all lookin at me like I was supposed to take care of him. Like he was my problem or somethin."

"So what did you do?"

"I was shoutin like crazy for him to quit comin towards our lines, but the crazy motherfucker just kept right on comin!" said Wells apologetically.

"What happened?"

"I opened up on im. Lit im up. Emptied a full magazine, changed mags real quick n emptied another full magazine up his ass," he said in a rather unrepentant way. "I greased the motherfucker."

"God! And what did he have in the backpack? Did you check afterwards?"

"He probly dint have nothin in the pack. But you cant be takin no chances. You know what am sayin? They was blowin us up all over the goddamn place with their motherfuckin tricks."

"So what happened to the kid?" said Brent, mesmerised.

"Couple of old Vietnamese women came out of the village n took him away. Dressed in black pyjamas n wearing them pointed hats what they wear."

"How did the other marines feel about it?"

"We was a band of brothers, man. We was all motherfuckin John Wayne when we had to be. You know what am sayin? You save their ass coz you know they gonna save yours some day."

"Yeah, I know what you're saying, man. You gotta stick together, right? Did they treat you any better afterwards? I mean, you were the only black guy in the squad, weren't you?"

"I was their goddamn hero. They was all shakin my hand n pattin me on the back, offerin me cigarettes. Those white boys sure as hell dint give me no more shit after that. I can tell you that, some," he said, laughing.

"Yeah, I'll bet," said Brent, loving every word of it, like the kid who had just met his comic-book hero. "And what did you think about their army? I mean, the guys that you were fighting against properly, the North Vietnamese Army. Were they any good?"

"They was damn good! Hell, yeah! You gotta shoot every one of them motherfuckers afore they stop comin at ya. They just keep right on comin at ya til they all motherfuckin dead."

"Did they get close to you? I mean, in the firefights, with all of the firepower that you guys had, how did most of the marines get killed?"

"They always gonna get yo ass somehow. When yer gun jams—specially if you got one of them new motherfuckin M16s—or you out of ammunition, or you shakin like shit tryin to change yo magazine or somethin. They was right on top of you at times and we was overrun. Specially at night. That's when they chose to fight us most of the time. They knew they could lose ten men just to kill one of us n they was still gonna win the goddamn war. And they was right."

"It sounds like hell. How many of them did you kill? Can you remember?"

Wells stared at him with a sad expression on his face.

"Brent, I don't wanna talk no more about the war. War's over, man. We all done with that shit."

Putting his full weight on the walking stick, Wells slowly stood up and limped off to his room, his tongue sticking out, panting for breath and coughing loudly.

Faye was very upset about Wells' story concerning the young boy, so Brent tried to explain things to her.

"That's exactly what the Viet Cong guerrillas used to do. They came out at night and controlled the villages and terrorised the people. They stole food and took children. Most of the villagers hated the VC just as much as they hated the Americans, but there was nothing they could do about it. They just wanted to get on with their lives, but they were caught in the middle of it all."

"Are you saying that the VC were responsible for killing the boy?"

"Probably. They used tactics like that all the time against the people in the villages."

"I don't understand what you mean," she said, looking confused. "He was a young Vietnamese boy, wasn't he?"

"Yes, but his family might have been Catholic or anti-communist or just not interested in taking sides. Maybe they were unwilling to help the guerrillas. The VC would then have used the boy, set him up, knowing that he would be killed. You remember that film, *Apocalypse Now*, don't you? We watched it together in the restaurant at the guest house in Kanchanaburi. I think it was the second night

90

we were there."

"Oh, yes, so anyway, what about it?" she said, trying hard to recall the movie.

"Colonel Kurtz reportedly goes insane out in the jungle. And when Willard comes to kill him, Kurtz tells him the story about how his Green Beret's team go into a Vietnamese village to inoculate the children for polio. Yeah?"

"Yes, I think I remember. He's the one with the bald head, sitting in the dark cave, isn't he?"

"Yeah, so anyway, after Kurtz and his special forces team leave the village, the Viet Cong guerrillas come with machetes and hack off the inoculated arms of the children and lay them in a pile."

"But that's so horrible, they're just innocent little children. How could they do that to their own people?"

"The Vietnam War wasn't about winning territory. It was about winning hearts and minds."

"How can you win somebody's heart by doing something as awful as that?"

"You don't have to. All you have to do is win their mind. The instant that you become scared of them is the instant that they start to control you. Now you can understand what happened to that young boy. That's what Kurtz was talking about: the horror of war. That's why they said he was insane."

"Was Kurtz insane?"

"How can anybody who takes part in a war call you insane? I don't think Kurtz was insane. He just knew the reality of war. And the reality is that wars are won with brutality. How can you seriously say that someone is insane when you have the total insanity of war all around you? He realised the truth, the horror, the sheer horror of it all, as he put it."

Faye lowered her head and sighed, thinking about Wells' stories and Brent's fascination with the whole thing.

"I need to go for a walk and get some fresh air, Brent," she said, feeling down.

"Do you want me to come with you?"

"No. I just want to be alone for a while."

She went to the park and sat on the grass by the lake, closing her eyes and focusing her mind, telling herself she had to toughen her hide and stop dwelling on matters that were outside of her control.

Walking around, she passed by an alley and saw two Vietnamese women pouring boiling water from a kettle onto something in the gutter outside their house. She approached and watched what they were doing.

They grinned at her while motioning to the vermin being exterminated below. On the ground lay a small wire-mesh rodent trap with a baby rat inside, desperately clawing at the bars. Before Faye could react, the women continued to pour the steaming water onto the rat as it squirmed and writhed around, squealing. Faye was horrified, appealing with them to let her take the cage across the road to the park so that she could release the animal there, but her efforts were in vain, and they finished it off with a final dousing.

She walked off feeling very angry, trying to understand the mentality of Buddhist people when it came to the way they treated animals.

Intending to cook a meal for Brent, she browsed through the indoor market with its rows of tiny cubicles, crammed full of goods so tightly stacked that it was difficult to see what they had for sale.

Squeezing past the vendors on either side and ducking under the clothing that hung down in the narrow aisles, she came into the centre where they sold the vegetables and the meat. On one of the stalls there was a large bowl of frogs, taking their dying breath. They had been skinned, and their long elongated faces had been cut off. Still alive, but unable to see, they jumped around helplessly, their throats gaping, like young birds wanting to be fed. Some of them lay motionless, perhaps dead or just too distressed to move. She felt sick and walked quickly out of the market to get some fresh air, no longer interested in cooking a meal.

Making her way to the leisure centre that she had joined, she booked a yoga session for the afternoon and hung around, chatting with a few local girls until it was time to go in.

Brent was nowhere to be seen when she returned to the room, but she didn't have to wait too long. He showed up in a happy vibrant mood.

"Hi, Faye. How is my princess feeling? Are you ok?" he said as he walked in.

"Hi, Brent," she replied, trying to sound as cheerful as he did.

"What's upset you this time, then?"

"No, nothing, really. I was going to cook a meal, but I couldn't stand walking around that market."

"Oh, well, that's excellent news."

"Why?"

"Because I've made you a big pan of beef stew."

"Brent! But you know that I don't eat meat," she said, pulling a long face.

"No problem. I'll eat the meat, and you eat the veggies."

"Oh don't be ridiculous," she huffed, folding her arms.

"I'm just joking with you, Faye. Pumpkin soup with garlic bread. Made it before while you were out. How does that sound?"

"Are you still joking with me?"

"No. It's all cooked and ready to go. Come on, let's go and sit on the terrace. I thought we could eat it up there."

They went up the final level of stairs to the rooftop terrace. Faye sat on one of the deck-loungers at a coffee table, surrounded by pots of tall flowers and plants that stood against the railings on all four sides.

Three short walls and a concrete plinth covered by an elevated tin roof made up the rudimentary kitchen over in the corner, where Brent put the finishing touches to the food on a little gas cooker.

"I've bought some nice cheese to put in the soup, Faye," he said, placing the tray in front of her. "And guess what else I bought?"

"Some decent butter?"

"No," he replied, walking over and opening the door on the fridge. "A bottle of red wine."

"I'm impressed," she said, smiling. "You know, I think you'd make quite a good husband, Brent."

"Oh shit!" he blurted.

"What's wrong?"

"I forgot to get the glasses."

"Never mind, we can use the coffee mugs instead," said Faye.

"No, that's not good enough. Wait here. I'll go downstairs and see if I can get some."

Faye discussed Buddhism with Brent and told him how they treated animals in Vietnam, seemingly caring and loving towards them when they were pets but callous and uncaring when they were merely vermin or food.

"You're right," said Brent, pouring the wine into the glasses that

93

he had managed to borrow. "They do seem to have two faces, especially for the dogs. I read this crazy story not long ago about a Vietnamese man who had invited some guests round for dinner one day. And guess what was on the menu?"

"Dog meat," she replied, as though she already knew the answer.

"That's right. But not just any old dog meat. Dog meat from poor old Fido!"

"Are you trying to say that he ate his pet dog?"

"That's what the story said."

"Well, it must have been a joke or something. People don't do that. They don't eat their pets. He could have bought dog meat down at the market. It's quite common in Vietnam."

"Well, this guy did. And I can show you the magazine article if you don't believe me."

"Why on earth would he eat his pet dog, Brent?" she said scoffingly. "That's a ridiculous story. You don't seriously believe that, do you?"

"Wait until you've heard the full story, Faye. This wasn't just any old dinner party. This was a dinner party designed to impress. The man who had been invited to dinner was a high ranking official, somebody with power. So the guy who butchered his dog was obviously hoping to get promotion or something. We call it kissing arse. Do you know what I mean? Apparently, it's seen as a great honour in Vietnam when you sacrifice your pet dog for someone to eat."

"Whatever next!" she remarked, looking astounded.

"By the way, you know how you were asking me about Buddhism and reincarnation? Well, talking about dogs and that remark about kissing arse has just made me realise where I get my fetish from."

"I didn't know you had a fetish. What is it?" she said naively.

"Sniffing bottoms," he said with a guilty look on his face. "I've been wondering for years why I have this urge to sniff bottoms, and the answer has just been revealed to me. That's what is known as instant karma, Faye."

"Is this another one of your jokes, Brent?" she said, smiling.

"No, honestly. In my previous life I used to be a saint."

"A saint?"

"Yes, a Saint Bernard," he said, trying hard not to laugh.

"Well, you're not sniffing my bottom, Brent, if that's what you're trying to suggest. So you can forget all about it, thank you."

They opened the second bottle of wine, gazing at the stars through the warm air of the night. Darcy and his girlfriend Leah came up to the terrace with their friend Norman. They had invited him knowing that he rarely socialised, hoping that the break from his monotonous life glued to a computer screen and his obsession with conspiracy theories might do him some good. He lived in the room opposite theirs and was the reclusive suspicious kind who rarely, if ever, laughed or joked. He wore thin round glasses, and his short, neatly combed black hair, parted and slicked to one side, together with his thin, tight lips, gave him the air of a Second World War Gestapo officer. He took a chair and sat slightly to one side, quietly observing Faye as she laughed and joked with Darcy.

Dave, the guy renting the room opposite Wells, came up the stairs carrying a crate of beer and took it over to the fridge.

"Wells doesn't think he can make it up without having a heart attack, so he's not joining us," he said. "Help yourself to the beer."

"I can't get my head around that one, Leah," said Brent, continuing the discussion. "You're saying that God has always been there, like there was no beginning. I mean, how can something have always been there? That's nuts crazy. It's just not possible. That's enough to drive you insane if you think about it."

"It's difficult to understand because everything that you have ever known has always had a beginning and an end," she replied.

"I prefer the idea of Buddhism. I think we evolved," said Brent.

"Isn't that a bit of a contradiction? You told me that you'd seen a ghost, and you believe they're real," said Faye.

"Yeah, ghosts are real, for sure. Damned thing scared the shit out of me. Why is it a contradiction, anyway?"

"If we had evolved then where did we get the spirit from?"

"We got it from the liquor shop, didn't we?" he said, laughing to himself.

Faye smiled. She liked Brent's dry humour. It made her feel good.

"Seriously, Brent. How can you have a spirit if you evolved?"

"We developed arms, legs, eyes, ears, everything else, so why can't we develop a spirit?" he argued.

"And what would be the purpose of humans evolving a spirit?" she replied, smiling.

"I don't know. I haven't really thought about it. I suppose it might come in handy, one day."

"One day? What, such as the day you die, for example?" she said, laughing loudly.

"Are you taking the piss, Faye?"

"Probably," she said, laughing even louder.

"What about you, Norman? What are you? Atheist? Buddhist? Sadist?" said Darcy.

"Well, actually I'm thinking of suing my parents," he said with a serious expression on his face.

"What for?" said Leah.

"As much as I can get, plus both of their houses."

"No, I mean for what reason?"

"For putting me on this wretched planet."

"They gave you the gift of life!"

"Do you think so?" he said glumly. "No, in my opinion I think they gave me a life sentence in hell on earth, actually."

"Have you always been miserable?" said Dave.

"Well, how would you describe it then?" replied Norman.

"Listen Norman, the sky isn't always filled with grey clouds. The sun always shines through sooner or later."

"Have you got that, *sunshine*? And don't forget, there's always the pot of gold at the end of the rainbow. That's worth living for. Isn't it?" said Darcy, impersonating a violinist.

"Life is definitely not all doom and gloom," said Leah.

"In my opinion, we're not just a product of evolution. This has been planned for us. We're all here to suffer. I can see that you're wearing a cross around your neck, Faye, so maybe you would like to explain it."

"Explain what, Norman?" said Faye.

"Well, let's start with you."

"Me?"

"Yes. I mean females, girls, women, the opposite sex. Why didn't He make them equal to men?"

"Well, first of all, I think you'll find that *He* is actually a *She*, and that's the reason why She made females superior to males and not as equals," replied Faye, trying to lighten up the conversation with humour.

"You're wishing on a star if you think that God is a female, Faye," said Darcy.

"God transcends gender. He's omni-everything," said Brent.

"Are you frustrated about not being able to get a girlfriend? Is that what it is?" said Leah, smiling.

"What makes you think I don't have a girlfriend?" said Norman, repeatedly rubbing his fingers across his forehead, as if to erase the frowning.

"Bitches are just as capable as men. They can do anything that we can do," said Dave.

Norman revelled in the argument, gesturing with his hands to get his point across.

"But this isn't about physical strength. When do you ever see women approaching men to chat them up and ask them if they'd like a drink, or a dance, or a ride home? Never. They're wired differently. They've got a different software program running in their head."

"So you're saying that if there is a God, then He obviously wanted some drama on the job. Otherwise, He would have made men and women harmonious with each other. Yeah, I can see your point. So, bottom line is, He's… er, *She's* a bit of a trouble maker. Case solved, Leah?" said Darcy, turning to look at his girlfriend.

"Let's put it this way," said Norman. "We're definitely not in heaven, are we?"

"I'm quite enjoying it actually," said Dave. "Maybe you just expect too much, Norman."

"Wait until you're an old man. See if you can still say the same when you're eighty. You won't be sitting with any young females when you're that old."

"I reckon that will depend on how rich I am when I'm eighty," replied Dave, kissing his girlfriend.

"Totally," agreed Darcy.

"We have to grow old. That's the way it is," said Leah. "It happens to everyone. I guess we start to die from the moment we're born, in a way."

"That's the way it is because we're in hell, and we're here to suffer," said Norman. "Look at that old woman who sells the lottery tickets. She's further proof that I'm right."

"The hunchback with the bow legs who gets around on a walking frame? Yeah, she's well past her sell-by date," said Dave, laughing.

"If you think about it, we could have been created to show our age in a different way, so that we all got to keep our youthful looks and physiques."

"You mean, everybody still looks young regardless of how old they really are?" said Leah.

"Exactly," said Norman. "You reach eighteen and then you stop aging in appearance. No wrinkled skin, no grey hair…"

"So how would you know someone's real age?" said Faye.

"Age wouldn't be of any real importance, but they could have different coloured eyes: blue eyes at eighteen, green at twenty-eight, brown at thirty-eight…"

"I think Hitler was working on something like that, wasn't he?" said Brent.

"Great idea, but the fact is that we evolved. There is no God and this is heaven and hell for everyone, depending on their circumstances," said Dave. "I stopped believing in God after my sister died of cancer when she was young."

"How old was she?"

"She was fourteen."

"Just because someone dies young doesn't mean there isn't a God," said Norman.

"How could God let a young girl die like that?"

"It depends which way you look at it. Like I just said, we've all been given a life sentence in hell. She was released early. Simple as that. If anything, God was being kind to her."

"That could fit, actually," said Brent.

"Fit what? Your head?" said Faye.

"Yes. At least it will do tomorrow."

"Why?"

"I'm shaving all of my hair off tomorrow and buying that orange robe that we saw."

"Oh, Brent, stop it!" she said, laughing.

"What are you laughing at? I'm serious."

"Brent has just seen the light," said Dave. "And Norman is the prophet, lighting the way with his dim torch."

The hour was getting late, and so they retired to their room. Turning the light off and the air conditioning on, Faye told Brent to go to bed and face the other way while she undressed and slipped into her pink pyjamas.

Faye tried to sleep, but Brent was restless.

"What are you doing, Brent?"

"I'm going asleep. Why?"

"I can feel your foot touching mine. Stop it."

"Ok."

"Are you on your side of the bed?"

"I don't know. Pass me the tape measure."

"What?"

"I said pass me the tape measure. I'll check whether I've crossed the halfway mark or not."

"If you can't behave yourself, Brent, then I'm sorry but you'll just have to sleep on the floor," she said, bashing her fluffy pillow to flatten it and pulling the blanket over her shoulders.

"Are you tired, Faye?"

"Why are you asking me that, Brent?"

"There's something on my mind. I just thought you might like to talk about it with me."

"I'm not interested in talking about sex, Brent, if that's what you want."

"No... no, it's not about that," he said, pausing to think. "Have you always been like that, Faye?"

"Been like what?"

"I don't know. I suppose... how can I put it, something like just not interested in having a bit of fun in bed."

"What do you think I am, Brent, some kind of Saigon taxi-girl or something?"

"No, of course not," he replied, laughing. "I was just wondering whether these traditional Vietnamese women have had some kind of influence on you. Like, *we're not married, so we can't do that sort of thing because, heavens above, what would the neighbours think?*" he said, affecting an aristocratic accent.

"I was raised as a Catholic if that's any help."

"I know. Don't get me wrong, you're a nice girl, Faye, a really nice girl."

"Thank you."

"Do you want to have children one day, Faye," he said after a moment of reflection.

"Is that what's on your mind, Brent?"

"No. Well, yes, and no. I mean, kind of, yes."

"What's bothering you?" she said, turning over to face him.

"I'm just so worried that I wouldn't be a good father. And I saw something today that really put me off ever wanting to have children anyway, I think."

"What did you see?"

"I saw a young girl, no more than about eight or nine. She had no arms. I felt embarrassed, guilty, sad. She was walking towards me and smiled at me, but I couldn't smile back. I think I pretended not to notice. That's a pathetic thing to do, isn't it? I felt like shit. It pissed me off and ruined my day for a while."

"It's very sad, I know. But it's not your fault, and you can't blame yourself for it. There are quite a few deformed people in Vietnam. They blame it on the chemical weapons that were used against them during the war."

"I know. Agent Orange. But I don't know how I would be able to handle it if I ever had a deformed child like that. It really worries me to think about it because I really want to have a family."

"We can ask God for a healthy child, Brent."

"We? You mean—"

"Brent, go asleep. It's getting late," she said, turning over to face the other way and pulling the blanket up.

They slept until noon the following morning, and after coffee, Faye went off to do her yoga. Brent hung around the house, getting to know the other tenants and organizing a rooftop party for the evening.

Darcy and Brent kicked off the party around mid-afternoon, but the girls were busy doing their own thing, and most of the bottles had already been drunk by the time they decided to join. The lads set off to replenish the stocks, saying they would be back shortly.

They returned after sunset and enticed Wells into joining the rooftop bash, taking hold of his arms and helping him to climb the stairs. Leah and Faye were sitting closely together, laughing and chatting endlessly, while Norman sat to one side with his laptop resting on his knees, busily updating skeptics with unsubstantiated evidence about the conspiracy theories that he was obsessed with.

"Hey, Darcy, we're dying of thirst over here. I thought you said you were going to get some more booze," shouted Leah.

"Yeah, relax, honey. Reinforcements are on the way. Have you got the cash card there?"

"Brent, what are you doing? Why have you been such a long time?" said Faye.

"Yeah, sorry about that. We got talking to a couple of guys down at the pub. It's one of their birthdays today. You know how it is," he replied drunkenly.

"Well, could we have some red wine, please, if it's not too much trouble?"

"Hey, Leah. Will you wear something special for me tonight, darling?" said Darcy, grinning.

"What, like a fancy dress party, you mean?" she said.

"No, it's a bit more private than that, babe. I'll let you in on it later."

Leah's eyes glinted with expectation, even though she hated being referred to as darling. She tried to imagine what it could be. Her mind wandered, seeing visions of black lacy lingerie and other items of intimate feminine apparel. After all, their relationship had not been going too well recently, not since she had insinuated to him that she thought he might be gay, or at least bisexual. This could be a moment for them to let cupid fly.

Her mind wandered further and was now firmly stuck in the clouds, dreaming of a candlelit dinner on a table for two, quietly secluded in the corner, a single bottle of rosé on the white linen, a single red rose in the glass vase. An English rose for a night, shining in amour.

Brent and Darcy headed back to the bar, promising to return soon with the drinks.

They returned with a couple of scrotes, Stoner and Fungy, whom they had met earlier that day, and they were all in a jovial mood, heavily drunk.

Leah was disappointed that her idea of a tête-à-tête at the restaurant didn't look like it was going to happen and made herself some spaghetti in the kitchen.

She sat down at the table opposite Brent and quietly ate the food. Stoner was starving and made a remark about the spaghetti.

"That reminds me of the time I dumped a tape worm in the bog a few months back," he said. "Must have been at least ten feet long if you stuck all the pieces back together. Never even knew I had it in my stomach until I swallowed some tablets by mistake. Probably got it eating raw pork when I was in Hanoi."

Leah glared at Darcy, throwing the spoon in the bowl and pushing the meal to one side. She was glad that dinner in a restaurant had never happened. It would have been an embarrassing scene anyway. She was well aware of drunken Darcy's penchant for breaking wind as loudly as he possibly could, especially in restaurants and in earshot of other people. All the same, she was curious about what it was that he wanted her to wear and offered hints.

Darcy had been waiting for his moment to deliver the punchline to maximum effect, and having his audience at hand, he pulled a used cork from a wine bottle out of his pocket.

"I thought you wanted me to wear something for you?" said Leah.

"I do," he said. "Here it is."

"A cork? What is it, some kind of lucky charm? You want me to put it around my neck, or something?"

"Not exactly, babe. The fact is, you farted in bed last night and I had to literally crawl on my hands and knees, gasping for air, to open a piggin window. I thought I was going to pass out before I got there."

The amusement left Leah's face, and she stood up quickly, pushing her chair back.

"Is that right?" she said angrily. "Well, I am disappointed. I thought you wanted me to wear a strap-on dildo so that you could fulfill your lifelong desire of being banged up the arse, you fat slob."

The lads thought it was hilarious, but Darcy didn't look too amused, especially now that Leah was standing over him, slapping him round the head. The embarrassment had turned full circle and he was beginning to regret his little prank.

Norman folded up his laptop and mumbled some excuse about how he had something important to attend to, smiling weakly and leaving the party.

"I can play the first three notes of 'God Save The Queen' on a trumpet," said Fungy, taking another bite of his baguette and another swig of the vodka, adding even more breadcrumbs to the rim of the bottle.

"So what?" said Stoner, taking the bottle of vodka out of his hand.

"So the trumpet just happens to be up me arse while I'm playing it," he replied, expressing pride in his achievement.

"That's really impressive," said Faye sarcastically. "You don't look like the musical type. Have you ever thought about entering one of those talent competitions?"

"Do you think three notes would be enough to get me through the audition?" said Fungy, barely able to speak properly, his mouth full of omelette baguette and his head full of grog.

"Well, I suppose you could always eat more beans and practice more. And tell me, do you and Stoner share the trumpet the same way that you share everything else?"

Stoner stared at Faye with a horrified look on his face, his mouth agape.

"Whatever happened to that old trumpet, Stoner? Did we leave it in that last squat what we had in Leeds?" said Fungy, taking another swig of vodka from the bottle.

"Are you not going to eat that spaghetti?" said Stoner.

"No, I'm full," replied Leah.

"Pass it over here, then," he said. "Shame to waste it."

Stoner and Fungy were a couple of carefree, couldn't-care-less English drifters, the type who thought nothing of sleeping rough but thought of everything when it came to scrounging enough money for the next drink. Alcohol was their priority.

Apparently, they were both on the verge of travelling north to take up teaching jobs that they had been offered and would be on their way just as soon as they had the price of a bus ticket.

They were shabbily dressed and unshaven. Fungy's hair was greasy and unkempt, and he had sleep in the corners of his eyes. He was also a heavy smoker and had badly stained yellow fingers and teeth. His dirty fingernails were actually so long that they could only be described as claws. Owing to the open sores on his face, arms, and legs, he was probably a heroin user too.

Stoner seemed a bit different. He wasn't as street as Fungy, and from the tone of his voice and the level of language that he used, he seemed a bit more sophisticated. Probably, he had been educated well, had come from a respectable home that wasn't short of money, and had chosen to live that way just for the kick of seeing how far he could take somebody for a mug. He more than likely hated the idea of working for a living, too.

Leah knew why Darcy had allowed them to latch onto him. They were entertaining with their stories and could talk incessantly. He saw them as drinking buddies. She saw them as what they actually were.

Faye was not happy at all about the company that Brent had brought back either and stood up, telling him that she was going to lie down for a while. She gave Leah a warm hug and then went downstairs to her room.

Dave and his girlfriend Suri joined the party, followed shortly after by a guy who seemed to appear from nowhere. Nobody knew him. He was in his early thirties, had fairly short black hair and sported a thick horseshoe type moustache that didn't really seem to fit his callow face. Being slightly built and medium height, he nevertheless had a habit of puffing his chest out, adopting a very macho stance with a wide, confident-looking grin on his face. He wore dark blue combat pants, light brown desert boots and a multi pocketed beige shirt with both sleeves rolled up. Wrapped around his neck and tucked inside his shirt was a black and white chequered cotton scarf.

"Oi, Dave, are you not going to introduce us to your mate then?" said Darcy.

"I thought he was Brent's mate," he replied.

"No, never seen him before."

"Just call me Mac," said the stranger.

"Live here, do you?" said Darcy.

"No. I used to. I just came round to see the woman."

"So what do you do?"

"I'm in the military," said Mac, speaking in a very clipped manner, like a witness who was providing evidence in a court of law.

"Oh, really. Army, is it?"

"I can't say too much. I'm still active. Returning to The Middle East soon."

"One of the boys?" said Dave.

Mac grinned but said nothing.

"Hey, Mac, can I ask you a question?" said Dave, staring at him suspiciously.

"That would depend," replied Mac.

"Depend on what?"

"Operational protocol, codes of practice, and such. Anyway, what was the question?"

"You've fired an AK-47, right?" said Dave.

"Only in action. It's the enemy's favourite assault rifle," he replied, grinning.

"Tell me something. The selector lever on an AK-47 has three positions: safety, single shot, and fully automatic rapid fire, yeah?"

"That's correct," said Mac, continuing in his contrite voice.

"So when you take the lever off safety, which position does it move onto next? Single shot or fully automatic?"

Mac wiped his brow with the rag that was draped around his throat and stared at him.

"That's classified information," he eventually replied.

"I fired an AK-47 down at the Cu Chi Tunnels firing range a few weeks ago," said Darcy. "I put it straight onto rapid and emptied the whole magazine in one go. Man, it was gone in seconds. I was hoping to fire an RPG as well, but they didn't have any."

"What's an RPG?" said Leah.

"Rocket Propelled Grenade. You hold it on your shoulder and fire it like a bazooka. I heard that in Cambodia you can buy a water buffalo off a farmer and blow it to pieces with one. Don't know if it's true or not."

"Oh my god!" shouted Leah. "How sick is that? Are you serious? I'm beginning to wonder just what it is that I see in you, Darcy boy."

"My grandfather was in the original special forces unit, SOE, during the Second World War," said Dave. "His mission was to infiltrate a Japanese held island in the Pacific, destroy a supply dump, and kill all the Japs."

"Yes, I know that kind of operation perfectly well. Was it a success, or was he compromised, the way we normally are?" said Mac in his serious tone.

"He destroyed everything, blew everything to pieces, killed all of the Japs, and then made his way to the beach ready for extraction by submarine."

"And he came out looking like a hero," said Mac.

"No. As he waited on the beach, in the dark, a coconut fell forty feet from a tree and hit him square on the head, killing him instantly. He thought that he was safely far enough away from the trees, but he hadn't noticed that this particular tree was arched over like a banana, as bent as your dick, Mac."

"Ha! Leave him alone, you rotten bastard," said Darcy, laughing.

"I have to split," said Mac. "Got business to take care of."

"Walter Mitty, you have to go," said Dave in a low voice.

"What?" said Mac.

"I said what a pity you have to go."

Faye grew restless alone in the room and decided to go for a walk. She wandered down the maze of alleyways until she came to the heart of the backpacker area. It was Saturday night, and both ends of Bui Vien Street had been cordoned off to traffic.

Throngs of people packed the street, slowly weaving their way around each other as they passed in opposite directions.

In between the hotels, restaurants, and bars, the sidewalks had been filled with small tables and stools by the local Vietnamese, who rented every available space to set up their beer stalls after the shops had closed.

She stopped outside a makeshift bar where a large portable speaker had been set up, blasting out loud music for the young Vietnamese who paid a small fee to pass the microphone around and sing karaoke. She spotted Norman sitting by himself, drinking coke and looking miserable. He noticed her and waved, trying hard to force a convincing smile. He stood up and walked over.

"Hi Faye, how are you?"

"I'm fine, just out for a stroll."

"Are you with Brent? I mean, are you alone?"

"No, he's back there getting drunk with his mates."

"You don't sound at all happy, Faye."

"I'm ok," she said, glumly, lowering her face.

"It's very noisy here, isn't it? Do you want to walk a bit further down there?"

"Yes, alright."

"Have you eaten yet?"

"No, not yet."

"There's a quiet bar at the end of the street, Faye. I think we should go and get a drink and some food."

They passed by some young, scruffy, barefoot Vietnamese kids doing their fire-breathing act, spitting fuel from their mouths onto a burning stick, sending flames high into the air to earn a few coins; and an illusionist, with a very young child standing on a box in the street, performing cheap tricks in a magic show. Further along, some musicians were jamming with a guitar and drums, playing rock covers. The whole street was buzzing.

"Here we are then," said Norman as they arrived at the open-fronted bar. "We can still sit outside, but at least we can have a conversation without having to shout. I find those other bars are just too noisy. Don't you?"

"Yes, I suppose they are," she said.

"So... here we are, Faye."

"Yes, here we are."

"So… would you like to eat something? I mean, food that is, I wasn't trying to suggest…"

"Those kebabs look nice," she said, pointing to the food stall next to the bar. "I think I'll go and have a look at what they've got."

"No, you stay there, Faye. Let me do it for you. I mean, go and see what they've got, you know? I wasn't trying to…" he said awkwardly.

"Is that calamari? I think it is," she said, smiling.

"Yes, they've got all sorts of food. I'll get some okra and tofu as well. How does that sound?"

Norman returned and sat down next to Faye, waiting for the food to arrive. Rubbing his forehead, he alternated between staring at his feet and looking around the room.

"Do you have a girlfriend, Norman?"

"Well, interesting that you should say that, Faye, because I want to ask you something."

"I meant, do you have a Vietnamese girlfriend?" she said quickly.

"Actually, you know, I've had a lot of girlfriends here in Vietnam, but I don't think they're the right type for me, Faye."

"Why not?"

"It's just such a different culture. They expect you to look after their entire family: parents, brothers, sisters, long lost relatives. And their family is always as big as your wallet. If you've got a penny left over they will find something for you to spend it on. It's very frustrating, Faye. It really is."

"Maybe you should try another country then."

"Or maybe I should meet someone like you, Faye."

He smiled at her, and she replied in kind. But she was smiling out of pity. She had noticed the way he always sat with his legs closed tightly together with his hands resting on them, his thumbs tucked inside his clasping fingers.

Thick plumes of greyish smoke billowed off the barbecue grill as the woman at the kebab stall next to them brushed more oil onto the pork cutlets. Their food arrived and they moved aside the drinks to make room for it.

"Try one of these, Faye," said Norman, passing her a grilled chicken's foot.

"Oh my god! It looks like a child's hand," she said, rejecting it.

"As I was saying, Faye, don't you think that you should be with someone who is a bit more responsible?"

"What do you mean?"

"I mean, well, Brent is a nice guy of course, but don't you think

107

he's a little too immature for you? You're a smart, educated girl, Faye. Is he really the best match for you? That's what you have to ask yourself."

"Can you think of anyone who would be more suitable for me?"

"Well, as you know, I'm looking for a nice girl to be with."

"I thought you were a misogynist, Norman."

"No, of course I'm not! I'm all for equality. In fact, I think that women should pay for men. They've been selling us their bodies for millennia, in one way or another. Give them the jobs, let them do the work and earn the money. Then they will have to pay us for sex. That's what I say. No offence, of course."

"You have a very low opinion of women. Don't you?"

"I've been in South East Asia too long. That's what it is. I can't trust women anymore. Not that I ever did, though, come to think of it. By the way, I just want to add something to the conversation that we had about heaven and my opinion about us being in hell here on earth. No, I mean, I understand that even if God doesn't exist and there is nothing after you die, then there could still be a kind of heaven for you when you're dead."

"What do you mean, exactly?"

"Well, heaven is a place—*I assume*—where there is no suffering, everything is bliss. So when you're dead, and that's it, no afterlife, then I suppose you would be totally at peace, wouldn't you? You would be dead, in a hole, and you wouldn't experience anything. Which in a sense is totally free from suffering. Wouldn't you agree?"

"Yes, I suppose so. Can we go now? I've got a bit of a headache."

"Oh. You've got a headache. Well, I suppose…"

"Could you make the bill, please?" said Faye, turning to speak to to the waitress.

"Faye, I—"

"It's ok, don't worry about it. I will pay."

"If you'd let me finish, I was going to show you how much of a gentleman I am. I was going to say let's split the bill fifty-fifty."

Back at the party, the boys had bought a small bag of grass, and they were all in the mood for getting smashed.

"We need some skins to roll one up. You got any, Brent?" said Fungy.

"Cigarette papers? No, we haven't got any. Me and Faye don't smoke fags."

"You don't smoke fags? What, not even little ones?" said Stoner, smirking.

"Got anythink we can use? Like some thin paper from inside a book or a dictionary?" said Fungy.

"Wait a minute. Yeah, Faye's got a little bible that she travels with. There are tons of blank pages in it," said Brent.

"Yeah, sweet. Go and get that."

"No, hang on, that's a bit disrespectful," said Brent.

"Dude, they're just blank pages, and that's why the Good Lord put them in the book. He thinks of everythink."

"No, listen, I know I've been getting in touch with my spiritual side since I came to Asia, but if Faye ever found out then I would *literally* be getting in touch with it! Know what I mean?"

"We don't need papers. Give me that empty coke can there. I'll make a bong out of it," said Stoner.

Pressing a dent in the side of the can, he took a sharp knife and pierced a few holes in it. Fungy mulled up some of the marijuana which Stoner then placed in the dent. Holding the can to his mouth, horizontally, sealing his lips around the opening, he drew in the smoke as he lit the weed with his lighter.

Holding the smoke in his lungs for as long as he could caused him to make guttural noises, smirking without being humorous. He exhaled and put the bong on the table. Fungy reloaded it with double the amount and took a couple of direct hits that blew his head off. Brent followed and made a complete zombie out of himself as well.

Stoner was in top gear with his story telling, but nobody was really listening. Fungy's eyeballs were rolling around in his head, and the stars up above were starting to spin out of control for Brent. He made his way down to his room.

Brent was alone. He turned the lights off, opened the wide doors to his balcony, and lay down.

Lying on his bed, he stared at the ceiling and watched the fan wobble as it spun around with his head, creaking with old age as it shifted the warm air.

Through the narrow gap in the curtains, something caught his attention across the alley at the small unlit room on top of the building opposite. He thought he saw something move. He stared into the darkness intently, unsure whether the flashes of light were just tricks of the mind brought on by smoking marijuana.

109

He could see that the door to the room, which led onto a small terrace, was open and again thought that he glimpsed, fleetingly, a pale, shadowy figure.

His mind wandered, obsessed with his fascination of the afterlife. He closed his eyes and thought again about what Leah had said to him about God: There had been no beginning; God had always been there.

He tried to imagine something capable of having an existence without having a beginning: something that had always existed. But it was too much, too complex for him, and it began to destroy his head. He dismissed the whole notion of it as impossible.

Opening his eyes, he saw a young Vietnamese woman in the room opposite. She was wearing a white Ao Dai, an ankle-length traditional dress, and she was standing with her back to him, holding a mirror, combing her long straight black hair.

She switched off the main light and sat on the side of her bed, her face concealed, her slender figure silhouetted by the glow from the red light emanating from the small Buddhist altar in the room.

She was inviting, and he wanted to reach out and touch her. She was close, but he wanted her closer.

Brent closed his eyes and drifted asleep, letting his mind lead him to The Zen Master, for only he had the knowledge and knew the truth.

Chapter 13

The Zen Master

You must scale this three thousand foot vertical rock face, follow the path of enlightenment and enter the black hole, said the voice in Brent's head. There you will see a tiger. Do not be afraid of the tiger. It will know everything about you, for it has witnessed all of your actions and listened to all of your thoughts.

Entering the black hole, he saw the tiger, old and wise-looking, waiting for him in the darkness. He approached it slowly, his head bowed, his bare feet piously taking gentle steps forward as it purred.

With each step he took, the tiger's face seemed to morph, its eyes narrowing, its whiskers growing longer.

It growled, and he approached no further. Kneeling before it, he did not dare look into its eyes. In the darkness, out of the corner of his eye, he glimpsed its face, the face of an old man with long flowing white hair and beard.

You have come in search of knowledge, said the master. My way intrigues you and yet mystifies you. You can not understand how I have always been here, for everything you have ever known has had a beginning.

I can not believe that your being had no creation. Where did you come from? said Brent.

How is it possible for me to have come from somewhere when I have always been here?

You are deliberately trying to confuse me.

No, replied the master. You are confusing yourself. Before you can begin to understand, you must open your mind and free it from the constraints that you have placed within it. Let me explain something to you. There was a man who had two daughters. They were twins, identical in every way except that one of them was born without arms. When they were young girls, the normal child wanted to learn how to draw pictures and paint, but the father steadfastly refused to teach her. As they grew older, the normal child wanted to learn how to write, but again the father steadfastly refused. And as the years passed, the normal child wanted to learn how to play musical instruments, but once more the father steadfastly refused. Now you must give me your thoughts about the father.

I think he was uncaring. He neglected his children and didn't show them any love. He was not a good father, said Brent.

You have drawn your conclusion from your inability to think. Therein lies a great weakness in you. It will be your downfall if you fail to learn the lesson that I am teaching you. The father had so much love for both of his daughters that he could not bear to see the pain in the eyes of the child whom he could not teach.

I need you to explain where you came from. I want to know, said Brent.

You would like to believe that there was something before my existence came to be, just to ease your mind. Would you not?

Yes, I would. You say that you have always been there, but that is not possible.

You are correct. There *was* something before my existence, said the master.

What was there before you existed? Tell me.

Before I existed there was nothing.

Nothing? You just said there was something!

Close your eyes, think of nothing, and tell me what you see.

I see darkness, flashes of light, stars.

Take away the flashes of light. What do you see?

Darkness, stars.

Remove the stars. What do you see?

Darkness.

Now you must remove the darkness.

I can't remove the darkness.

What do you see?

I see a vast expanse of darkness, so black, so dark, no light.

Think again. What do you see?

Nothing. I see nothing.

Describe again what it looks like.

Blackness. Total darkness. Nothing.

Do you understand that you have just described nothing?

Yes, of course.

Then you must surely understand that nothing is something.

How can nothing be something?

You have just described what nothing looks like.

You're confusing me!

Words can not describe that which does not exist.

It exists in my mind!

What exists in your mind?

Nothing!

Can you not see how confused you are?

Brent screamed loudly, sitting bolt upright on the bed, sweat coursing down his face, his head groggy from the dream.

The room was in complete darkness, and he began to panic, with no recollection of where he was.

He slowly put his feet onto the floor and stood up, holding out his hands in front of him, gingerly edging his way around lest he fall down a hole or stumble over the edge of something.

Totally blind, he fumbled around until eventually he touched a wall. Sliding his hands up and down on the wall, he cautiously edged his way forward. Taking another step forward, he heard a sound that made him freeze. Was that the sound of a bolt being drawn on a rifle, he asked himself. He raised his hands as if to surrender.

Opening the door and taking her key out of the lock, Faye entered the room and turned on the light.

"Faye!"

"Brent! What on earth are you doing?"

"I'm… yes," he said, totally dazed, lowering his arms.

"Brent, are you alright?"

"Of course," he replied, sounding very unsure.

"I think you should sit down, Brent, because you don't look alright. Have you been smoking drugs again?"

"I need a drink, Faye. Is there any water?"

"It's all gone," she said, looking in the fridge. "Sit down. I'll go and see if there's any in the kitchen."

The party on the terrace had finished, and apart from Wells, everybody had left. He was slumped in the deck-lounger staring into the distance, no doubt recalling haunting images of firefights in the far-off jungles all those years ago during the war. He didn't notice as she walked over to the fridge to get the water.

She went down to the bathroom and soaked a small flannel to

wipe Brent's face, which had lost all of its colour and turned pale.

Closing the balcony doors and drawing the curtains, Faye switched off the lights and got undressed. She changed into her nightie and got into bed, moving closer to Brent and placing the palm of her hand on his forehead.

"Was it a nightmare?" she said.

"I don't remember much about it. I just remember climbing something really high and being scared of falling."

"Brent, I've noticed that you've been spending a lot of time down at Wells' room over the past few days. You're not using heroin, are you?"

"No, of course not. Why do you say that?"

"You just don't look the same anymore. And you've been sick in the toilet again, haven't you?"

"What do you mean I don't look the same anymore?"

"Your eyes, your complexion. You can't hide it, Brent. You do understand that heroin addicts need someone to lean on when they run out of money, don't you? You might just find yourself paying for him if you let yourself fall into that trap. The woman told me that he borrows from her all the time until he receives his next government handout."

"I'll stop going down there, Faye. I promise."

Chapter 14

Cu Chi

The next morning revealed another hot sunny day in Saigon. Faye showered and went up to the terrace to make some coffee.

"Put your jeans on, Faye," said Brent.

"What for?"

"I'm taking you to the Cu Chi tunnels today, and I reckon it's going to be pretty grubby down there."

"I don't think I want to go down the tunnel. I don't like tunnels. Maybe I will just wait for you outside."

"No, Faye, listen. This is a must do. Trust me, you'll love it."

"What about the spiders and snakes?"

"Don't worry about the spiders and snakes. They'll be too busy chasing the scorpions."

"Don't say that!"

"Faye, come on, get your jeans on."

"*Please!*"

"Sorry. Faye, *please* go and put your jeans on."

"I'm drinking my coffee, so you'll just have to wait, Brent."

Brent paused and reflected on the situation, smiling to himself.

"What are you grinning at?" she said.

"Well, it's not very often that I'm trying to get you to put your jeans *on,* is it?"

They hired a motorbike for the day and set off for the town of Cu Chi, about thirty miles to the west of Saigon.

It was a busy double-lane highway, at times narrowing down to just one lane on either side, and the ride was hazardous.

Oncoming vehicles, large trucks, and buses blasting their horns pulled out to overtake each other, forcing their motorbike onto the gravel by the side of the road. Driving in Vietnam was like playing one big game of Chicken.

There were two tunnel sites, and the one they were heading for was past the town, further out at Ben Duoc. Brent had chosen this site because it was authentic, unlike the one at Ben Dinh that had been modified to facilitate tourists.

They walked through the rubber plantation with its rows of neatly lined trees, each one slowly yielding tiny drops of white latex, seeping from a scar into a small bowl.

The close proximity of the tall trees standing together shaded the land, apart from a single beam of bright sunlight that shone onto the ground ahead. Being superstitious, Brent saw it as a sign, a pointer, and walked towards it. He rummaged through the foliage expecting to find something left over from the war but found nothing.

During the Vietnam War, the area had been a heavily contested battlefield, and the tunnel complex had been a vast network, stretching a combined two hundred miles, connecting the hamlets together for the Viet Cong fighters via the underground.

Brent and Faye continued until the plantation gave way to jungle, and they came to the main entrance to the tunnels. They were the only visitors.

Choosing not to hire a Vietnamese guide, they entered the tunnel at one of the original trapdoors, a perfectly concealed small removable cover on the ground, eighteen inches long and twelve inches wide.

Brent lifted the cover, placed it to one side, and awkwardly squeezed his way in, dropping down about four feet. He moved horizontally into the tunnel and called for Faye. As she lowered herself down, Brent grabbed her legs and pulled her in.

Dim lights, strung every twelve feet, barely guided the way as they arduously crawled on their hands and knees moving slowly forward.

It was dark, claustrophobic, airless, and extremely hot, and after crawling for some distance, Brent came to a point where the tunnel diverged and took the one leading off to the left.

He called out to Faye to check that she was alright but heard no reply. Turning around, he could see that she wasn't there and so made his way back, repeatedly calling her name.

At the point where the tunnels branched, he looked around but couldn't see her. He shouted her name again but got no answer.

Straight ahead of him, barely visible in the dark, he saw her. She had passed out and was lying face down.

Scurrying over to where she lay, he grabbed her arm, shaking it and calling her name to get a response. Grabbing hold of her ankles, he dragged her backwards. Sweat ran down his forehead and stung his eyes. His shirt was sodden and stuck to him awkwardly.

He pulled her back to the point where he had turned left and she had turned right. Climbing over her, he took hold of her arms and dragged her, inch by inch, back down the tunnel to where they had entered.

Completely exhausted, he finally made it to the entrance and sat Faye in an upright position, gently slapping her face. She rolled her eyes, took in deep breaths of fresh air, and came around.

Having recovered some of his strength, Brent squeezed past Faye and clambered out of the tunnel, telling her to follow.

Lacking energy and still feeling sick, she couldn't quite make it out and got stuck halfway. Brent stood behind her and stooped down, wrapping his arms around her lower chest and yanking her out.

Gently laying her on the ground, he lifted the back of her head and held a small bottle of water to her mouth, pouring some of it onto her face to clean off the dirt.

Brent sat down to get his breath back, removing his sodden shirt and using it as a rag to try and wipe the sweat off himself. He looked at Faye, lying there with her arm across her forehead, her eyes closed.

"Are you alright, Faye?"

She nodded her head slightly but didn't speak. He offered her some more water and closed his eyes, listening to the total silence of what was once a scene of carnage.

"I don't suppose you want to give it another go, do you?" he said.

"Is that a serious question?"

"Well, we've come all this way. I just thought..."

"I'll wait here for you," she said quietly.

"No, it's just that I really wanted to show you what's down there, but... anyway. How about the rifle range? Do you want to go and shoot some of the guns that they've got left over from the war?"

"Only if you're the target, Brent," she said, sitting up. "Maybe we should just go back. There are dark clouds gathering and it might start raining soon."

Helping Faye to stand up, Brent took her by the arm, and they walked out of the plantation.

As they set off, Faye put her arms around his waist and asked him to drive the motorbike slowly, as she was still feeling dizzy and nauseous.

They made it back to Saigon just before the rain came pelting down, quickly flooding the streets again.

Dave was standing in the doorway as they walked into the house. Faye walked straight past him to go and have a shower in her room, leaving Brent to chat with his mate.

"Did you guys get to see the tunnels then?" said Dave.

"Yeah, kind of."

"What did you make of it?"

"Er, yeah, it was ok. Bit of a drag if anything."

"I was there a couple of weeks ago. Same spot. Went all the way down, three levels. Must have gone at least forty feet underground. They've got huge rooms and everything down there. It's incredible."

"Yeah. Hey, listen, I need to grab a shower. I'll talk to you later, ok?"

"Yeah, mate. Catch you later," said Dave, removing his shoes and rolling up his pants to wade through the water.

"Hey, Brent. How you been doin?" said Wells as Brent walked past his room.

"Yeah, pretty good. How about you?" replied Brent.

"Come on in, man. You wanna smoke some?"

"Er… no, I think I should…"

"Well, why don't you come right on in and talk to me some? You know I get kinda lonely sometimes. Have been since I lost the only friend what I had in the platoon, when we was ambushed. You know what am sayin?"

"Well… I suppose I could stay for a while. Faye will be in the shower for ages anyway."

"Close the door, man. Sit over by the table right there," said Wells, fixing up a needle to inject himself.

The days passed by, and Faye knew for sure that Brent was still going down to Wells' room and smoking heroin while she was out. He denied it, but she could see how he had lost his appetite and was eating less every day, the dark bags under his eyes and his sallow face.

Saturday morning, Brent woke up to see Faye folding her clothes and neatly packing them into her bags. He stared at her for a while, trying to remember if they were going somewhere together that he had forgotten about.

"Where are we going today?" he said.

"We aren't going anywhere. I'm moving out, back to the hostel," she said without looking at him.

"Why?"

"Because you're turning into a heroin addict, and I don't want to be around to watch it happen. That's why."

There was nothing Brent could say or do to make her change her mind. He knew that, and so he closed his eyes to spare himself the disappointment that was about to hit him.

"I hope you come to your senses soon, Brent. Call me if you do, I won't be too far away."

The sound of the door closing made him open his eyes. He stared at it for a long time, hoping that she would walk back in with a big smile on her face and somehow forgive him and nurse him to better health. But he was fooling himself.

He got out of bed, and without bothering to shower, went straight down to the ground floor and knocked on Wells' door.

Chapter 15

Hooked

Knowing that he was in a mess, Brent weighed up his options, carefully considering which course of action to take next. He figured it was pointless chasing after Faye and questioned himself whether she was worth it anyway. After all, wasn't he in South East Asia where girls were plentiful and readily available? And wasn't he just wasting his time with Faye, given the fact that she left him sexually frustrated all of the time?

The following morning he bought a ticket and headed back to Cambodia, arriving in Phnom Penh that afternoon. He hadn't smoked heroin since the day before, so he spent the rest of the day in his room, feeling sick and going through mild withdrawal symptoms.

Feeling slightly better the following day, he hung around the guest house until the evening and then made his way to the mall where he sat by himself drinking beer.

"I always knew you would come back."
"Oh, hello, Jack. How's tricks? Good to see you again," said Brent, turning to look at him.
"Couldn't be better. On your own tonight?"
"Yes, I've just got back from Saigon. Pull up a chair."
"And how is your charming girlfriend? Faye, isn't it?" he said, taking a seat.
"Faye, yes. Yes, she's fine, just fine."
"You're not getting along too well with her, are you?"
"What makes you say that?"

120

"And I take it she's not here with you, either. Still in Saigon, is she?"

"I, er… yeah, I think she is."

They talked for a while, mainly about what Brent and Faye had been doing since they left Cambodia. Jack showed especial interest in Faye, in particular her whereabouts and her intentions for the immediate future.

"Brent, how about if we meet tomorrow? I should imagine you're not doing much. I have some business to take care of right now. Do you still have my number?"

"Yes, it's on my phone."

"Give me a call tomorrow," said Jack as he stood up and left the table.

"Yes, I will. See you tomorrow then."

Brent wasn't well, either physically or emotionally, and he decided to head back to his room and rest. Lying on his bed, he reflected on the previous few weeks in Saigon and felt ashamed for allowing himself to be so easily led down the path to ruin that he had been on.

He rose early the next morning and went jogging, stopping off at a bustling market to get some fresh fruit. As he was leaving, he walked past a row of ducks and chickens, tethered and waiting by the side of the dirt street to be slaughtered. They were untied and thrown, one by one, to the man behind who busily slit their throats, collecting the blood in a bowl. Almost dead, they were individually thrown into a cauldron of boiling water, stirred briefly, and then scooped out and put in a small machine that spun them rapidly, removing all of their feathers. The naked carcass was then chopped for selling, the whole process taking less than two minutes.

That evening, he walked past the restaurant where he and Faye had dined on so many occasions, stopping for a moment to reminisce. He saw Kun Thea sitting with a fat western man and smiled at her as she turned to look at him. She gestured with her hand for him to join them, but he shook his head and walked on.

Entering the mall, he was just about to take a seat at one of the quieter bars when his phone rang.

"Don't sit at *that* bar. Look to your right, on the other side of the pool table, across the hall."

"Jack, I was just about to call you," said Brent, turning to look where he was sitting.

Brent walked over to his table.

"I'm drinking a mix. What's your poison?" said Jack as Brent sat down.

"I think I'll just stick with the beer. What's wrong with the bar over there, then? It's not as busy as this one. Is it too quiet for you?"

"I won't be seeing you for a while, Brent, so here's to a good one," said Jack, raising his glass.

"Can I get a jug and some ice?" shouted Brent, looking over at the barmaid. "You won't see me for a while? Why? Are you going somewhere?"

"I promised to take a boy on holiday. He wants to go to Thailand."

"A boy? What boy?"

"He's over there, playing pool."

"When are you going?"

"Rith!" shouted Jack. "Rith! Come here."

A young lad, very dark skinned with bad acne and broken teeth walked over to Jack's table and stood next to him.

"Say hello to Brent."

"What are you taking *him* for?" said Brent, looking at the emaciated youth with a gormless expression on his face standing next to him.

"I was going to take Sov, but since I told him that you were back in town he's suddenly changed his mind and wants to stay here."

"You told Sov that I was here?"

"Yes, unfortunately. We were all set to go, and he was really excited about it. I can't understand him sometimes. But it's my fault, I shouldn't have mentioned your name."

"Does Sov want to see me?"

"I take it you don't think very much about this boy here?" said Jack, looking at Rith.

"Well, I suppose it depends on what you're taking him for, I guess."

"I thought you already knew what my taste was. Same as yours, Brent. Wouldn't you say so, or haven't you been brave enough to indulge yet?"

"Indulge?"

"Have you been to Thailand?"

"Yes, that's where I met Faye. We were there not long ago."

"It's the perfect place to lose yourself, isn't it?"

"My grandfather is buried there, in Kanchanaburi."

"*Is he really*," said Jack slowly, his voice filled with a touch of anticipation. "Is he really. That's very interesting."

"Yes, he was—"

"Rith, go away," said Jack abruptly. "Go over there. I'll speak to you later."

"Money!"

"You've had enough money. Now fuck off!" shouted Jack.

"I'll be back in a minute," said Brent, standing up. "I need a piss."

Jack was talking on his phone as Brent returned and sat down at the table.

"No, you can't talk to Brent right now. We're busy," he said, then paused briefly.

"What?" said Jack, pausing again. "No, he can't come to see you tonight. I've just told you, he's busy."

He paused again, closing his eyes and shaking his head slightly.

"Alright, I will ask him. Now put the phone down, and don't call again. Yes, yes, I will. Now hang up."

"Was that Sov?" said Brent as Jack put the phone in his pocket.

"Damned nuisance, that boy. I don't know why I put up with him sometimes."

"What does he want?"

"Now he wants to go to Thailand," sighed Jack.

"Well, why don't you take him then?"

"He wants you to go along as well. He said I'm too boring, and he finds you more attractive, more interesting, apparently. I told him it's too late anyway, that I'm taking somebody else."

"You mean that boy that was here before? Rith, or whatever his name is."

"Yes, Rith. Would you like to come along? I know a nice little secluded spot on one of the islands. We can have some fun."

"Nah, not for me, I don't think," said Brent.

"What are your plans then? Chasing after Faye again?" said Jack, rather sarcastically.

"I haven't really got a plan, to be honest. Any way the wind blows, I guess."

"Blow him," he replied, almost inaudibly.

"What?"

123

"No, nothing, I was just talking to myself. Look, I have to go. I promised Sov I would bring him a pizza. How about if we catch up tomorrow?"

"Yeah, sure, no problem."

After Jack had gone, Brent paid up and moved over to a smaller bar on the other side of the mall. Sitting by himself in the corner, he was approached by a middle-aged western man.

"Got yourself involved with *Martey Heng* then, have you?" he said, slamming a bottle of whiskey and a tiny single-shot glass on the table.

"What did you say?" said Brent.

"Lamb to the slaughter," he continued, knocking back the grog and refilling the glass.

"Martey Heng? Who's Martey Heng?" said Brent. "And who are you?"

"Doesn't matter who I am," he said in a sullen tone.

"Listen pal, don't just walk up to my table like that and start giving me a load of drunken old shit. Alright?"

"Your table? This isn't your fucking table, you prick. You're not in fucking England now," he sneered, sitting down and swigging more whiskey.

"You'd better watch yourself, mate. I'm not in the mood for taking shit off some washed-up expat like you."

"You're the one who needs to watch himself. *Martey Heng* is looking for your type."

"Martey Heng? Who the fuck is Martey Heng?" said Brent, becoming annoyed.

"Martey Heng is a fucking anagram."

"I haven't got a clue what you're talking about, pal, so why don't you just leave it out and go bug somebody else instead?"

"You're obviously not an English teacher," he said sarcastically, knocking back another shot of whiskey.

"And you are, I take it?"

"What else is there for a foreigner to do in fucking Cambodia, apart from driving around all day in a fucking SUV, pretending to do some good deeds for some fucking NGO or other?"

"Yeah, whatever. So Martey Heng is an anagram. Sounds very interesting," said Brent, showing a complete lack of interest.

"*Silent* equals *Listen. The eyes* equals *They see*."

"What?"

"Do you like riddles?" he said, staring at Brent with a manic grin.

"I prefer jokes. Do you know any, or are you just one hell of a gross one?"

"That was almost humorous in itself," said Fox wryly. "No, I'm afraid jokes are boring, and most of them aren't even funny. No, let's see if you can get what I'm talking about."

"I'm not interested in playing stupid games with you."

"You'd rather play dangerous games, would you? We might have something in common after all."

"What are you talking about?"

"That man that you were talking to before."

"What man?"

"*Agent Rhyme,*" he said, taking another shot of whiskey.

"So who is *he* then?" said Brent, sounding bored.

"He's *Garth Yemen. Agent Hermy.*"

"What is this? Some kind of *Who Done It*?"

"You're getting warm," he said, giving Brent an encouraging look and slugging more whiskey.

"Why don't you just fuck off?"

"*Angry theme!*" he continued. "What's the problem? Too much *math energy* required to work out what I'm saying?"

"What is it that you're looking for?" said Brent impatiently.

"I know him. We used to... let's say *work together*. Until he found out what my real intentions were, that is. I had a finger in all of his pies. He just didn't realise it. *Great hymen,* by the way. Of course, I knew all along what *his* real game was."

"You're talking about Jack, right?"

"Yes. *A green myth,* in case you haven't picked it up yet."

"They're all anagrams of *Germany*. Right?" said Brent.

"Oh! Nice try!" he said, slowly clapping his hands. "You're not as dumb as you look. But no, not quite. Actually, they're all anagrams of *The Grey Man.*"

"I don't know what you're talking about. I gotta go. See ya," said Brent, standing up to leave.

"He's got everybody fooled, including you," he shouted, sculling another glass of whiskey as Brent walked off.

The sound of Brent's phone ringing early the next morning woke him up. He looked at the screen. It was Jack's number.

"Hello?"

"Brent, what are you doing today?"

"I don't know," he said, yawning. "Why, what's up?"

"I'm going to Thailand. Fancy coming?"

"Not really. I've only just got off the bus from Vietnam."

"Well, I'm heading to the airport soon with Sov. The flight leaves at eleven-thirty."

"You're going with Sov? I thought you said you were taking that other lad."

"No, I'm taking Sov. Are you sure you don't want to come along?"

"Well... I don't suppose there's much for me to do here," said Brent.

"Listen, I've already told Sov that you'll be going, so why don't you get yourself down to the airport?"

"You've told him I'm going?"

"He's all excited. Listen, we will be in Bangkok only for a day or two before we head out, so I suggest you get your skates on. Give me a call when you land. Ok?"

"Can I speak to—"

Jack hung up, leaving Brent to consider his next move. He hadn't planned on returning to Thailand, but then again he hadn't really planned anything. He was drifting aimlessly.

He decided to weigh it up over a beer and headed for the bar.

The drink eventually convinced him that it wasn't a bad idea, so he walked down the street and bought a ticket for the following day.

Chapter 16

Where Fate Leads

Brent landed at Don Muang airport around midnight and joined the queue for foreigners—or *farangs,* as the Thais were so fond of calling them. He hated the word, as it was more often than not accompanied by a derisive tone of voice.

Leaving the air-conditioned comfort of the airport, the hot air hit him in the face like a blast from an oven, and the familiar smell of Bangkok and the steady rumbling of traffic nearby instantly reminded him of being in Thailand again.

He walked down the causeway and stood by the main highway among the local people and workers waiting for buses, concentrating hard on the approaching vehicles, hoping to identify the fifty-nine, which passed nearby to his intended destination, Banglumpoo. But in the dark, the dimly lit numbers and the glare from headlights made it difficult to see. Minibuses and pickups weaved in and out among trucks, coaches, and other vehicles, making good use of the four lanes of steadily flowing traffic, and he expected the usual frustration of waiting, only to see them all turn up together, some failing to stop due to the congestion.

Groups of people readied themselves as three buses appeared in the distance. He shielded his eyes from the lights and focused on them intently. One of them was a fifty-nine, and now it was a case of guessing where it would pull over, whether it would remain last in line as it currently was, or overtake and stop ahead of the others.

He stepped off the pavement, signalling the driver with his arm outstretched and then turning to grab his backpack, jostling with the Thais as the buses pulled in randomly.

Personnel eager to get to and from the airport pushed each other aside in the stairwell as they boarded. The bell rang, and the driver revved the engine as Brent threw his heavy bag onto the steps and grabbed the handrail, squeezing past the doors as they folded together.

Thick black exhaust fumes blasted out from the side as the decrepit vehicle set off, the driver noisily crashing into second gear then wiping his brow with the towel that hung around his neck.

The seats on either side filled quickly, as did the ample floor space in between which accommodated those who had to hang on and be crushed.

Eventually, as people got off, he was able to sit on the bench seat at the rear and enjoy the draught coming in through the open windows as the bus gathered speed.

The journey would take more than one hour, and as the other passengers left, he found himself alone. A small kaleidoscope of rotating colours drew his attention to the front of the bus where the driver had made a little shrine to his deity, draped with a wreath of small yellow flowers, sitting in front of burnt-out incense sticks. Above it hung a picture of the Thai king.

He got off at Democracy Monument and made his way to Khao San Road nearby. It was almost two in the morning, and there were people everywhere, revelling and enjoying the night in the numerous bars and restaurants that lined the street.

He decided not to check into a guest house until later, as there was every chance that he would be charged for that night and not the coming day.

At the end of the street, on the pavement, there was a small makeshift bar with a couple of tables and chairs and an icebox full of cans and bottles.

He sat down and ordered a beer, calling over a street food vendor as she walked past, pushing her vending cart. He hadn't eaten since he left Phnom Penh, and the tray of Pad Thai stir fried noodles and prawns would see him through until breakfast later on.

Dawn broke, and as the last few revellers staggered back to their lodgings, he headed off, crossing over one of the many canals that crisscrossed Bangkok. The unpleasant smell of drains that emptied into the black stagnant water filled his senses as he ambled towards the cheap guest house that he had stayed at last time.

Turning off the street and heading down a short alleyway, he arrived to see Chuenchai, the old lady that ran the place, sitting outside on a bench, eating a bowl of rice and some dried fish. Her house was situated opposite the rear wall of a temple, down a narrow passage lined on either side with plants and flowers. She smiled warmly and greeted him in Thai.

"Sawatdee Ka."

"Sawatdee Krab. Good to see you again. How are you?" he replied.

"Yes. You go where?"

"I went to Cambodia and then Vietnam. And then I went back to Cambodia again."

"You stay how long?"

"In Bangkok? I'm not sure. I've just come to see somebody. Maybe one day, two days. Do you have a room for me?"

She nodded and continued eating her food.

"Can I put my bag in the room?"

She nodded again and gestured with her hand, pointing towards the stairs, handing him a key from her pocket.

"I clean room later," she said.

"Let me help you. Just give me the sheets and I will do it myself."

She finished eating her breakfast and then gave him fresh bedding from the cupboard.

It was an old two-storey traditional Thai house made of teak, one of the few that still remained in Bangkok, and Chuenchai had lived there all of her life.

Brent walked inside, past the long wooden couch that she slept on and the boxes of junk that she had accumulated over the years. He climbed the stairs to his room.

There were four rooms downstairs and six upstairs. His was very basic, like a wooden cell, consisting of a single bed, a small table, and a ceiling fan. But it was cheap, and he liked the homely atmosphere.

He laid his backpack on the table, changed the bed, and swept the floor. The early morning sun shone fiercely through the window, and the room was already turning into an oven. There was no curtain to draw, so he raised the lever to open the opaque glass slats. The wire mesh was full of holes, and he would have to prepare for mosquitoes.

He unpacked his bag, got undressed, and wrapped a towel around his waist. The thin plywood walls of the room shook as he slammed the door shut and went downstairs for a shower.

He squatted down in front of a large earthenware pot filled with water and washed in the same manner as Thai people, dunking a small bowl into the basin, scooping up the cold water, and pouring it repeatedly over his head and body.

Feeling refreshed, he refilled the pot, went back to his room, and lay down. The fan rattled noisily as it spun around, wobbling from side to side directly above him, making him feel uneasy. He got off the bed and turned it down to the lowest setting.

He picked up his phone and checked the time. It was still quite early, and he asked himself whether he should contact Jack or wait until later. He decided to call him later and set the alarm on his phone in case he fell asleep.

Later that day the alarm sounded, and Brent awoke with a start, jumping out of bed as though he were late for his own wedding. He sat down for a moment to clear his head and then got dressed and went downstairs.

Chuenchai was sitting outside in the narrow passage in front of her house talking to a policeman. Brent asked her if he could make some coffee. He felt a bit self-conscious when he saw the officer, dressed in his dark grey uniform, but there was nothing to be concerned about, so he made a strong hot drink and sat down at the far end of the ledge. They paid no attention to him, so he called Jack, who answered straight away as though he had been waiting impatiently to speak to him.

"Hello," said Jack abruptly.

"Hey, Jack, how's it going?"

"Brent! Where are you?"

"I'm right here, in Bangkok."

"So you made it. That's good to hear. I was expecting you to call last night."

"I didn't land till late. The flight got delayed."

"I see."

"Yeah, so, anyway, how is Sov? Is he enjoying his trip to Thailand?"

"Where are you staying?" said Jack.

"I'm near Khao San Road."

"Give me your address. I'll come down there and pick you up."

"I don't know the address of this place. It's not on a street. It's off Ram Buttri, somewhere."

"Ok, meet me at the Songkran Hotel, instead. It's on Soi Kraisi. I'll wait there for you."

"Yeah, no sweat. See you soon," said Brent, hanging up.

The police officer stood up and handed some paperwork to Chuenchai before leaving, staring at Brent as he walked past.

Brent was curious and asked her what was going on. She informed him that the police made regular checks on the guest houses and hotels to ensure that all foreigners had been registered properly.

Feeling a little easier, he drank the rest of his coffee. The mug was rinsed and left hung out to dry. It was time to visit Jack.

He walked up to the main road, flagged down a tuk-tuk, and headed for the hotel.

When he arrived, Jack was sitting outside a small bar on the other side of the street, facing the Songkran Hotel. Brent saw him and went over.

"Hey, Jack."

"Hello Brent. Good to see you again. Sit down, have a beer."

"Is that where you're staying?" said Brent, pointing at the hotel.

"No, it's a bit too tacky for me," he replied.

"Yeah, it looks a bit run down, doesn't it?"

"It's where the ladyboys and prostitutes take you. They let you have visitors in your room, if you know what I mean."

"How is Sov? You said you were bringing him with you. Is he having a good time?"

"Yes. Are you having a beer? I could murder another one," said Jack.

"This is your favourite bar then, is it?"

"I come here now and again. It brings back memories, gives me a special feeling. An existential feeling."

"Check that out!" said Brent, looking at the hotel.

"You're not even listening, are you?" said Jack, talking to himself.

"Is that a chick or a ladyboy? Hot as hell, whatever it is."

"You're a gift," he replied in a low voice.

"You know, before I left Phnom Penh, I met this drunken crazy guy at the mall. Told me that he knew you."

"What was his name?"

"He didn't say. He wasn't there very long. He seemed a bit cuckoo, but he was pissed out of his head, rambling on about anagrams and shit, so—"

"What did he look like?"

"He's about fifty, around five feet ten, a bit skinny, scruffy blond hair. His face is a bit gaunt, looks like he might be ill or something. Stares at you with a wicked grin and a mad look in his eye. Drinks whiskey like I drink beer."

"So he knows me, does he?" said Jack.

"He said something about a grey man, whatever that is. Think he might have been referring to you."

"A grey man, did he?"

"Do you know him?"

"Yes. He's drinking himself to death, has been for some time. What else did he tell you?"

"He said he used to work with you."

"I wouldn't call it that," said Jack, laughing slightly. "No, he's an informer, what you just referred to: a Grey Man."

"What do you mean, an informer? Inform on what?"

"I took him to the same place that I showed you, in Phnom Penh."

"The house where I met Sov?"

"Yes. Most of them are Australian, ex military—special forces—or former police officers."

"The Grey Man, you mean?"

"Yes. They dupe you into thinking they're one of you. That drunken loser that you were talking to in Phnom Penh pretended to be interested in the young girls, but it turned out that he was working against us, ratting on us to the police."

"Hey, about Sov," said Brent. "Does he—"

"Listen, I have to go. I will contact you later," said Jack, standing up to leave.

Brent was in the mood for drinking and ordered another beer. A plump middle-aged man wearing shabby clothes, looking like he was still hungover from the night before, came out of the Songkran and sat down at the table next to his.

Brent watched as the young barmaid brought the man a cheap bottle of Thai whiskey, a glass, and a small bucket of ice. His hands shook as he poured himself a drink, knocking it back in one and refilling the glass until he felt sufficiently satisfied.

"Morning," said Brent, catching the man's attention and raising his glass.

"Ah, not quite. Almost," he replied, pushing his round wire-rimmed spectacles up his nose and looking at his watch. "It has just gone past twelve o'clock noon."

"You sound like you're from Germany."

"Yes, and you?"

"England, Manchester."

"And what are you doing in England?"

"I rescue people," said Brent, laughing. "For the Fire Brigade."

"I see. My name is Wilhelm. And you are?"

"Brent."

"Yes, nice to meet you, Brent."

"What do you do? Are you retired?"

"I am a pharmacist. I work for six months in Germany, and then I come to visit here for the other six months."

"Sweet! Nice lifestyle. And you stay here in Bangkok all the time?"

"No, just some of the time. I have an apartment in Pattaya also."

"And you're staying over there, in that hotel, are you?"

"Yes, I stay for one month, and they make discount for me."

"What's it like? Is it a good place to stay?"

"It was ok before, but now it is not so good. I think I must try to find new place to stay."

"What's the problem? I heard there are lots of ladyboys and loose girls going in there. Are they causing too much shit?"

"Not so much, but I am told one more man has killed himself also, while I am in Germany."

"Another suicide in the hotel? How?"

"Ja, they tell me he has taken too much heroin. They find him on the bed in the room."

"Overdosed on heroin!"

"I don't like this. You know, for me this is not so good. Maybe I take this room where he die."

"Do you know what I mean!" said Brent. "Sleeping in the same bed that some lemon has just squeezed himself on. Fuck that. How hard does that hit the spot on the creepometer? Hey man, do you believe in ghosts? Can you imagine turning over in bed and there he is, fucking staring at you?"

"Yes, thank you," said Wilhelm, his hands shaking worse than ever as he poured another whiskey.

It was getting late, and Brent decided to head back to the guest house, choosing to walk so that he could find somewhere to eat.

Stopping at a small greasy Chinese restaurant on the corner of a soi, he watched an old Thai woman standing outside cooking a dish.

Flames rose high in the air as she threw a handful of hot chili peppers into a large wok, stirring them vigorously. The fumes took his breath away and made his eyes water, causing him to cough. He no longer felt hungry and moved on, wandering the streets and getting lost, eventually ending up around Soi Cowboy. The street was similar to Patpong Road, and he considered going into one of the clubs to look for a girl, but he had spent most of his money at the bar already and decided to head back.

Later that evening, he received a phone call.

"Brent, how are tricks with you?" said Jack.

"Yeah, Jack, what's happening?"

"Nothing much. Sov has been asking about you, so I thought I'd give you a bell, see how you are. I was just wondering what your plans were for tonight."

"I'm pretty smashed right now. Been drinking all day with some German guy."

"Listen, I can fix you up with a room at the Songkran if you're interested."

"Er… yeah, so…"

"Don't worry about the cost. This one's on me. How about if I send a taxi round to your place to pick you up?"

"I'm a bit fucked right now, Jack. I ended up on the whiskey. Didn't realise how strong it was either. Think I might have to get an early night."

"Look, it's still early. Have some coffee and lie down for a while. You'll feel much better in an hour or so."

"I've got a monster of a headache. Honestly, I don't think I can make it, Jack."

"You don't want to let Sov down, do you? He's travelled a long way just for you Brent. I hope you understand that."

"How about if we go to Kanchanaburi?"

"And?"

"I could meet you there. It's a quiet place, and I was thinking of going anyway. Like I told you, my grandfather is buried there and—"

"Yes," said Jack abruptly. "That sounds like a good idea. When will you be leaving? Are you heading off tomorrow?"

"If I feel up to it, yes."

"Get in touch with me when you arrive."

"Yes. So, you'll meet me there? You and Sov?"

"Perfect. Look forward to it. Ciao," said Jack as he hung up.

Brent packed his bags the next morning and bade farewell to Chuenchai, pressing the palms of his hands together in front of his face and bowing his head slightly, just as he had done upon arriving.

Walking past the rear of the temple, he repeated the action and uttered a short prayer of good fortune before making his way down the alley to the main road.

Standing on the jetty by the Chao Phraya River, he watched as the long, narrow, single-deck ferryboat quickly came alongside, overshooting the dock. The driver revved the engine loudly and reversed the boat, bringing the stern inward at an angle towards the waiting passengers, who cautiously climbed on board as it bobbed in the churning water.

Lowering his head under the cabin's door frame, Brent made his way inside. There were seats vacant, but he chose to stand towards the rear so that the spray from the river wouldn't come through the open sides and hit him in the face, knowing that they would be moving fairly quickly.

The boat heaved up and down, zigzagging from one side of the wide river to the other until he came to his destination on the far side, where he was forced to make the hazardous step of jumping onto the jetty as other people boarded.

The train station was nearby, and in three hours he would be in Kanchanaburi. He bought a ticket and tried to make himself comfortable on one of the wooden benches, which were the only form of seating available.

The carriage was old, and it was hot and stuffy. He lifted the wooden shutters up to release the catches and then lowered them, allowing a slight breeze to flow through the open windows.

The carriage jolted as the engine coupled up to it. The lights came on, and the small ceiling fans revolved into action.

Halfway to Kanchanaburi, the train stopped at Ban Pong, the town where the Death Railway had started from in 1942.

Brent knew very little about his grandfather's experience during his captivity on the line, but the thought of crossing his grandfather's path and being in the places where he had been gave him a strong feeling of connection. His thoughts turned to Faye and how she had told him of the feeling she experienced as she walked down the Via Dolorosa in Jerusalem.

Brent arrived in Kanchanaburi and headed for the town centre, strolling through the other allied war cemetery on his way.

He found some digs and lay on the bed, thinking about Jack. He was about to send a message but hesitated. He thought he could feel the presence of someone standing next to him and quickly left the room.

Later that evening he called Jack, arranging to meet the following day.

"I see you've shaved your head, Brent. Are things getting a bit too hot for you?" said Jack.

"Morning. Yeah, I've been getting into Buddhism just lately. I like the idea of it, the meditation, the way it seems to make sense, and everything."

"You need to be careful. Too much sun on your head can be dangerous."

"Yeah, don't worry about it. Anyway, what are you doing today? I want to check out the tiger temple. Fancy coming along? We could rent a bike for the day, have a look around," said Brent. "Have you been to Hellfire Pass? I wouldn't mind going back there again, too."

"You get a bike for yourself. I'll follow you on mine. We can meet up later. There's something I need to do first."

"Yeah, sure. I want to go back to my room to change my clothes before I go, anyway. I've got an orange shirt and a matching pair of slacks that I want to wear. What time do you want to set off then?"

"Going in disguise because you're afraid of being eaten by a tiger? Is that what the camouflage is for?" said Jack sarcastically.

"Well, I can think of better ways to go. Let's put it that way. Anyway, I heard that you can buy food at the temple, so I reckon the cats should be pretty cool with me if I look like a monk and I'm feeding them. Somebody said they sedate them as well. Don't know if it's true, though."

"Remind me to take a few shots when we get there. I'll see you back here in a couple of hours."

Chapter 17

A Strange Message

Faye had been waiting for Brent to contact her, unaware that he had already gone. She took a stroll down the alleyway to the house and saw Wells sitting outside. His jaundiced sunken eyes stared straight through her into the distance as she approached.

Panting, with his tongue hanging out of his mouth, he grunted as she spoke to him, causing the long column of ash to fall off the spent cigarette stump between his fingers.

The landlady came to the gate and informed Faye that Brent had moved out some two weeks previously, and she had not heard from him since.

It was around noon, and Faye decided to go for lunch. Sitting outside a quiet restaurant, she noticed a man standing at the entrance to one of the narrow alleyways, those passages that extended throughout Saigon knitting together the main roads and side streets.

He seemed to be staring at her. She turned her face and feigned interest in something else, but when she looked at him again he was still staring at her.

She thought that she had seen him before but couldn't quite recall where. He was about six feet tall, fairly stocky, and quite physically fit, even though he looked about sixty. He wore a light grey shirt, neatly rolled up at the sleeves and tucked in at the waist, and his dark grey slacks and black leather shoes almost gave him the appearance of wearing a uniform. He lit a cigarette and crossed the street.

"Hello Faye," he said in a dull tone.

"Hello... I don't think we've met before," she said nervously. "How do you know my name?"

He took a drag on his cigarette and stared at her without replying, his cold, steel-blue eyes penetrating hers, making her feel uneasy.

"You're waiting for Brent, aren't you? You should go home, Faye. Back to England. This part of the world is no place for a young girl on her own."

"I'm not a young girl. I'm twenty-six, and I'm not on my own."

A faint smile cracked his granite face. An image shot through her mind and she remembered where she had seen him.

"You're the man who took Brent somewhere on the back of your motorbike in Cambodia. Aren't you?" she said.

"Did he tell you where we went?"

"No, he wouldn't tell me. So where did you take him?"

"Somewhere quiet. A safe house for types with that kind of bent. He got a taste of things to come. He didn't tell you about that young boy, did he?"

"What young boy?"

"The one who was abducted in Spain twelve years ago when he was three."

"Why are you telling me this?"

"I just want you to understand."

"Where's Brent?" she said anxiously.

"I couldn't say. Maybe you should contact his family and ask them."

"He doesn't have much of a family."

"No. He's pretty close to his grandfather, though. Isn't he!"

She stared at him, feeling confused.

"Maybe I can help you, Faye."

"Help me? How?"

"I can take you to the place that he went to. You could talk to the people there. Maybe they can throw some light onto his whereabouts."

"You mean the house that you took him to in Phnom Penh? You could take me to the place where the boy lives?"

"Yes."

"Why should I trust you?"

"Why should you not trust me? Brent was a close friend of mine. I'm just as concerned about him as you are, Faye."

"If I went back to Cambodia, would you contact the police and get them to help us look for him?"

"Yes, if that's what you want. I know a very good police officer who would be more than happy to assist you. He's the head of that district."

Faye looked at him intently and then lowered her face.

"I'll have to think about it," she said.

"Let me give you my number," he said, handing her a business card. "Please, call me when you get to Phnom Penh."

She stared into the distance with a troubled look on her face and didn't reply.

"I will wait for you, Faye. We can make this work. You and me, together. Let me buy lunch for you," he said, calling the waitress and handing her a fifty.

"I can pay for myself, thank you," she replied curtly.

"No, Faye, please. Let me help you. I insist," he said, forcing the note into the waiting girl's hand.

"I said I can pay for myself," said Faye, snatching the money out of her hand and putting it on the table in front of him.

She felt upset and confused.

He stared at her with a pitiful look on his face.

"I'm sorry, Faye. I didn't mean to annoy you. I just wanted to help you, that's all."

She cringed as he placed his hand on her shoulder.

"Can you just leave me alone now?" she said.

"Yes, of course. I'm so sorry. I will be leaving for Cambodia tomorrow morning, so promise me you'll take care walking the streets. Especially late at night."

She didn't reply.

"Goodbye, Faye."

He lit a cigarette and slowly walked away, staring at the ground, his left hand resting on his hip.

The days dragged on and still no word from Brent. She tried to contact him every day, but her calls and messages got no response. She wasn't able to get in touch with his parents as Brent's mother had died of cancer some years before, and his father was now an alcoholic drifter with whom he had lost all contact. Faye knew of no other family members that she might contact either.

The last message that she had received from Brent was more than two weeks old. It read that he had met some guy, an old friend, and they had gone travelling somewhere.

She typed another message and sent it to his phone.

Brent, where are you now?
Feeling lonely
Can you get in touch with me soon?
Love you
Faye

She stared at the phone, feeling dejected. Had she lost him? Had he met another girl? She scrolled through their photos, reminiscing about the great times and laughs they had shared.

The phone beeped, indicating that she had received a new message. The sound alone gave her hope and made her sit upright. It was Brent's number. She opened the message quickly.

Brent?
Where?
Are you now feeling lonely?
Can you get in?
Touch with me soon
Love you Faye

She found the message strange but was nevertheless relieved and happy that Brent had finally got in touch with her. Judging by the way that he had interpreted her words, it sounded as though he was having a good time with his drinking buddy or something.

As she was typing a reply, her phone rang. It was Brent's number again. She answered it quickly with a jubilant voice.

"Brent!"

There was no reply.

"Brent!"

Still no reply.

"Brent, can you hear me? Where are you? I've been worried like crazy."

Nobody on the end of the line spoke. Faye heard the faint sound of music playing in the background and pressed the phone close to her ear. The music grew louder. She listened intently and thought that she recognised the song but couldn't quite recall the title.

"Brent! Are you there? Speak to me. Please!"

There was still no reply. She was becoming confused and upset and couldn't understand why he was refusing to speak to her. Maybe it was a prank, a joke to go along with the garbled message that he had just sent. Or perhaps he was injured and unable to talk.

As she listened, she thought she could hear someone breathing, very faintly.

"Brent, are you injured? Make a sound, any sound, so I know that you're listening."

Still, nobody spoke. Tears began to well up in Faye's eyes. She was about to make one more plea, but before she could speak, the phone hung up. She called his number straight away, but the line was engaged. After trying repeatedly to get through, she eventually realised that her number had been blocked and gave up.

Faye switched off the light and lay down on the bed. It was late in the evening. The phone call had been another one of life's pendulum rides of hope and expectation that quickly fades into disappointment. It was the essence of life, as Brent had once told her.

She closed her eyes and cast her mind back to that conversation, recalling how Brent had sat before her with his shaven head, expounding his newfound knowledge of oriental philosophies and his interpretation of what life meant.

She hadn't eaten dinner yet, but the call had taken away her appetite anyway, so she read the messages that Brent had sent her prior to the long spell of silence.

She thought long and hard about Jack, and although he made her feel uneasy, she couldn't think of any alternative and reasoned that she would have to return to Phnom Penh if she wanted to find Brent.

Chapter 18

Mandy

Faye woke early the next day and boarded a minibus for Chau Doc, a town in the Mekong Delta. From there, she took a ferryboat up the river and crossed the border into Cambodia.

She bought the entry visa at the border, paid the usual bribe for some excuse such as not having a photo on her visa application form, and then proceeded through immigration, where they took her fingerprints and scanned her face onto their computer.

As the boat cruised steadily along the brown stained river, winding its way past the thick mangrove swamps that lined the banks, she sat on the deck and tried to chat with other travellers, but her mind was not at ease, and she found it difficult to make herself sound interesting.

Moving to the back of the boat, she sat alone and let her mind wander off into the distance of Vietnam, where she had last seen Brent.

Docking at Phnom Penh, she made her way back to the area that she had stayed at before, calling in at the places she and Brent had stopped at, hoping for any news of his whereabouts.

Having failed once more to contact Brent, Faye sat on the bed in her room and deliberated over meeting Jack, realising that her options were now slim and that he was probably her only chance.

She picked up her phone and sent him a message. He replied straight away, arranging to meet her later that evening.

She went to the mall and found a quiet spot to sit in, ordering a glass of beer just to take the edge off things and help her relax.

It wasn't long before she found herself being approached by local Cambodian men, who regarded all western women as depraved and immoral and an easy score.

Feeling uneasy, Faye moved to a table near the street, closer to other westerners.

A young boy passed by on the other side of the road. They made eye contact and smiled at each other. As he walked off, he turned to look at her, motioning with his hand for her to follow him. She blushed and looked over her shoulders at the people sitting around her.

She felt exposed and vulnerable and smiled warmly as a young female walked up and started chatting to her, seizing the opportunity of companionship.

"Hi," said the girl.

"Hi, how are you?" replied Faye.

"Pretty cool! Cool and pretty!" she said, laughing. "You too! Are you alone?"

"Yes, I got here today. How about you?"

"Yep. It looks like my girlfriend has left me, so I think I should guess so," she said, pouting her lips.

"Where are you from?"

"I'm from Hong Kong. My name is Mandy."

"Hi Mandy, I'm Faye. Have a seat, join me for a drink."

"I'm very sad, so I must buy a lot of beer to get drunk."

"You say your girlfriend has just left you?" said Faye, ordering a jug of beer and two glasses.

"Yes, but I don't know why she has gone. I very much have a broken heart now, but I am strong so it is not a problem," she said, tears welling in her eyes. "If your mind is strong, all difficult things will become easy. If your mind is weak, all easy things will become difficult. Chinese proverb. Do you know about true love, Faye?"

"Yes, I understand," she said, putting her hand on Mandy's shoulder.

"Do you have a lover, Faye?"

"Kind of, yes."

"A girl?"

"No, his name is Brent. I've come here to catch up with him. We got separated back in Vietnam, so hopefully he's here in Phnom Penh somewhere."

"What do you mean *kind of*?"

"I suppose we're just good friends really, but I've grown attached to him. We're more like an item if you know what I mean."

Their conversation was cut short by a Cambodian girl who approached Faye, informing her that a man had requested her to join him at his table. She looked over to where the girl was pointing and saw Jack sitting alone in front of a restaurant. She acknowledged the request and asked Mandy if they could see each other later, explaining that she had made an arrangement to meet somebody. Faye paid the bar tab and left.

"Hello Faye, glad you could make it," said Jack.

"Yes, hello."

"Please, sit here, Faye. I prefer people sitting to the right of me. I don't know why, of course. That's just the way it is."

"Yes," she said.

"I must say, you're looking very attractive this evening if you don't mind me saying so."

The Cambodian girl who passed the invitation to Faye came to the table.

"I sit here," she said, pulling out the chair and sitting down.

"No!" he barked. "You don't sit there! This is a private conversation. Now go away. Go and play pool or something."

"I drink one beer," she replied.

"Get a glass, take the beer, and leave. Do you understand?" said Jack curtly.

"Maybe I should leave as well," said Faye, standing up.

"Sit down, Faye. She's not worth being concerned about. She's nothing more than a bar dog. You came here for a reason. Do you remember?"

"Yes. So can you help me to find Brent?"

"All in good time, Faye. All in good time. I take it you'll be sticking around for a while. Finding Brent isn't going to be easy, you know. There's a lot of groundwork that needs to be done before we get to uncover what happened to him."

"I need to find Brent, so I'll stay for as long as it takes. And I *will* find him, with or without your help. You can rest assured of that."

"That's the spirit, Faye. Good girl. I have a feeling we're going to get along just fine, you and I."

"Are you going to contact that police officer like you said you would?"

"Of course. Stop worrying, and try to enjoy yourself, Faye. I will get in touch with you tomorrow. Ok?"

"Yes. I have to go now," she said, leaving quickly.

Faye left the mall and started walking back to her room when a motorbike driver pulled alongside and asked her if she needed a ride. She looked at her watch. It wasn't that late in the evening, so she asked him if he could take her around the city to see some special places. He didn't speak much English, and so she decided to try somebody else.

There were drivers everywhere, sitting on motorbikes and tuk-tuks outside the mall and all along the adjoining streets, so she carried on until it was fairly quiet, choosing one at the end of the line where it was dark.

The man had a friendly face, and emboldened by the beer that she had drunk, she approached him confidently, asking him as though her request was normal and commonplace.

"Do you speak English?" she said to the man sitting on the motorbike.

"Yes. What name hotel?"

"I don't want to go to a hotel. Can you take me to see a boy? I want a boy."

"Boy?"

"Yes, a boy. Do you know?"

"Boy where?"

"I don't know where. Can you show me where I can find a boy? Drive around the city, go to the house with girls for boom boom. Do you understand?"

"You want boom boom with girl?"

"No, I want a boy."

"You want boom boom with man?"

"No. I'm looking for a boy."

"You go one?"

"What?"

"You have friend?"

"No, I'm alone."

"Ok, I take you."

Faye thought about it for a moment.

"Never mind," she said.

She turned to walk away, realising the danger that she would put herself in being alone.

"Ok, I take you, no problem."

"No, I've changed my mind. It's getting late now. Maybe tomorrow. Thank you."

"No problem, I take you to find boy, don't worry," he said, desperate to get the fare.

"How about tomorrow? Will you be here?"

"Ok, up to you. Now you go hotel?"

"No, I'm fine. I'm staying just over there."

She walked away, turning out of sight as quickly as possible, hardly able to believe what she had just done by asking a complete stranger, a Cambodian man, to take her around the brothels to look for a boy when she was all by herself. She began to question her own sanity.

The following day turned out to be uneventful. Jack had not contacted her yet, and the chance of getting in touch with Brent seemed impossible.

That evening she headed for the restaurant where she and Brent had spent their last night together before leaving for Vietnam.

Sitting at the same table, she closed her eyes and pictured him in her mind, recalling how he had made her laugh so many times and the way he had held her hand as he talked of the future. A future that he wanted to share with her.

She opened her eyes to see Mandy standing in front of her wearing a new multi-coloured blouse, short denim hot pants, little pink socks, and white trainers on her feet. They blended perfectly with her long black hair and olive skin, making her look extremely cute and sexy.

"Hi, Faye! So nice to see you again. How is it?"

"Wow! Mandy, you look great. I'm fine. Would you like to join me? I'm just about to have dinner."

"Sure. You know, I was hoping to see you again, Faye. I went shopping today. Can you tell?" she said, laughing.

"Of course, and you've had your hair done as well."

"Yes, they made it a little bit wavy, like yours. And check out my nails!"

"Woh! Each one is a different colour. That's so today, Mandy. They look great, but it must have cost a mint!"

"But I'm worth it, right?"

"You bet!" she said as they laughed together.

"Do you think it's too far out there?"

"Not far enough. You should have done your toes, as well."

"I did. But I only wear trainers outdoors. I get blasters if I wear my sandals."

"Blisters," said Faye.

"Blisters?"

"Yes. Why don't you wear socks with them?"

"Socks with sandals? No, Faye, that's way not cool. And what will everybody think?"

"I understand, Mandy, I really do. But isn't it crazy how people are prepared to suffer just for the sake of having the approval of others? Anyway, we can have deep conversations later. Let's get a drink in."

They ate dinner and drank cocktails, talking and laughing and sharing their travel stories and experiences. Faye talked of her days at university and her job as a care assistant, while Mandy enthused about her work as a fashion designer and travel writer. They finished their drinks and decided to go to the nightclub across the street, The Art Of Darkness.

Admission was free, and there was a two for the price of one offer on the Margaritas and Mojitos until midnight. Mandy took hold of Faye's hand and led her through the black curtains at the entrance, down the narrow hallway, and into a dark and crowded space.

They ordered drinks and stood next to a table, sharing it with some young Cambodians who tried to talk to them, shouting to make themselves heard above the excessively loud music.

After another cocktail or two, Mandy linked arms with Faye and led her onto the dance floor. They swayed in rhythm through the white flashes of the strobe lights, making eye contact and coming closer together in sexually suggestive gyrating moves, holding each other by the waist.

They danced until they could dance no more and drank until they could drink no more. They left the club laughing and joking.

"What should we do now, Faye?"

"I can't think. How about you?"

"Can I ask you something, Faye?"

"Yes, sure."

"You know, I really like you, Faye. Do you know what I mean?"

"And I really like you too, Mandy," she said, giving her a hug.

"No, I mean, I really *like* you. I felt like we connected when we

147

were dancing together. Do you feel the same way?"

"Of course. We're good friends, and I hope we always will be, Mandy."

"Can we be more than just good friends?"

Faye looked at her, thinking carefully about how to respond.

"You mean lovers?" she said cautiously.

"Can we, Faye?"

"Oh, Mandy, you're so sweet," she said, holding her closely. "But I'm just not like that."

"Yes, it's ok. I understand," said Mandy, smiling softly, her eyes watering slightly.

"Can I buy you one last drink?" said Faye.

As they chatted together outside the mall, a motorbike pulled over. It was the driver that Faye had been talking to the day before.

"You want boy?" he said.

"I'm not sure," replied Faye, feeling slightly embarrassed.

"What does he want?" said Mandy.

"He's asking me if I want to go for sex with a boy."

"Do you have girls?" said Mandy.

"You want boom boom with girl?" he replied.

"Yes. Do you have?"

"Ok, no problem. I take you."

"Will you come with me, Faye?"

"Do you think it's safe? I mean, we don't know who he is or where he's going to take us."

"Let's not worry too much. Don't miss opportunities; time doesn't come around again. Chinese proverb," said Mandy.

"If you don't do stupid things, you won't end up in tragedy. Chinese proverb," replied Faye.

"Ok, you don't worry. Come," said the driver, smiling broadly and patting his hand on the rear of his motorbike seat.

Faye got on the bike, and Mandy sat behind her, wrapping her arms around Faye's waist as the driver set off. It was a short journey, and they found themselves down a dark deserted side street across the river in the poorer part of town.

He pulled up outside an unlit building and told the girls to get off the bike. Killing the engine, he led them down an enclosed alley to the rear and banged on the door. A middle-aged woman opened up and they went inside.

It was a novel experience for Faye and Mandy, and they sat expectantly but slightly apprehensively on a couch, looking amused as the girls came into the room while the driver spoke to the woman.

Mandy told her what she was looking for and was taken to another room where a young Cambodian girl who was twenty-four and quite attractive sat on the edge of the bed. The woman explained that the girl was the only one available for what she wanted, and so Mandy agreed on a price and accepted the offer.

Closing the bedroom door behind her, the woman returned to Faye and asked her what she was looking for. Faye brazenly told her that she wanted a boy, someone around the age of fifteen. The woman informed her that there weren't any boys staying in that house, but she could take her to one not far away.

Faye knocked on the bedroom door where Mandy was. She opened it, wrapped in a large white towel. Faye explained that she was going somewhere and told Mandy to wait there for her until she returned.

The woman took Faye outside and down a winding dirt path to a small group of shanties nestled together among some trees.

She opened the twisted wooden door on one of the huts and went inside. A young boy sat alone in the dim glow of an unshaded light bulb that hung down and rested against the bamboo wall. Faye walked over and smiled. She had lost the anxiety that she felt earlier and sat down next to him on the rattan bed frame, asking his name. He didn't seem nervous or shy but said nothing, just smiled. The woman spoke to him, and he told Faye his name.

Taking out her phone, Faye showed the boy some pictures of Brent and asked if he had seen or spoken to him. He looked at the photos and said definitely that he didn't recognise him. Faye asked the woman if there were any other boys that she could talk to, but she was told that he was the only one.

They left and went back to the house. Faye sat on the couch and waited until Mandy's desire had been sated, passing the time by chatting to the girls who worked there and watching curiously as men came and went, rejecting their offers by telling them ridiculous lies about how she was just waiting for her boyfriend to finish, unable to think of a better explanation for being there.

Mandy came out of the room and they left the house, returning to the mall on the motorbike. They paid the driver handsomely and sat outside a bar, contemplating the evening. Neither of them spoke. Mandy was wrapped up in the moment and gazed into the distance, smiling contentedly. Faye's mood shifted between a sense of achievement and a feeling of disappointment. She had been bold about asking for the boy, but she was still left with the frustration of being no closer to finding Brent.

The next day, Faye received a message from Jack saying that he wanted to meet her and would call her later that morning. She had already made arrangements to see Mandy, and so she headed for the restaurant to meet her.

As the afternoon wore on, Faye received a phone call.

"Meet me at the bar in the mall," said Jack.

"Why do we always have to meet in the mall? I'm bored with that place already," replied Faye.

"Alright, tell me where you are, and I'll come down there."

"I'm with my friend outside The Alley Cat Bar & Grill down by the riverside."

"I need to talk to you alone."

"Why? What's the big secret?"

"This is between me and you, not the entire world. I will be at my bar on fifty-first street. I've got some news about Brent. Show up if you want to hear what I've got to say," he said curtly, before hanging up.

"Who was that?" said Mandy.

"Just some creep who claims he can help me find my boyfriend."

"Blessings come in disguise."

"Chinese proverb?" said Faye.

"Of course."

"He wants to meet me alone later on at the mall."

"That's alright, I can do my own thing. We can meet afterwards if you like."

"We can go together," said Faye.

"He might get angry."

"I've got an idea. You walk in first and sit at a different bar, nearby. I will phone you just before I meet up with him. Don't hang up. I want you to listen to the conversation."

"So I will have a good excuse for ignoring everyone because I will be *talking to you*, right?"

"At least pretending to. How good is your acting?"

"I was in movies in Hong Kong, fighting the bad guys. I practice martial arts. For real, Faye, I can show you the films that I was in. Have you seen Mai Dim Sun's *Chew Kok*?"

Faye stared at her.

"You're joking, right?" she said, looking serious.

"Of course not! Why?"

"*My dim sons?*"

"Yes. Mai Dim Sun is one of Hong Kong's most famous film directors. I was in that movie, *Chew Kok*. I'm surprised that you've never heard of him."

They smiled innocently at each other.

"Ok, don't forget to mute your phone so that no noise comes from your end."

"Got it," said Mandy.

Placing her phone in front of her on the table by the side of her bag, Faye sat down next to Jack. He was drunk and in a bad mood, and she felt intimidated, wanting to leave immediately.

"Do you have some news about Brent?" she said.

"I might do," replied Jack abruptly.

"What do you mean *you might do*?"

"I mean I might have some news about Brent. That's what I mean."

"Either you do or you don't."

He stared at her coldly.

"What would you say if I told you that I know exactly where he is?"

"I would say that's the best news I've had in a long time, and let's go there right now."

"Yes, I suppose you would."

"Are you teasing me?"

"Why not? I mean, after all, isn't that what you're doing with me?"

"I don't know what you're talking about."

"Yes you do. Or maybe you're doing it subconsciously and don't realise it," he said, slurring his words slightly and raising the beer bottle to his mouth.

"Doing what, exactly?"

"Flirting with me."

"In what way am I flirting with you?"

"The way that you pout your cherried lips, flutter your painted eyelash—"

"I don't wear makeup," she said abruptly. "You're letting your imagination run away with you."

"Don't get me wrong, Faye. Being seduced by a woman who is trying to get what she wants doesn't bother me at all. In fact, I'm quite used to it by now."

"You expect something from me then. Is that what it is?"

"People normally do receive payment for services rendered, Faye," he said, staring at her coldly. "That's just the way it is."

"So what do you want from me?"

"Nothing much, Faye. Just a bit of respect and trust. Dare I mention the word friendliness? I'm not the bogeyman, Faye. I just want to help you, that's all."

She frowned and looked deeply into his eyes.

"Do you have any news about Brent, or are you just playing games with me?"

"He's in a monastery on the other side of town."

"What's he doing there?"

"Being reclusive, I should imagine. That's normally the reason why people become monks, isn't it?"

"This is ridiculous," she said angrily. "You're just making up one big story after another."

"Am I? Have a look at these," he said, taking out his phone and showing her a set of pictures. "He seemed very depressed, told me that he needed to forget his past, that he wanted to go somewhere and meditate, start a new life, become a different person. I suggested the monastery. I think he's found peace with himself now."

Faye looked at the photos of Brent in the grounds of a temple, wearing loose-fitting saffron-coloured clothing, his head shaved bald.

"Can you take me there?" she said.

"You won't be able to go inside the monastery. The monks only allow males to enter, but the police officer that I told you about owns a hotel nearby, so you can stay there while we arrange something. You'll be perfectly safe. What do you say?" he said, changing his tone and talking to her more politely.

"Will the police officer be at the hotel?"

"He's very busy down at the station most of the time, but I can get him to meet you at the hotel if you like," said Jack in a reassuring voice. "You need to relax, Faye, and start trusting me. There really isn't anything to worry about, you know. We've found Brent for you. You should be pleased with yourself."

"So I will get on the back of a motorbike and follow you to the hotel, and then we will meet the policeman at the reception. Is that right?"

"Absolutely. Are you ready to leave now?" he said.

"Yes, let's go, Mandy," said Faye, picking up her phone and placing it in her bag.

"What did you say?"

"Oh, I'm sorry. I thought your name was Andy. I was mistaking you for somebody that I'd met earlier. It's Jack, isn't it?" she said, smiling.

Ending the call with Mandy, Faye hailed a driver, got on the back of his bike, and followed Jack as he headed off towards the outskirts of town, six or seven miles away.

They pulled up outside a modern upmarket property, standing alone on the corner of the street at the end of the block. Jack drove his bike straight into the large foyer and parked it next to the others by the reception desk.

Faye paid the driver and waited outside, stalling for time until she caught sight of Mandy approaching on the back of a bike in the distance. Mandy waved to acknowledge that she had seen her and tapped on the driver's shoulder for him to turn the corner and stop. After the driver had gone, she took a circuitous route and walked to a small coffee shack where she could observe the building but remain inconspicuous.

Faye went inside the hotel. A young Cambodian woman welcomed her warmly, offering her a seat on an intricately carved wooden couch and then returning to bring her a glass of warm green tea.

"Where is the police officer?" said Faye.

"He's on his way. I've just called him. He should be here any minute now," replied Jack.

"Can you take me to see Brent after I've met him?"

"I will have to arrange a meeting with the abbot first, let him know who you are and why you've come here. I'm sure there won't be any problems, but it's always best to follow protocol, isn't it?"

"When do you think we can go there?"

"I've sorted a suitable room out for you, so if you want to get some rest, I will go and speak to him, fix things up for later. How does that sound?"

A middle-aged Cambodian man dressed in a light brown uniform with a peaked cap entered the lobby and shook hands with Jack, who stood up to greet him. He turned to Faye and introduced himself.

"Hello, how are you? My name is Mr Somnang," he said with a broad smile.

"Hello, nice to meet you. I'm Faye," she said, standing up.

"Welcome to my hotel. I hope you have a good stay with us. Mr Jack has told me that you come here to meet your friend?"

"Yes. Apparently, he's joined the monastery and become a monk. So this is your hotel! I take it that you're also a policeman?"

"Yes, I am the district chief of police. What is the name of your friend?"

"His name is Brent. He's from England. Do you know him? Have you seen him?" she said, taking out her phone and showing him some pictures.

"No, I have not met this person. Do you have your passport or some ID?"

"My ID or Brent's ID?"

"Your ID."

"The guest house where I'm staying has my passport, but I have my international driving licence. Is that ok?"

"Yes. Please, show it to me."

"And what is the name of your guest house?" he said, handing back the licence.

"I can't remember exactly," she replied, not wanting to give Jack any information. "It's a Khmer name, a strange name. It's not far from the Royal Palace. That's all I know, really."

"I must return to my job now. Is there something you would like to ask before I leave?"

"Do you have a number that I can contact you on?"

"Yes. I am busy most of the time at my office, but you can call me on this number."

"Thank you," she said, taking the card and putting it in her bag.

"I am sorry, but I am very busy, so now I must go. Please enjoy your stay with us."

"Thank you for your help, Mr Somnang," she said as he turned to leave.

"Let me show you to your room," said Jack, picking up the key from the reception desk.

"Maybe it would be a better idea if I went back to my guest house and came here tomorrow morning," she said.

"No. There's a chance that I can get Brent to come here tonight. I will speak to Mr Somnang later this evening to see if he can go round there and talk to them. Come, follow me."

"Mr Somnang said that he doesn't know Brent and that he hasn't seen him. I think you're lying to me."

"Brent has changed his appearance and lost a lot of weight since he joined the monastery due to the strict regimen he has been placed on. Mr Somnang simply didn't recognise the photo that you showed him. Besides, apart from official ceremonies, the police have very little contact with the monks, and anyone who seeks sanctuary at the temple is granted complete anonymity."

"So how were you able to find Brent so easily then?"

"What makes you think it was so easy? Phnom Penh is my home, Faye. I've been here a long time now, and I know a lot of people. Look, I've gone to a lot of trouble to help you, and all you seem to do is cast doubt on me. And now you're calling me a liar. I think the least you could do is give me the benefit of the doubt. You'll be perfectly comfortable staying here, and I've arranged to have dinner sent to your room with enough food for two. I understand your reservations, Faye. I really do. Let me buy you a drink at the hotel bar. We can have a chat and get to know each other better."

They walked up the winding staircase to the first floor and sat at the bar. A group of men walked past Faye and went into a private room at the back, and as the door opened, she watched as they joined others, sitting around tables playing poker and roulette. The girl behind the bar asked Jack what they would like to drink.

"I think I'll have a double HeadBanger. No, wait. Make that a triple," said Jack.

"A tipple WallBanger?" said the Cambodian waitress.

"*Triple*. Yes, but with extra vodka and a splash of gin. It's called a HeadBanger. Not too much ice, either. What will you be having, Faye? It's on me, of course."

"Just a beer, please."

"Are you sure? The cocktails are top shelf here, if you know what I mean. Are you sure you wouldn't like to try one of those, instead?"

"Beer is fine, thank you."

"You must be feeling quite excited, are you? When was the last

155

time you saw Brent?"

"I think it's been almost a month now. You've spoken to him just recently then, have you?" she said, drinking the beer straight from the bottle.

"Yes. Last night, actually. He's quite a changed person, Faye. I hadn't seen him since he came to Thailand. That was about one month ago as well, come to think of it. He was full of life back then. I don't know what's got into him lately. Something must be eating away at him."

"Does he know that I'm here?"

"No, not yet. I thought we'd keep it a surprise. Who knows, it might just raise his spirit."

"Do they have a toilet I can use?" said Faye.

"Yes, over there, on the left."

Jack told the waitress to accompany Faye to the bathroom.

"Your friend Mr Somnang must have a very high-paying job," said Faye as she returned to the bar. "It's a very posh hotel."

"Yes, absolutely," replied Jack. "Would you like another drink?"

"No, thank you, this one is beginning to taste bitter."

"You must be hungry. Let me show you to your room, and I will have dinner sent up."

"And then are you going to get in touch with Brent afterwards?"

"Yes, straight away."

They left the bar and walked towards the elevator.

"I've chosen a room for you at the very top," he said, pressing the key for the eighth floor. "There's a group of Chinese businessmen arriving tonight, and it's going to get busy. They like to party, and it tends to get rather noisy. They will be staying for a couple of days."

As Jack unlocked the door to Faye's room and showed her inside, a Cambodian man, adjusting his belt, came out of the room opposite with two young women and got into the lift.

"You'll find everything you need here. There's more beer in the fridge if you want it, and there's a telephone over there if you want to call reception. Just dial zero and tell them what you need."

"Will they have any headache tablets?" she said, sitting on the edge of the bed. "I feel a bit light-headed."

"Yes, of course. I'll get them to send some up with your meal. Help yourself to the water. It's in the fridge," he said as he left the room.

After a couple of minutes, Faye opened the door and checked the hallway to make sure that Jack had gone. Feeling dizzy, she took out her phone and fumbled with it, her vision blurring and her hands shaking as she called Mandy.

"Mandy, where are you?"

"Faye! Are you alright? I'm outside the hotel in a coffee shop. What's going up? Is it happening? I've been hanging on just waiting for you to call me."

"I'm ok, Mandy. Are you ok? I love you so much for looking out for me. You know that, don't you? Jack said that Brent might come round tonight."

"Are you feeling safe, Faye? You know I'm very worried about you right now."

"I should be alright if I keep the door locked. There's a good movie on tonight, and I've got a few beers in the fridge. I'm feeling a bit excited about Brent coming round, but I think I should keep my feet firmly on the ground about that one."

"Do you want me to come round there?"

"I think it might be better if you didn't, Mandy. I don't know what it is, but there's something about Jack that doesn't fit, and I don't want to drag you into anything. But if you could meet me tomorrow, then it would be super sweet of you."

"I can feel it too, Faye. Something is not right about that place. You know, I've been sitting here looking at that hotel, and the Feng Shui is all wrong, and the harmony is out of sync."

"I don't know about that... but, I..."

"Faye, are you alright? You don't sound well. What's wrong with you? Your voice has slowed down. You sound like you're really sleepy, or something."

"It's ok, Mandy. Will you meet me here tomorrow?"

"Of course I will. Tell me your plan."

"If Brent doesn't show up by about ten or eleven in the morning, then I will leave."

"So I will be here waiting for you at this coffee shop tomorrow morning. Ok, promise me that you will be careful, Faye."

"I will... and..."

"Faye! Are you sure you're ok?"

"Yes, I just feel a bit drowsy, that's all."

"Ok, good night, Faye. I will go back to my guest house now. See you soon."

"Yes," she said faintly, as the phone slipped from her hand and she passed out on the bed.

Feeling confused and nauseous, she woke up to the sound of men and women arguing and fighting in the room opposite. It was totally dark outside, and the clock on the wall showed two in the morning. She searched for her phone but couldn't find it, noticing that the top three buttons of her blouse were undone as she checked her top pocket.

Her door had been securely locked on the outside, and there was no way of leaving the room. Her banging on the door and shouting brought no response. She walked over to the window to see if there were any means of escape, but there were none. She searched again for her phone, looking under the bed and even in the bathroom. But it was nowhere to be found.

The sound of the padlock being undone made her step backwards. She looked around for an object that she could use as a weapon, but her mind was too clouded to think straight. Jack opened the door and walked in, closing it quietly behind him and locking it.

"I have some news about Brent. He said that he doesn't want to see you ever again. He said that he had disgraced himself by performing sexual acts with a boy and that he must serve his penance with the monks."

"You're a liar. Why did you lock me in the room?"

"For your safety. There's a lot of drinking and gambling going on downstairs, and some of the people staying in that room opposite are mafia. I had to make sure that you were safe. It's not uncommon for girls like you to be kidnapped, Faye. By the way, are you feeling alright? Can I get you anything?"

"Yes, you can get me a taxi. I want to leave, right now!" she said angrily.

"Brent asked me to take good care of you, Faye. In fact he made me promise. Of course, I said that I would. We were close friends, you know."

"Let me go! I want to go. I have to leave," she screamed as she pushed past him towards the door.

Jack grabbed hold of her arm and spun her around before she could get to the door, covering her mouth with his hand as she screamed loudly for help. Tears welled in her eyes as she fought to get free from his grasp, but he was too powerful, standing behind her

158

with his arms around her. She bit hard into his hand, sinking her teeth into his fingers, causing him to momentarily release his grip. She made another attempt at getting to the door, but he grabbed her hair, and she fell backwards onto the bed.

Jack stormed out of the room, slamming the door shut and putting the padlock on, leaving Faye on the bed crying inconsolably.

She was desperate for help, but her mind was still groggy, and she could think of no way of getting out or contacting anybody.

It was four in the morning when Jack returned. He unlocked the door and opened it cautiously. Faye was standing in the corner when he entered the room.

"I didn't appreciate the way that you treated me when I came to see if you were alright, Faye. I don't understand why you felt the need to attack me. I was simply bringing you news about Brent, that's all."

"Yes, I know. I'm really sorry about that. I hope I haven't caused any serious injury. I was confused. It was just a misunderstanding. Are you alright? Here, let me have a look at your hand. I trained as a nurse before I went to Uni."

"You bit so hard that you drew blood. I thought I was going to lose a finger or two."

"I'm so sorry, Jack, honestly. It was just a mad moment. It must have been the drinks that we'd had earlier in the bar. Please, sit down next to me on the bed. Let me fix it for you."

"I want to look after you, Faye. And I will, just like Brent asked me to. I'm going to take good care of you. I promise. You're like the daughter that I never had."

"Do you have any children, Jack?" she said, holding his hand as she inspected the wound.

"No. I missed all of the chances that came along, and now it's too late."

"I'm glad that you told me about Brent. I always suspected there was something odd about him, something strange. And now I know the truth. We talked about having a child, but there's just no way that we could ever be together, not after what you've said. No way."

"I realised he was no good when he came over to visit me in Thailand. I'm sorry if I've ruined things for you, Faye, but I think it's best for you to know just what kind of guy Brent was."

"*Is*," said Faye.

"Is what?" said Jack.

"To know just what kind of guy Brent *is*," she said, smiling at him as she corrected his manner of speaking.

"You're too nice, too sweet, to let somebody like him into your life, Faye. You need a stronger man, somebody who will protect you."

"Well, it looks like I've found one," she said, smiling at him again. "Do you have a medicine cabinet? I need to put something on that cut to stop it becoming infected."

"Yes, there's one downstairs. Tell me what you need. I'll go and get it for you."

"I will have to go and look what there is myself, see if there's any antibiotic ointment and a sterile dressing. Hold your hand under the cold tap until I get back, but try not to touch the cut," she said as she made a move for the door.

"Sit down, Faye."

"I'm just going to get something to treat that cut on your finger."

"I said sit down. SIT DOWN!" he barked as she continued heading for the door.

"Why won't you let me go and have a look at what medical supplies you've got? I'm the only one who knows what to use. You don't know what to look for."

"What makes you so sure about that? You'd be surprised at what I know."

"So we can go together then."

"No. You stay here."

"Why can't I go with you? I've been stuck in this room for hours. I need a break. I thought you said you were going to take care of me."

"That's why I want you to stay here. I told you, there are mafia roaming around the place. They're drunk, and it's not safe for you out there. They will be leaving soon, so when they do, I will let you know."

"I will bring some breakfast up for you. Do you want tea or coffee?" he said, heading for the door.

Faye stared at him coldly.

"I said do you want tea or coffee with your breakfast?"

"I don't want anything," she said quietly, lowering her head.

Jack closed the door behind him and put the padlock on. Faye sat on the edge of the bed, crying and holding her head in her hands. She was drained, physically and emotionally, wanting to scream, jump

160

out of the window, anything.

Jack returned around six-thirty, unlocking the door and placing a tray of food on the small table next to Faye's bed. He had been drinking in the bar since the night before and was heavily drunk.

The dinner that he had promised to send her never arrived, and although she was faint from hunger, she refrained from eating the breakfast or drinking the coffee, too paranoid and concerned about her safety.

Jack told her that he would be back shortly and then left, padlocking the door.

Faye searched the room again, desperately trying to find her phone. She searched the place thoroughly, but it had gone. She picked up the hotel phone and called reception.

"Hello, may I help?" said the girl on the desk.

"Yes, I want to speak to the owner, Mr Som... Som, something."

"You want to speak with manager?"

"Yes. No! Not the manager—the owner," said Faye impatiently. "*Own?*"

"The owner, the police man."

"Who?"

"Police," she said, raising her voice. "I want to speak to the police."

"Speak to the *please?*"

"*Police,*" said Faye, slowly pronouncing the word.

"You talk to Mr Jack, manager."

"No, I don't want to talk to Jack. I need to talk to the police. Can't you just put me through to the police?" she pleaded.

"No. Sorry, I can not do. Can only speak to manager, Mr Jack."

"Can I speak to somebody else?"

"What?"

"Can I speak to a tourist? Somebody in the hotel. Anybody."

"What tourist?"

"I don't know. Anybody!"

"What problem?"

"I'm stuck in my room. I can't get out. I can't open the door."

"Ok, I tell manager, Mr Jack."

"No, you don't understand! I need to speak to somebody, but not Mr Jack."

"I very sorry. All call from hotel room go to manager, Mr Jack.

You want to talk with manager?"

"No," she said, slamming the phone down.

Jack returned with more coffee. He came into the room and sat on a chair by the door.

"You haven't eaten your breakfast."

"I'm not hungry."

"You don't understand me, do you, Faye?"

"What is there to understand? You've got me locked in a room against my will."

"I just want to take care of you now that Brent has gone."

"What do you mean *now that Brent has gone*?"

"He's gone from your life, hasn't he?"

"Yes, I suppose he has."

"You suppose? He was having sex with a young boy. He—"

"Have you got proof that Brent was having sex with the boy?" said Faye angrily.

"I don't need proof. I know *his* type. I've met them before. He was a vile, sick person who had no morals, no decency, no worth, no right to be in society. He was a predator."

"And you're different, right?"

"I have a reason to be walking the streets. A good reason. He didn't."

"And what reason might that be?"

"To clean up the garbage, the filth. To rid society of the evils that exist. To make sure that our children are safe."

"That's very admirable, Jack. I'm impressed."

"You don't sound very impressed," he said, staring at her. "Let me inform you of an incident that happened recently. Maybe it will help you to understand what I'm talking about. A Japanese man bought a young Cambodian girl and kept her in his room for three days before strangling her. Her body was later disposed of by the local chief of police. The man paid one hundred thousand dollars for the experience."

"Really?" she said, her face turning pale.

"Yes."

"I'm sorry, but I can't believe what you're telling me. You're saying that the people are willing to sell their children and the police know exactly what's going on? Why should I believe that? How do you know it's true and not just a lie?"

"Because I was in the same building, in the room next to his, when it happened."

"And now he's in prison? You had him arrested afterwards?"

"No. Now he's dead."

"I don't understand. Are you saying that you knew he had the girl in his room?"

"Yes."

"Did you know what he was going to do to her?"

"Yes."

She stared at him, trying to make sense of the madness that she was listening to, trying to find the words that she needed to say.

"How could you do that?" she said slowly. "Why didn't you rescue her?"

"I'm not here to save people. I'm here to kill paedophiles."

"So why are you not in jail for murdering him?"

"Money. The price for the girl should have been seventy-five thousand. He unwittingly paid the extra twenty-five to cover my costs. He paid for his own death. And it wasn't murder. It was retribution."

"Can you stop talking? Just stop! I don't want to hear this."

"Tell me something. When you were in Vietnam did you visit My Lai?" he said, pressing hard.

She stared at him with a desperate look on her face and sighed, tears forming in her eyes.

"No, I've never heard of it. What is it?"

"It's a village, near Quang Ngai."

"Why do you want to know if I went there?"

"During the war, in 1968, American forces concluded that My Lai was a Viet Cong stronghold and sent in ground troops to destroy it. More than five hundred unarmed civilians, poor rice farmers, old men, women, children, and babies were murdered, their livestock shot, their hamlet of simple bamboo and straw dwellings torched and razed to the ground. Alongside the American soldiers were army photographers. They were sent there to document the entire operation. One of the photographs taken shows a group of four women and two children embracing each other, crying, their faces fraught with anguish. Seconds later they were all shot dead."

"I don't understand your point," said Faye, smiling faintly, her lips quivering.

"My point is that the photographers weren't there to save the children. They were there to take photographs, and the children would have been killed regardless of whether the photographers were present or not. Do you understand?"

"Yes," she murmured weakly.

"Think about it carefully, Faye. About that—what should we call him—*tourist*, if you like, who came to Cambodia for the specific purpose of buying the girl and killing her for his sick, perverted gratification. Do you condemn me for terminating him? What would you prefer? That we let him continue?"

Faye stared at him with a determined expression.

"But the fact is that you enjoy killing people. Don't you?"

"Like I just said, some people deserve it," he replied. "Apart from the first one, that is. I still have regrets about that."

"So why did you kill him then?"

"It wasn't a man. It was a woman. Our team was inserted into an area at night on a covert mission in Iraq. She got in the way, so I took her out. But I realised later that I'd had alternatives."

"I see," she said faintly, staring at the floor.

"No, I don't think you do," he said, raising his voice. "You can't see me for what I am—my good intentions, my care and consideration, my feelings for you and others. You don't understand me. You can't see the real me."

"Believe me, Jack, I can. I can see exactly what you are. Exactly."

He stared at her, forcing her to turn her face and endure the agonizing silence.

"We could be together. You know that, don't you, Faye?" he said, softening his tone. "I can take care of you. We can have children. You'd like that, wouldn't you? And I've got money, so you don't need to worry about anything. We can go anywhere you want. We could stay here or live in Thailand, travel the world, anything."

She stared at him with a horrified look on her face.

"It sounds promising, but I would have to think about it. Besides, I don't know much about you, Jack. You haven't told me anything about yourself."

"What do you want to know?"

"So... I take it you're from the UK?"

"Originally, yes. Then I emigrated to Australia."

"And you were in the army?"

"Correct."

"And now you're running a hotel?"

"Among other things, yes. Do you want some of this coffee before it goes cold?" he said, totally uninterested in her questioning.

"No. Thank you. Among other things, you say? Other things such as vigilante paedophile hunter?"

"If that's what you want to call it."

"How old are you, Jack?"

"Sixty-two. Why?"

"Can I ask you a hypothetical question?"

"What is it?"

"If you were to be interned for the rest of your life on a deserted island and you could take just one person with you, a female, which one would you take? A female the same age as yourself or a young girl?"

Jack glared at her.

"I suggest we finish this conversation later," he said. "I have something to sort out. The Chinese will be leaving shortly, so when they do I will let you know."

Standing up and opening the door to leave, he turned around and stared at her.

"Don't try getting too smart, Faye. I don't like that in a woman."

As he padlocked the door, she ran to the bathroom, collapsing on the floor and vomiting into the toilet.

Chapter 19

Strangers In The Night

Mandy finished her morning yoga session around noon and hired a fast motorbike for the day. She skipped breakfast, deciding instead to have lunch with Faye later on.

It was a beautiful sunny day, and the sky was solid blue without a cloud to be seen. She laughed, throwing her head back and letting the breeze blow through her hair as she took off, thrilled and delighted and singing her favourite songs as she opened up the engine on the free highway ahead.

She was looking forward to meeting up with Faye and expected to see her sitting outside the coffee shop talking to Brent. Faye had spoken a lot about him, and she was keen to find out what he looked like in person, having seen only a few badly taken snapshots of him on Faye's phone.

Mandy revved the bike as she passed the hotel and pulled up in front of the coffee shop.

She sat outside under a large sunbrella, ordered a drink, and took her phone out.

The waitress brought the coffee and a small glass of green tea, placing them on the table with an ashtray. She walked over to the television that hung on the wall and switched it on, turning the volume up and changing the channel to an American news agency.

The cafe was empty, and apart from a young child collecting plastic bottles and discarded soft-drink cans, the road was deserted. She phoned Faye, but there was no answer.

Mandy had been there almost two hours, and after repeated attempts at trying to contact Faye, wondered whether she should go over to the hotel and ask the receptionist what was going on.

The hotel was across the road, almost opposite the cafe, and she noticed the phone number written next to the name on the awning above the entrance. She tried to call the number but realised that her phone was out of credit.

"Excuse me," she said, turning around to speak to the waitress. "Is there anywhere I can buy a phone card to top up my phone?"

"No. You want phone?" she replied, taking her phone out of her pocket and offering it to Mandy.

"You're so kind. Thank you."

"Ok, no problem," replied the waitress, smiling.

Mandy called the number and spoke to the girl on the desk.

"Hello, do you speak English?" said Mandy.

"Hello, yes, Hotel Somnang. May I help, please?" said the receptionist.

"Hi, I'm trying to get in touch with my friend. She's staying at your hotel. Her name is Faye."

"What number room, please?"

"I'm sorry, I don't know the room number."

"You wait moment, please. You call manager, hotel. His phone number—"

"Oh, hang on, let me write it down," said Mandy.

She turned to the waitress and asked to borrow a pen.

"Ok, what's his number?"

"You call 0585695023," said the receptionist.

"Thanks."

She called the mobile, and after a lengthy delay, she finally got through to a man at the end of the line.

"Yes?" he said in a stern voice.

"Hi, I'm trying to contact my friend. She's staying at your hotel. She's from England. Her name is Faye."

"Who are you? What's your name?"

"I'm a friend of hers, from Phnom Penh."

"She's not here anymore. She checked out this morning."

"Checked out! Did she say where she was going?"

"She said she had to go back to England urgently."

"Really? Are you sure?"

"Yes, I'm sure."

"Are you sure you know who I'm talking about?"

"I just told you. I'm sure."

"Did she leave a... Hello? Hello?"

Mandy gave the phone back to the girl, thanked her, and offered to pay for the call. She ordered another coffee and stared at the hotel, feeling disheartened at what she had just been told, questioning whether it was true, refusing to believe it. She felt like going over there to see for herself, but the curt response that she had got from the manager dissuaded her. She struck up a conversation with the waitress to take her mind off it, buying her a drink and asking if she would like to go on a date sometime.

It was late in the afternoon, and Mandy decided to head back into town, feeling that there was nothing more she could do there. Taking the keys out of her bag, she sat for a minute, staring at the hotel before getting on the bike. As she was about to leave, the waitress walked over, holding out her phone.

"I think maybe for you," she said, passing the phone to Mandy.
"What is it?"
"Message."
"Let me see what it says."

Sorry about not contacting you earlier
Had to leave early to get Brent to the airport
He's very ill
Had to get him back to England asap
Faye

Mandy checked the number. The message was sent from Faye's phone. She thanked the waitress, gave her the phone, and wished her well before starting the bike and slowly driving off.

Pulling up outside the mall, she went to the bar, ordered a beer, and sat alone, watching the sun sinking to the ground as though it were the beating heart inside of her. She felt numb, sad, and alone, and yet she didn't want anybody to comfort her. All she wanted was Faye. But she was gone.

The girl behind the bar must have sensed her mood and put on some blues music. Mandy smiled at her and asked for another bottle of beer.

As the alcohol started to take effect, she began to mellow out, and as one of her favourite tunes came on, she sang along, quietly repeating the words.

"Strangers in the night, exchanging..."

Strangers in the night. Strangers in the night. She repeated the words over and over in her head, but for some unknown reason the words seemed to haunt her. She thought about Faye and how she had sent the message to a stranger instead of sending it to her personally. Maybe Faye had thought that she had bought a new mobile and had changed her number.

Mandy put the bottle to her lips but stopped short of taking another sip. Something didn't fit, wasn't right. She just knew it. She thought about the message again, how Faye had checked out early that morning to get to the airport and then had managed, somehow, to get hold of the waitress's number.

"Oh my god!" she screamed, jumping up from the table and running towards her motorbike.

"Hey! You pay money!" shouted the bar tender.

"Oh, I'm so sorry!" said Mandy, returning to the bar hurriedly.

"You drink two beer, yes?"

"Yes, how much do I owe you?"

"You look," said the waitress, passing her the bill.

"Ok, keep the change," said Mandy, handing over a note and rushing outside.

Speeding down the road, it was almost dark when she approached the coffee shop. Slowing the bike, she cruised up and down in front of the hotel, revving the engine loudly like some kind of fighter pacing to and fro, waiting for their opponent to step out.

Faye heard the roar of the engine and ran to the window. She could just about see the bike as it pulled up in front of the coffee shop, but it was too dark to make out who the driver was. She tried to open the window, but it was stuck fast, and the security bars that covered it prevented any chance of breaking the glass.

As Mandy debated what to do next, something caught her eye. On the top floor, a light flashed on and off repeatedly. She watched it carefully and noticed that the light came on for three short flashes and then three longer flashes followed by three short flashes, repeating itself over and over. She recognised the distress signal and calculated that the room was on the eighth floor at the rear of the building.

The rescue mission was on, and she didn't have to wait long before going into action. She saw her chance when a group of drunken Chinese men emerged from the lobby and stood in front of the hotel to get some fresh air. Walking over, she started chatting to them, and as they went back inside she linked arms with the two in the middle, acting the part of the call girl, laughing and flirting.

Four of the men went back to the casino, and the other two got in the lift with Mandy.

They stepped out onto the third floor and walked over to a room. As one of the men fumbled in his pocket looking for the key, Mandy made an excuse about having left something at the coffee shop. She threw her arms around the men, hugging and kissing them, explaining that she would be back shortly. Taking the stairs, she slowly walked down until she was sure they had entered their room, listening carefully for the door to slam shut before doubling back and quietly climbing the stairs to the top floor.

On the landing, there were two rooms to the left, one on either side, and two rooms to the right. She noticed one of them had a light on with a padlock on the door and walked over, standing outside and listening momentarily before tapping on the door. There was no response, so she softly called Faye's name.

"Faye, Faye, are you in there? Faye, can you hear me?" said Mandy in a hushed tone.

"What?" said Faye in a slurred, almost incomprehensible voice.

"Faye, it's me, Mandy."

"Mandy? Oh God, Mandy!"

"Keep quiet! Don't shout. Faye, you have to keep your voice down. Stop shouting."

"Mandy, please, help me. Mandy, you have to get me out of here. For God's sake, Mandy, please!"

"Stop shouting! Faye, you've got to stop making all that noise. You're going to bring Jack up here. He will hear you. Just calm down, ok?"

"Mandy, he's going to kill me!" she cried.

"Faye, are you hurt? What's the situation in there? Has he tied you up? Can you move around?"

"No, I'm alright. I just want to get out of here. Mandy, I'm going insane! Please, do something," she sobbed, yanking the door handle backwards and forwards, trying to break the padlock.

"Stop it! Stop doing that," said Mandy, grabbing hold of the door handle and pulling it towards herself. "You're making a hell of a noise. For God's sake, Faye, get a grip of yourself. You're going to attract attention and bring Jack up here."

"Please, just get me out of here," she cried, slumping to the floor.

"Faye, listen to me. Do you have a phone in the room?"

"What?" said Faye, whimpering.

"A phone. Do you have a phone?"

"No, Jack took my phone."

"I mean a hotel phone. Is there a phone?"

"Yes, over by the table."

"Ok, listen carefully. I want you to call reception and tell them that you want to speak to Jack. Can you do that?"

"Are you serious? Mandy, he's going to kill me, for Christ's sake! And you just told me to keep quiet in case Jack comes up."

"Faye, if you want to get out of here, then you're going to have to do exactly what I say. Do you understand?"

"Yes. So what's your plan then? What do you want me to do?"

"Just go over to the phone and tell reception that you have something important that you want to say to Jack. Get him to come up here. Ok? Do it now."

"Are you sure that's what you want?"

"Yes. Do it now."

"Yes, alright," she said, standing up and walking over to the table.

Faye picked up the phone, her hands trembling as she composed her thoughts.

"Hello, may I help?" said the receptionist.

"Yes, I want to speak to Jack."

"Mr Jack, manager?"

"Yes."

"Please, you wait moment. He call you soon."

"Thank you," said Faye, putting down the receiver.

Jack was in the bar with Brad, his American friend who had arrived the day before.

"Hey, Brad, can you help me handle the bar tonight?" said Jack. "We're short of an experienced hand at making cocktails and stuff, and I think it's going to get lively tonight."

"Sure, no sweat, buddy. What are you having?" said Brad, walking behind the counter.

"Do me a Harvey, would you?"

"A Wallbanger?"

"Yes—and some! Stick a shot of gin in there with extra vodka.

Make it a triple Headbanger. Not too much ice."

"One triple Headbanger coming right on up," said Brad, flipping a glass into the air.

"Mr Jack, Room 804 want talk to you," said one of the staff members as she walked into the bar.

"Room 804?" he replied, sounding surprised.

"Yes."

"I'll be back shortly, Brad," said Jack as he made his way to the reception desk.

Faye stared at the phone, listening to it ring.

"Mandy, what should I do?"

"Stay calm, answer the phone, and tell Jack that you want to see him up here, right now," said Mandy quietly.

Faye walked over and picked up the phone.

"Hello?" she said, trying not to sound nervous.

"You want to speak to me?" said Jack.

"Yes."

"About what?"

"I don't know. I mean… I'm just lonely, and I thought that it would be… I guess, nice to have somebody to spend the evening with. The air-con isn't working too well, and I'm feeling a bit hot. I just thought…"

"Wait a minute, I will come up and check it. Do you need a drink?"

"No, I'm fine," she said, hanging up the phone.

"What's happening?"

"He's coming up!"

"Ok, get ready! Stand by the door."

Mandy briefly explained what she intended to do and then dashed to the elevator, staring at the indicator panel flashing in the upward direction, the numbers increasing as the lift made its way up from the first floor.

She stood on the second step of the stairs next to the lift and readied herself, knowing that she had only one chance to get it right and that timing was of the utmost importance. She closed her eyes and drew in deep breaths, holding the palms of her hands outstretched in front of her and drawing in the energy of Chi.

The bell sounded, the doors parted, and Jack exited the lift, walking out and turning right to go to Faye's room. Mandy braced herself, waiting for that vital sound of the padlock being undone before stepping out into the corridor.

"Excuse me!" she said, stepping forward and looking at Jack.

"What?"

"I've come for something."

"Who the fuck are you?" said Jack in an angry tone.

"I've just come to pick somebody up."

"*What*?"

"After I've put somebody down, that is."

"*What the…*"

As he turned to face her, she launched herself like a javelin, hurling towards him with her legs extended, the sole of her right foot hitting him squarely in the chest, the heel of her foot slamming into his heart with massive force. He reeled backwards, smacking his head on the wall, collapsing and sliding down in a heap on the floor. The vibration unhinged the picture above him, and it fell, the heavy frame cracking him on the skull. Faye was already out of the room as Mandy picked up the painting of Dante's *Inferno*, smashing it over Jack's head for good measure before they both ran down the stairs.

At the ground floor, Mandy looked at the lift and noticed that it was on its way down, the arrow indicating that it had just passed the third floor. They ran across the street and started the bike, dirt spewing violently from the rear wheel as they raced off. Jack staggered out of the hotel clutching his chest with his left arm, running towards them, trying to grab hold of Faye as their motorbike shot past. She felt his fingers slip off her shoulder as she leaned forward, gripping Mandy's waist as tightly as she could.

Pulling up outside the mall, they got off the bike and embraced each other. Faye tried to control her emotions, covering her face to hide the tears as Mandy led her past the tables to a quiet spot in the corner of a bar.

"Faye, are you alright? Let me look at you. Sit down and try to relax," said Mandy, putting her arm around her shoulder and ordering two bottles of beer. "Do you want to call the police?"

"I don't know what I want, Mandy. I don't know what to do."

"Do you need to go to a hospital?"

"No, I think I'll be alright. I'm just tired and confused. Maybe we should get out here in case Jack comes looking for us."

173

"You don't need to worry about him, Faye. I've got him measured alright. He's nothing but an old man. See that girl over there, the big one with short hair, wearing black, standing outside the nightclub? She's my sparring partner down at the Taekwondo gym. If Jack is stupid enough to come looking for you then I swear he will be leaving here on a stretcher."

Mandy opened her bag and took out a small packet.

"Take one of these, Faye. It will make you feel better," she said, handing her the tablets.

"You saved my life tonight, Mandy. I hate to think what would have happened to me without you. You were so brave. How about you, are you feeling ok?"

"You bet! I'm so amped up right now I could blow a marathon to Hong Kong and back without even stopping. I'm still running on high octane adrenaline with a red-hot turbo kicking in."

"I think I know how you feel," said Faye, cracking a smile.

"What do you want to do, Faye? Do you want to stay here for a few drinks, or do you want to go back to your room and get some rest? How about something to eat? You must be starving."

"I'm too sapped of energy to even think straight, Mandy. But I guess that I should go soon."

"Yes, let's finish these drinks, and then I will take you back to your room."

Mandy gave Faye a spare phone that she didn't need and then took her back to her guest house.

"Here's my number. If you need anything just call me," said Mandy, throwing her arms around Faye and hugging her tightly. "Seriously, day or night, I'm right here for you. You know that, don't you?"

"You're too beautiful, Mandy. You know that too. Don't you?" she replied, embracing her warmly.

Faye tried to sleep, but she was too troubled by the drama that had unfolded round at Jack's hotel. She couldn't take her mind off the stories that he had told her, especially the harrowing account of the girl who was bought by the tourist and held captive in his room for three days before being murdered. Had it happened in room 804? Had she been staying in that very same room? Why had Jack told her those stories? Her mind ran riot. A shiver ran through her, and she hurried into the bathroom. Slamming the door behind her, she stood under the steaming hot shower, running her hands over the top of her head as if to wash away the memory of it.

As the bathroom filled with steam, she thought that she heard a sound coming from the bedroom. Had she locked the door to her room? She couldn't remember.

Staring at the gap at the foot of the bathroom door, she saw what looked like a shadow briefly flicker across it. She froze, too petrified to move, staring through the haze of the steam.

Reaching out, she tried to move a shower curtain aside, her hand wafting away the steam as she tried to get hold of something that didn't exist.

She tried to quietly slide the bolt on the bathroom door, noticing that it was unlocked, but the clasp was missing, and she couldn't lock it.

Standing there motionless for what seemed like an eternity, the hot water in the tank eventually ran out. Shivering with cold and realising that she couldn't stay there all night, she stepped out of the shower and slowly took a towel off the rail, wrapping it around herself. Unfolding another towel, she held it in front of her chest as she quietly opened the bathroom door. There was nobody in the room. She walked to the door and checked that it was locked and then picked up the remote control for the television, taking the sound off mute.

Mandy came around to see her the next day.

"Hi, Faye, how are you feeling, honey bee?"

"I can't explain how I feel, to be honest. I couldn't get to sleep last night, so I took another one of those tablets that you gave me, and now I'm somewhere between altered states of reality and illusion. Do you understand what I mean, Mandy? Does that make sense?"

"Yes, baby."

"I'm glad it makes sense to you, Mandy, because it doesn't make any sense to me. Nothing makes any sense to me now."

"You'll be ok. Guess what we're going to do today?"

"I'm hopeless at guessing. Tell me."

"I'm taking you down to the Seeing Hands massage parlour. There's one next to Wat Phnom."

"I've never heard of it."

"It's just the best massage you'll ever get. The people who work there, the ones who give you a massage, they're all blind. Most of them are victims of land mines that exploded."

"Land mines?"

"Yes. There are millions of them all over Cambodia still, so watch where you're walking! Come on, let's go."

Soft instrumental music played quietly in the background as they lay next to each other on separate raised beds and drifted into the realm of the bliss for the next two hours, almost falling asleep.

Leaving the parlour, they went into the Wat. Mandy paid respect to the Buddhist and Taoist statues, standing before the one of the genie, Preah Chau, to which she asked for protection for herself and Faye, blessing it and making a donation afterwards.

"I can't feel myself," said Faye.

"You're not feeling yourself today?"

"No, I mean I can't feel my body. That massage has left me feeling completely numb. I feel like I'm floating through the air on a cloud. It's the strangest sensation I've ever had."

"I told you it was the best massage, didn't I?"

"You know, I was so looking forward to seeing Brent when I went to that hotel, Mandy. I can't tell you how much I needed to see him. I feel so shell-shocked about it all now."

"Distant water can not put out nearby fire, right?"

"Chinese proverb?" said Faye.

"Yes."

"And that horrible creature, Jack. I think he might have done something bad to Brent, but I don't know what to do about it."

"I think you should rest your mind for a little while, Faye. You will feel better in a day or two and then you will have clear thoughts. You will make the correct decision when the time is right."

"Yes. You know, I'm so glad I met you, Mandy. I really am. I would be so lost without you right now," she said, holding her tightly.

"We were meant to be together, Faye. It's our fate. We will be sisters for a very long time."

They strolled around the gardens for a while, enjoying the peaceful atmosphere, feeling completely at one with the ambience.

"Should we go and see what those children are doing over there, Mandy?"

"They're selling birds, I think," she said as they went over to get a better look.

"What for?"

"Good fortune. You buy a bird, let it go free, and you will get good karma. Lucky for you," said Mandy.

"Look at all those poor tiny little birds cramped up in that small cage. There must be hundreds of them in there."

"You buy?" said a young Cambodian street kid, her bare feet black with grime, gesturing towards the sparrows in the cage.

"How much do you want?" said Faye.

"The birds are trained to return to the cage for food, Faye. So you're pretty much wasting your money if you release them."

"It's ok. It will help the children. And at least the bird will get to fly around for a bit," said Faye, handing over the money and taking hold of the sparrow.

"Let's walk down to the river. You can release it there."

"Here, Mandy, take the bird," said Faye as they stood on the riverside. "I want you to bless it and set it free. Maybe that way it won't return to the cage. Tell it to fly across the water and stay on that side."

Mandy took hold of the bird and held it in her hands for a while, talking to it before throwing it high in the air. It flew across the river and into the distance beyond without returning.

They continued walking along the riverfront, looking at Cambodian fishermen and their families living in their boats anchored at the water's edge, cooking under a tin-roof shelter on the deck and washing themselves and their clothes in the murky brown water.

"I think I will head back to my room and have a nap," said Faye. "I'm pretty much done."

"Yes, ok. I'm going to check out some meditation courses. Do you want to meet later?"

"Sure. We can have dinner and then go dancing if we both feel up to it. I just need to catch up on some sleep. I'm going to jump in a tuk-tuk. Do you need a lift?"

"No, I'm good. I want to walk around for a while. Should I come to your place and pick you up, later?"

"Yes. Around eight?" said Faye.

"Ok. Later."

That evening they dined on the terrace of the former Foreign Correspondents Club, a three-story colonial-style building overlooking the Tonle Sap River, before exploring some of the girlie bars nearby.

They went inside The Candy Bar and saw dozens of Cambodian girls sitting around and approaching western men as they filed in looking to pick up some meat for the night.

Faye and Mandy soon grew bored of it and decided to go to the mall.

Being the Water Festival, it was especially busy that night and everyone was in party mode. In the centre of the mall, a stage had been constructed where various events were happening, and rock bands jammed. The bars that lined all three sides were heaving, and revellers danced, drank, and partied on. The two girls found an empty table at the rear and sat down.

It wasn't long before some more space junk walked up to them, inviting himself into their scene.

Chapter 20

Whiskey Tango Foxtrot

"Hello Faye, I heard you're looking for a boy," said a man, pulling up a chair and sitting next to her, placing a small glass and a bottle of whiskey on the table.

"What? Oh, God, not another one."

"You don't need to worry. I'm not going to harm you. It's just that I know too many people around here, and I know what's going on. Who's your friend?"

"Who are you would be a better question to start with, wouldn't it?" said Faye.

"Whiskey Tango," he said with a manic grin, showing off his brilliant white dentures. "WTF, to you. Hope you don't mind me joining you, by the way. Not that I care too much if you do. Great party atmosphere tonight, isn't it?"

"WTF? Are those your initials, or something?"

"Yes, if you like. Or how about *What The Fuck*? Actually, it's Whiskey Tango Foxtrot. It's a little moniker that was given to me when I was in the army. I like a drink and a scrap, and you can ask Jack about the foxtrot bit. I'm sure he would be more than pleased to let you in on that little secret. And don't pretend that you don't know him. I've been watching you very closely ever since you arrived," he said, knocking back a shot of whiskey. "You can call me Fox."

"What do you know about Jack?" said Faye.

"I know that you should stay away from him. Let's put it that way."

"Why do you say that?"

"You're looking for your man, aren't you? That's why you came here."

"How do you know?"

"I met the prick. Right here at this exact table, if I'm not mistaken. Gave him a warning too. He didn't listen, either. You won't find him, you know. He's gone. You can bet your lovely arse on that one," he said, topping up his glass.

"Yes, I am looking for a boy. You're quite right. Do you know where I can find one?" said Faye nonchalantly.

"Of course I do. But first of all, who is your delightful little friend?"

"Her name is Mandy."

"*Hello* Mandy," he said lecherously, raising his glass. "Fancy a drink with me?"

"I can't drink whiskey. Maybe I will just stick with the beer."

"So, Mandy, confuse us, say something like *if nothing change then everything stay same*," he said, putting on an accent to caricature a Chinaman.

"No, I don't think Confucius said that," replied Mandy.

Fox roared with laughter.

"That's just fucking brilliant, Mandy, you little minx."

"He's having a laugh, Mandy. Just ignore him," said Faye.

"I think you're very rude. Never do to others what you would not like them to do on you," said Mandy.

"Absolutely. Yes, *ab-so-fucking-lutely*. Totally agree with you on that one," he replied in a serious tone, downing more whiskey and staring at her with a disparaging look on his face. "Methinks the minx is one of the chinks, Faye."

"One of the chinks?" said Faye, glaring at him.

"One of the chinks in your armour. The armour that you think you've got so nicely wrapped around you, like the little English castle that you live inside, up there in your head."

"Maybe we should go, Faye. He's very rude," said Mandy.

"I can be as rude as I like because she isn't going fucking anywhere," he said scornfully.

"And what makes you so sure about that?" said Faye.

"Because."

"Because what? You think I won't just get up and walk away?"

"I don't think it. I know it."

"Why?"

"Because there's only one boy who knows Brent, and there's only one me who will take you to see that boy. That's why. But you can leave if you like. See if I care."

They stared at each other intensely.

"Well, maybe I will get in your lunar-lander with you one day and we will go and see him," said Faye sarcastically.

"Life is really simple, but men insist on making it complicated," said Mandy. "Will you dance with me, Faye?"

"Yeah, let's hit the dance floor," she replied, scowling at Fox as she stood up.

A band was playing on the stage, and after the two girls had left the table to go dancing, Jack walked up to Fox.

"What have you been saying to her?"

"What the fuck has it got to do with you?" said Fox.

"It's got everything to do with me."

"Get fucked, you stupid old cunt."

"You listen to me, you filthy fucking paedophile. I've still got enough dirt on you to put you away for the rest of your miserable stinking life," said Jack.

"So what's been stopping you then? Is it the fact that I can prove you're a murderer? Are you worried that your bent associates in the police will turn against you when they find out what I know about them? You're still smarting because I duped you when we worked together. Oh, by the way, I never did get around to saying thank you for entrusting me with that last case we worked on. She was just *so* cute. Did exactly what I told her and everything," said Fox, laughing to himself.

"You disgusting fucking pervert."

"I suppose being a cold-blooded killer is somehow better then, is it?"

Jack stared at him with total contempt.

"I should have fucking killed you when I had the chance," he said.

"Well, you always were a bit fucking slow, weren't you?"

Jack lunged at him and threw a punch, but Fox saw it coming and moved aside, standing up quickly and headbutting him, knocking him to the floor.

While their girlfriends looked on in disgust, drunken men laughed and cheered as Jack and Fox rolled around on the floor, wrestling each other.

They got to their feet and continued slugging it out until Fox picked up an empty bottle from a table and smashed it over Jack's head, knocking him for six.

Over by the stage, oblivious to what was going on, Faye and Mandy were having a dance of their own, wildly throwing their arms in the air as they rocked to the beat of the band.

Two guys lifted Jack off the floor and dumped him in a chair. He nursed his head for a while before staggering out of the mall and getting into a taxi.

The next day, Fox returned to the mall and put the word out that he wanted to talk to Jack as soon as possible.

Jack showed up not long after.

"I heard you wanted to see me," said Jack, holding a bottle in his hand. "Round two, is it?"

"Calm down, Jack. It's nothing like that. Why don't you pull up a chair and pour yourself a drink," said Fox, sliding the bottle of whiskey towards him.

"So what is it then?"

"I've got a proposition to make."

"*A proposition*," said Jack warily.

"You want that girl. Don't you?"

"What girl?"

"Faye."

"So what about it?"

"I can bring her to you."

"You think so?" he said, sitting down opposite Fox and putting some ice and whiskey into a glass. "She isn't *that* stupid."

"That's right. She's not," said Fox, taking a sip of whiskey and staring at Jack. "Who's running the operations these days?"

"What operations?"

"The Grey Man operations."

"I don't know. I'm not involved with them anymore. I do my own thing now. Why do you want to know that, anyway?"

"There's a couple of westerners been hanging around. I was talking to them earlier. One of them is looking for a boy, the other one a girl."

"And?"

"We do one last hit together like we did all those times before. Remember the first time we worked together and staked out that dirty cunt who was after a boy? He took our bait, and we brought the police in and had him arrested? Shit, we must have been holed up for three days doing nothing but getting blind drunk just waiting for him to make his move. Remember that one, Jack? We almost bailed out because the grog rations were about to run out," said Fox, laughing.

"What is this? Some kind of fucking joke or something?" said Jack angrily.

"What do you mean?"

"I mean, you will excuse me if I don't sing along to the tune of 'The Good Old Days', won't you?"

"Of course," said Fox sarcastically.

"You were doing it so that you could get your filthy hands on the kids. It was right there for you on a fucking plate! You weren't doing it to protect the children or take the philes off the streets. You were doing it for yourself."

"That's not altogether true, Jack. I was right there with you on taking those young-boy lovers out of the ball game. I hate those disgusting cunts just as much as you do."

"So we have to look the other way while you have your fun with the young girls that you're supposed to be helping, do we? Like, that's your reward for a job well done or something?"

"Let's not get too heated over this, Jack. Ok, so I wasn't exactly a proper operative, but then again neither were you. So I reckon you and I are pretty much on the same level. We both had our own private agenda for doing it. Wouldn't you agree?"

"What do you mean by that?" said Jack, scowling at him.

"That Scandinavian guy, the fat one down in Sihanoukville. Remember him? The one with the *orphanage* full of young boys? For some strange reason you wouldn't pass the case on to the police like we were supposed to. Even after we'd caught him red hot doing it. Said you'd take care of it yourself. Remember that one, Jack? You must have chopped him up and fed him to the fucking pigs after you'd finished with him, eh, Jack? He's still listed as a missing person to this very day," said Fox, grinning broadly. "Pour yourself another drink, Jack. Let's celebrate."

"I must be confused. Maybe it's the bruise on the side of my head or something. What the fuck are we talking about the Grey Man for? Weren't you making a proposition about bringing Faye to me?"

"That's right, I was. Slide your glass over. Let me top it up for you," said Fox.

"So what's your bright idea then?"

"Faye wants to meet that boy that you've got because she's looking for Brent. I can bring her out there for you."

"What's that got to do with the Grey Man?"

"Those two chancers that I just told you about. We can fix them up. You find out who is running ops and get in touch with them. Tell them you need a twelve-year-old girl sending out from the countryside to offer as bait for one of them. We can use the boy that you've already got to interest the other one, the queer. Ops know you, they know your history, your credentials. You had a good reputation with them. Remember, it was you that recruited me, and I always stayed in the shadows. Nobody from that organization knows me."

"You don't need to rub it in," he sneered. "I don't need reminding that I fucked up by recruiting you."

"Get over it, Jack. So what do you say? You want to do it or not? Up to you. You want Faye, or don't you?"

"And what are you getting out of it? What are you doing it for?"

"I thought you knew me better than to ask questions like that," said Fox with a sly grin on his face.

"You slimy cunt. You haven't got any morals whatsoever. Have you?"

"That's why we made such a perfect team. We're both on the same level," said Fox, refilling Jack's glass. "Think about it. A girl for a girl. Fair enough, isn't it? I mean, what sort of payment would you expect me to take? You need to broaden your mind, Jack. Do you know what the age of sexual consent was in England before 1875? It was twelve. Of course, life expectancy was a lot lower back then, so females started procreating at a younger age. And conversely, in a hundred years from now, when life expectancy will be much longer than what it currently is, the age of consent will be raised to twenty-one, and people like you, Jack, will be seen as disgusting child molesters for having sex with eighteen-year-old girls. It's called *the progression of civilization*, but I don't want to bore you with trivia such as that, so why don't you listen to the plan? When the two gentlemen show up, the queer one goes off with your boy, and the other takes the girl to a room. Soon as they're at it, your Cambodian policeman friend knocks on their door and it's *see you later*. The girl will be quietly handed to me, and I will take her for safekeeping for a couple of hours. Know what I'm saying?"

With a disgusted look on his face, Jack stared at Fox for a considerable time, mulling over what he had just said.

"We don't need the Grey Man for this one," he replied.

Fox's eyes narrowed, and he stared at Jack with a wry smile, lighting a cigarette and then sipping his whiskey. His ruse had worked perfectly.

"Of course, when your Cambodian friend walks into the joint, our two gentlemen will shit themselves and get their wallets out, which I'm sure you would agree is going to be a nice little bonus," said Fox.

"I want you to bring Faye out first, before those two feathered friends of yours turn up."

"I take it you know a young girl who is up for the job? A twelve-year-old?"

"Yes."

"I will talk to Faye tonight. Don't show your face around the mall, and stay out of the way. Give me your number. I will get in touch with you when I've arranged everything."

Fox drove around the area on his motorbike until he spotted Faye and Mandy sitting outside a pizza joint. Parking the bike across the street, he paid a kid to keep an eye on it and walked over to see the girls, giving them a big friendly smile as he approached.

"Good evening. How are you both? Do you mind if I join you for a little while? I have something to ask you," he said, putting on his best voice.

"Are you going to be rude again?" said Mandy.

"No, of course not. I really should apologise for that, actually. I don't know what came over me. Anyway, you've chosen a great place to eat pizza. It's my favourite too. Best in town, and they have a good wine list as well. I know the owner. She's a close friend of mine. Known each other for quite some time now."

"So what do you want to ask us?" said Faye, unimpressed by his suave act.

"I happened to see that boy, the one who knows Brent. He said that he would be very happy to meet you. I can take you there tomorrow if you like. What time will you be free?"

"I'm not sure whether I'm still interested in meeting him. Brent has obviously left me, so I guess that's the end of it," said Faye.

"The boy said he has some important information that he wants to tell you about."

"Really. What kind of information?"

"He wouldn't tell me. He said he only wants to speak to you about it. He's a bit shy, doesn't really like talking to men. He gets on a lot better with women."

"Is that right? Well, if I did go to see him I would want to take Mandy with me. That's if she agreed to go, of course."

"I wouldn't let you go without me, Faye," said Mandy. "And I will ask my friend who works at the nightclub if she will go with us too."

"You don't need to worry about anything. I just want to help you. Of course, it's not up to me who they let into their house, but I will speak to them, act on your behalf, and explain things for you. I suggest we go there tomorrow afternoon. How does that sound?"

"Why don't you bring the boy here?" said Faye.

"He doesn't like to leave his grandma, Sawatdee. They're very close. Inseparable, in fact. And she is old and frail. She never ventures past the veranda on the front of her house unless it's for a good reason."

"Well, we'll think about it. We're going to the mall tomorrow afternoon anyway, so we'll let you know."

"Yes, alright. So I will see you tomorrow then. Can I buy you two ladies a drink before I go?"

"No, you can't. But thank you anyway," said Faye.

"Well, it's been lovely chatting with you, and I will catch up with you both at the mall tomorrow then. Good night," he said as he left.

"Oh my God. Have you ever met a weasel like him before, Mandy?"

"I thought Jack was shit until he came along. That guy is one king-size creamy crap crêpe mister chocolate smoothie. Where is he from, Faye?"

"He sounds like he's from the UK, but I'm not sure where."

"Are we going to see that boy tomorrow? Do you think it would be a good idea?"

"I don't know, Mandy. I desperately want to find Brent, but I hate the idea of getting involved with those psychos that are out there. Who knows how I will end up. I just wish there was an easy solution to it."

"And I hope I never have to look at Jack ever again. He's got the eyes of a madman. It was like dealing with the devil when I came to get you out of that hotel."

"You certainly brought hell crashing down on top of his head, Mandy. There are no two ways about that one."

"He totally had both of us figured out the wrong way, didn't he?"

"But you put him in the picture, right?"

"You bet," she said as they laughed and slapped hands together.

Mandy had talked things over with Faye and decided to stay at her guest house, arriving the next day and checking in at reception. The girl at the desk registered her passport and visa details then handed her the key to the room opposite Faye's, wishing her a pleasant stay.

Jack was at the bar of the hotel drinking with his Cambodian friend, Mr Somnang, the local chief of police, informing him about the sting operation that he and Fox were planning for the two nonces. He phoned Fox and asked him what was happening.

"What's the situation looking like at your end? Did you get Faye to agree on coming out to see the boy?" said Jack.

"I'm meeting her at the mall tomorrow. There's every chance that I can talk her into it, but she wants to bring two of her friends with her as well."

"That's not a good idea. Talk her out of it."

"And what if I can't? It's going to be pretty difficult to get her to go out there all by herself," said Fox.

"You will just have to think of something then. What about the puff and his mate? Is everything set to go on that front?"

"I saw them earlier. They're ready and waiting for the word. Where is the girl? Is she at the house?"

"I will take her there when I'm sure that Faye has decided to show up. I want definite confirmation or the whole thing is off," said Jack sternly.

"You'll have to wait until I see her tomorrow. I will call you as soon as she agrees to go. Hopefully, it will be sometime after that in the afternoon."

They hung up. Fox poured himself another whiskey and relaxed on his bed, dimming the lights and flicking through the latest porn movies that he had bought the day before.

Later that evening, he received another phone call. He didn't recognise the number, so he let it ring for a while, assuming that it was from some Cambodian girl looking for some action. Eventually, he answered it.

"Hello," said Fox.

"Yes, hello. You are Tony?" said Mr Somnang.

"You can call me Tony, yes. Who are you?"

"I am Mr Jack's friend, the local police chief. I would like to speak with you."

"About what?" said Fox.

"Mr Jack has told me about your... your job tomorrow."

"My job?"

"Yes, with the two tourists who you will take to the house."

"That's right. And then you will turn up wearing your uniform. I can't see any problems. They will scare real easy when you start talking to them about doing jail time. Take my word for it. Did Jack talk to you about the money? I suggest we split whatever money you can get out of them equally, three ways. You might have to hold their passports until they get it together, but we can wait."

"I am phoning to inform that you will be arrested when you take the girl to your room."

"What are you talking about? I'm not going to be arrested. Did Jack not tell you the plan? I take the girl and entertain her for a couple of hours afterwards while you deal with the sex tourists somewhere private. Jack gets Faye. That's all he really wants."

"You must listen to what I am telling you. You will be arrested."

"Why are you telling me this?"

"Because Mr Jack has become... how do you say... a liarbilly."

"A liar Billy?" said Fox, confused.

"I am sorry. I speak English only a little."

"No, it's fine. Wait a minute."

Fox paused for a few seconds to think about what Mr Somnang had just said.

"A liability," said Fox.

"I am sorry?"

"A liability. You're saying that Jack has become a liability."

"Yes, exactly. A liability. He has changed, and his behaviour now is very strange."

"And he plans to have me arrested when I take the girl to my room afterwards? After he's got Faye?"

"Yes."

"And what about the two tourists that we're taking to the house?"

"Jack has asked me to take some of my colleagues from the station to arrest them. So you can see that it will be very difficult for me. I do not have answers for the questions my colleagues will ask."

"It looks like your friend mister Jack will have to be taught a lesson."

"But he is my partner, you understand? I need him for my

business operations."

"Leave it with me. I'll see if I can knock some sense into him."

"Yes, I hope so."

Hanging up the phone, Fox walked outside his apartment and sat on the balcony, resting his feet against the thick glass panels that formed the barrier along the railing, gently rocking himself backwards and forwards on his chair, staring out at the cloudless dark night beyond.

Thinking about Jack's plan to betray him, he lit a cigarette, drawing in the smoke deeply, rocking faster and more aggressively. Opening his mouth wide, as if to howl, he blew smoke rings at the full moon above him, seeing perfectly clearly how his plan would unfold.

Chapter 21

Punch Drunk

The travellers at Faye's guest house had organised a big party that night to continue celebrating the Water Festival. It was a large place, and there were about forty people of all nationalities staying there.

Faye and Mandy went outside and stood around the swimming pool, mixing with the crowd.

"Ok guys, we've got a fun party game here for you," said Paddy, a young backpacker from Ireland. "We've got a big bowl of home-made punch over there on the table, so here are the rules: You have to tell us who you most resemble in life. Now, it can be somebody real or not real, dead or alive, doesn't matter. If we think you don't fit the person you claim to be, then you get thrown in the pool. If you pass, then you get a glass of punch. Ok, any questions?"

"Yeah, over here," shouted Baz, an English guy. "How about if we name other people? That sounds like more fun to me."

"Ok, so who do you want to call out?" said Paddy.

"That guy over there. He must be Buddha."

"Why?"

"Look at that fat belly and that bald head. He's a dead ringer for Buddha."

"I take it you two are mates," said Paddy.

"Not anymore," said Jonny, laughing. "Ok, so now it's my turn. I name him Adolf Hitler," he said, pointing at Baz.

"Why is that, now?" said Paddy.

"Because the only good idea that Hitler ever had was when he put the gun to his head and blew his fucking brains out."

"Ok, so now it's time to vote, guys," shouted Paddy. "Who gets drunk and who gets dunk? Get a drink or get *in* the drink? First of all, let's hear it for Baz. Punch or pool?"

"POOL!" they all shouted, picking him up and throwing him in the water.

"And now for Jonny. Punch or pool?"

"There won't be any water left in the pool if you throw that fat bastard in there!" shouted one of the guys.

"POOL!" they shouted, pushing him in the swimming pool.

"Now, to be sure, I think you're all going for a swim tonight," said Paddy with his thick Irish brogue. "But let's see if you can prove me wrong, now."

"What about Scrooge over there?" a voice shouted.

"No need for a vote on that one," said Paddy. "I know your man too well for that. If we had to pay for air, he would be blue in the face holding his breath. Get yourself a drink and pour one for me while you're at it, now."

"*Achoooo!*" added another voice, feigning a sneeze at Scrooge.

"*Hey, Dude, don't look so sad,*" crooned Macca, singing to the beat of a song that was aimed at Scrooge.

"*D'You* know what I mean?" said Jules scoffingly.

"Hey, Fagin, what time does the sun rise? You fucking little cocksucker," retorted the guy that was referred to as Scrooge.

"Now calm down, the lot of yous! This is supposed to be a party game, not a tennis match of insults!" shouted Paddy.

As the scene degenerated and they all started pushing each other into the pool, Faye and Mandy decided to leave and go into the reception area.

A group of backpackers lolling around on couches and cushions watched some American traveller doing his stand-up comedy routine on the stairs in front of them.

"You guys wanna know how pasty looking my wife's skin is?" said the comedian. "You wanna know how fucking fat and ugly and white she is? Let me tell you. So she's sunbathing on the beach the other day, wearing her new two-piece black swim gear. And guess who comes along? Fucking Greenpeace in their high-powered speedboat. And what do they do? They tie a rope around her ankles and drag her ass out to sea, shouting 'save the Orca'. You know what? I might make a donation. Last I heard she was being chased by some Japanese ship with a fucking harpoon on the bow!"

The comedian's ex-girlfriend, wearing a black and white polkadot top, wedged inside the big armchair, wiped the grease from her mouth and started on another double cheeseburger. She feigned

191

boredom, but he could tell that she was having a whale of a time.

Faye looked at Mandy and frowned at the way she was laughing at the stand-up.

"Listen, guys, I just wanna tell you, you've been a great audience tonight, and before I go, I'd like to share a bit of my culture with you. You probably think I'm a fucking Mexican or something, but the truth is I'm a Native American, what you might call a Red Indian, and I was born in a teepee out on the plains, on the coldest winter's day you've ever seen. Now, the way my people name their new born little baby is like this: The father walks outta the tent the morning after the birth, and the first thing that he sees, well, that's what they gonna call their kid. I just wish that I could have been the first born, like my older brother, Wild Horse, or even my younger brother, Sleeping Dog. But you know what they say: That's life! Guys, I'm Steaming Turd, and you've been great. Thank you. Good night."

"Mandy, what are you laughing for? Everybody is so rude and sexist," said Faye. "I'm surprised he didn't start talking about his squaw or mention the word *paleface* while he was at it."

"I was laughing at him. Is he a Red Indian because he has a red face when nobody laughs at his jokes?" she replied.

"No, it's because he speaks with a fucked tongue."

"Faye!"

"What?"

"You just said a swear word!"

"No, I said *forked*," she replied, blushing slightly.

"Faye, that's the first time I've ever heard you swear," said Mandy, giggling.

"I didn't swear. I hate swearing."

"It's so cool to hear you swear, Faye, but I know it's not your style."

"Well, anyway, he was awful, and he deserves to be swore at. And you shouldn't encourage him, laughing at his nasty racist remarks."

Mandy put her hand on Faye's arm and gently massaged it.

"Is there something bothering you, Faye?"

"What do you mean?"

"You seem to be uptight and worried about something. Is it about Fox?"

"Yeah, I guess so," said Faye, lowering her face as she considered what Mandy had just said. "I can't get it out of my head. It's just that I so badly want to find Brent, but I don't know if I can bring myself to go out and see that boy. I'm just so paranoid about everything now. I really don't know what to do. Sorry if I seem a bit snappy, Mandy."

"Relax a bit. Let's enjoy the party and think about that later."

After the comedy act had finished, the guys used the microphone and speakers as part of the sound system for the karaoke show that came up next. The computer was put in a suitable place and provided the lyrics for anyone who wanted to sing a song.

Mandy and Faye went outside and helped themselves to another large glass of punch, laughing at the guys who were chasing the girls around the pool, hoping to catch them and throw them in again.

Returning inside, the two girls sat next to each other on a sofa in the lounge and talked some more about Brent.

"If you really want to go there, I can ask my Cambodian friend, and we can all go together, Faye. I think it would be safe enough."

Faye drank the punch and placed the glass on the small coffee table in front of them.

"Mandy, when you take a glass and put it next to another glass, of the same type, both touching each other, they will always stand in a straight line. But if you add another glass, then you will have to place it carefully, and position it, for all three of them to make a straight line. And the more glasses that you add, then the more effort it will be to make them form a perfectly straight line."

"English proverb?" said Mandy.

"No, I just made it up. I haven't got a clue what I'm talking about, either. This punch is stronger than I thought."

"I think I know what you mean, Faye," said Mandy, putting her hand on Faye's shoulder and drawing closer to her. "My friend isn't gay, she's just a bit... what's that word you guys use? Butch? Yes, she's just a bit butch."

"I didn't mean to be rude to your friend, Mandy. I don't even know how she ended up in the conversation, but..."

"What's he like, Faye?" said Mandy, cuddling up to her.

"Who?"

"Brent. You've never told me very much about him."

"Well, he's fit, very good looking. He works as a—"

"No, I mean, is there anything strange or different about him?"

"Strange or different? I don't know, really. He can be a bit qwerty sometimes, I suppose."

"Qwerty? I don't understand. What does that mean?"

"I mean, well, he's so fussy, so particular, sometimes. Everything has to be just so for him. I can just imagine him when he was a boy, playing with his toy soldiers. They would all have to stand in a perfectly straight line, in a certain order. Do you know what I mean?"

"Hmm, that's weird. A bit like the glasses that you were just talking about on the table. My God! This punch really *is* stronger than we thought, Faye," said Mandy, resting her head on Faye's shoulder and closing her eyes. "I think we should stop chatting for a while now and just chill for a bit."

Chapter 22

The Hit

The next day Faye and Mandy arrived at the mall around mid-afternoon. Fox had been waiting all morning for them to show up and was sitting at a place nearby, watching. He called Jack on his mobile.

"Where are you?" said Fox.

"At the hotel. What's happening?" replied Jack.

"Get over to the house. It looks like it's on."

"What do you mean *it looks like it's on*?"

"She's at the mall. I've got a hunch I can talk her into it."

"Has she agreed to go?"

"I haven't talked to her yet. I'm going over there now."

"So all you've got is a fucking hunch?"

"Listen, just get to the house and make sure that the boy knows what he has to do. I can see that she's up for it."

"Have you got those two perverts ready to go?"

"Yeah, they're waiting for the word."

"After you've brought Faye, you go back and bring them out last. You bring Faye out first—on her own. Have you got that understood?"

"And what about my reward? Where is she?"

"She will be in the shack behind the house, waiting for you. Don't worry about it."

"Keep her out of sight, and don't let her talk to anybody. One more thing," said Fox.

"What."

"Put a flimsy padlock on the back door."

"For what?"

"Faye suspects that the boy is being held against his will and that Brent might have been trying to rescue him. She will try to get him out of there if she can. Put a cheap lock on the rear door, nothing too strong, and make sure that nobody else is in the house when we get there."

Jack thought about it carefully.

"Tell Faye to stand at the side of the house, underneath the window, so that I can see her," he replied.

"Which window?" said Fox.

"There's only one. It's a small one, with bars on the inside. I'll put the boy in that room."

"Remind me. What's his name?"

"Sov."

"Ok, listen up. You tell him that he has to get Faye to come in there and help him escape. Understood?"

"I'll be waiting for you then," said Jack, hanging up.

Fox casually walked over to the two girls and smiled in a relaxed manner, asking very politely if he could join them.

"Hey! You know, I really think you should let me buy you both a drink," he said. "I will be flying to Malaysia for a business meeting tomorrow, and I really would like to apologise for my behaviour the other day. I will be there for a few weeks so we might not see each other again. This might be the last opportunity that I get. How about a cocktail each?"

"I think I will just have a beer," said Faye.

"How about you, Mandy?" said Fox.

"I will just have a beer too."

"Three beers it is then," he said, raising his hand to attract the bar maid's attention.

"So you're leaving tomorrow then, are you?" said Faye.

"Yes. I don't really want to. It's such a bind having to travel there, but a contract depends on it, so I don't really have any choice. And what are your plans for the immediate future? Will you be staying in Cambodia for much longer?"

"I'm not sure. I was hoping to find Brent, but I don't even know if he's still in this country or not."

"Yes. And what about you Mandy? What are your plans?"

"I don't have any plans. I'm just enjoying my free time."

The conversation died, and an awkward silence ensued.

"Am I bothering you?" said Fox.

"What do you mean?" replied Faye.

"I get the feeling that neither of you like me very much. I'm sorry, but I feel as though I should leave," he said, standing up and taking out his wallet to pay for the drinks.

"I thought you said that you were going to take me to see the boy," said Faye.

"The boy? Oh, you mean the one who knows Brent? Well, what time is it?" he said, looking at his watch. "It's getting late, but I suppose we could pay a quick visit. You seem unsure about it, anyway, as though you can't make your mind up whether you really want to find Brent. What's bothering you?"

"I don't know. I guess I'm just worried about my safety. I'm scared in case Jack might be there waiting for me."

"Jack? Oh, you don't need to worry about him," said Fox.

"Why not?"

"It might come as a bit of a blow, but Jack is dead."

"Dead? How?"

"Heart attack, a couple of days ago."

"Why didn't you mention it yesterday when you saw us outside the pizza place?"

"Well, if you remember, I was in a celebratory mood yesterday, and I didn't want to give you the impression that I was gloating over his death, even though I hated him. I thought that would have been a bit distasteful. Did you have much to do with Jack? I think you met him once, didn't you? Wasn't it here, in the mall?"

"Yes... no, I... so maybe we should go and see the boy then."

"Well, are you ready to go now? I only have an hour or so," said Fox, looking at his watch again. "I have to pack my suitcase for tomorrow, but I suppose we could do."

"Faye, my friend over at the night club isn't here yet," said Mandy, covering her mouth and speaking in a low voice. "That means we would have to go without her."

"Yes, I know, Mandy, but..."

"Faye!" begged Mandy, trying to caution her.

"You said that you've got the boy's phone number, didn't you?" said Faye.

"Did I?" replied Fox hesitantly.

"If I spoke to him, then I might go out there. What's his name?"

"Yes. Let me see if I can find his number," he said, taking his phone out of his pocket. "His name is Sov."

Fox called Jack's number.

"Hi, Sov. I've got Faye here. She wants to have a chat with you.

She's Mr Brent's girlfriend. You remember Mr Brent, don't you?"

He passed the phone to Faye, and after a lengthy pause, Sov came on the line.

"Hello?" said Faye.

"Yes," replied Sov.

"Hi, Sov. How are you?"

"Yes."

"Do you remember Brent? An English man called Brent?"

"Yes. My friend, Mr Brent. He come here."

"I don't want to sound impatient, but I really can't waste any more time like this," said Fox. "I have a lot to do. Maybe we can arrange something when I get back."

He took out his wallet and walked over to the bar to pay the bill.

"Faye! Don't go!" said Mandy.

"I have to go," said Fox, taking his phone back and making his way outside to his motorbike.

"No! Wait," shouted Faye. "I want to go and see the boy."

"Well, you really need to make your mind up," he said. "I really don't have any more time to waste like this."

"Faye! No! Are you crazy? For God's sake, don't do it," pleaded Mandy.

"Mandy, come on, come with me. It will be alright, trust me."

"No way. Faye, sit down. I'm not going with you. Can't you see what he's doing? Don't be so crazy!"

"Mandy, hurry up," said Faye, walking quickly towards his motorbike.

"I'm not going, Faye. You're making a big mistake."

As Fox was putting on his full face helmet and zipping up his jacket, Faye ran back, begging Mandy to go with her.

"No! I'm staying right here. Stop being so stupid. He's fooling you."

Faye turned around to see Fox putting on his black leather gloves and steering his bike carefully past the others, edging his way off the sidewalk. As he started the engine, she ran towards him and climbed on the back, turning to look at Mandy as he took off rapidly down the street.

"Oh, shit!" screamed Mandy, running outside and getting on her motorbike, fumbling through her bag to find the keys.

By the time Mandy had got her act together, Fox was way ahead in the distance, speeding down the boulevard.

Rounding a sharp bend, she came to a crossroads and stopped, looking left and right trying to catch sight of them. Fox had gone, and she didn't know where, so she decided to carry straight on, down the road that lay ahead of her.

Nearing the outskirts of town, the dirt roads that she was on were obviously leading nowhere, and she pulled over, switching off the engine. She had lost Faye, and there was nothing she could do about it.

Fox slowed down as he approached the house, turning off the road and parking at the rear. Faye got off the bike and stood around, looking apprehensive, noticing that everywhere seemed deserted and eerily quiet. Walking around to the front, Fox knocked on the door.

"Is this where the boy lives?" said Faye, trying to sound calm.

"Yes, but it sounds like nobody is home," he replied, repeatedly knocking on the door.

"Where is everybody?" she said, looking around.

Fox knocked loudly on the door.

"I think we might have to come back another day. It doesn't look like anyone is home," he said.

"I can hear somebody," said Faye.

"Where?"

"It sounds like it's coming from the side."

"Let's go and see."

"You! You!" cried Sov as they passed underneath the window.

"It's coming from that window," said Faye.

"Help me! You. Help me."

"Who is it?" she said, looking up at the darkened glass. "It sounds like a boy."

"Sov! Is that you Sov?" shouted Fox.

"Yes. You help me."

"Sov, I've brought someone to see you. Her name is Faye."

"Where my friend, Mr Brent?" shouted Sov.

"Brent isn't here," said Fox. "Can you open the door, Sov?"

"No, can not. You help me."

They walked to the rear of the house and stood in front of a small set of wooden steps leading up to the veranda.

"Look, they've put a lock on the door to stop him getting out. I'll have to smash it off. Wait a minute," said Fox, lifting up the seat of his motorbike and taking out a hammer.

"Why won't they let him go out? Is there something wrong with him?"

"No, there's nothing wrong with him," he replied, smashing the lock off the door.

"Are you sure it's alright to be doing this?" said Faye with a nervous laugh.

"Can you hold this for a minute?" he said, passing her the hammer so that he could force the door open.

Faye cautiously followed him as he entered the house. Next to a long couch, a dim lamp lit the room, but nobody was there. Fox walked around on the creaking wooden floor, opening the doors to the rows of small wooden box rooms and looking inside. They were all dark and empty. Faye stood motionless as he called out the boy's name.

"Sov. Sov. Can you hear me?" There was no reply. "Sov, where are you?"

Still, there was no answer.

"Where are you, Sov?" he said, louder.

Fox heard a noise coming from a room at the end of the dark corridor and gestured for Faye to follow him. She refused to go with him, so he took her by the arm and forced her to walk in front of him. She was terrified and didn't even realise that she was still holding the hammer.

Standing in front of the box room where the noise was heard, Fox pulled the visor down on his helmet, took the hammer from Faye's hand, and pushed open the door. The glow from a dim red bulb lit Sov's face as he sat on the edge of his bed. Gripping Faye's arm tightly, Fox shoved her into the room as Jack stood up from the chair in the corner and moved towards her. Using Faye as a shield in front of him, Fox swung the hammer over her shoulder, striking Jack on top of the head. She screamed loudly and hysterically as blood, brain, and fragments of bone sprayed in her face as Fox repeatedly rained down blow after blow on Jack's skull until he collapsed onto the floor.

Fox released his grip on Faye's arm, and she ran out of the room and down the hallway, catching up with Sov who had already bolted. Turning right into the back room, Faye threw the door aside and they made a hasty exit out of the building.

Stepping backwards to avoid the pool of blood that was forming on the floor, Fox hit Jack repeatedly on the head until he stopped quivering. Satisfied that the job was done, he calmly placed the hammer on the table and lit a cigarette.

Sov bolted down the dirt lanes, cutting in and out between the houses; Faye, still screaming and crying with panic, ran blindly onto the road and straight into the path of an oncoming vehicle. The driver of the car slammed on the brakes and swerved to the left, trying to avoid a collision, but Faye was hit with a glancing blow and knocked backwards, striking her head on the ground as she fell.

Fox walked out of the house and down a narrow path to the shack. Opening the door slightly, he stood outside and stared in at the young girl sitting on the floor. She looked at him without smiling and continued eating her mango. He pulled the door shut and walked back to the house.

Removing his gloves and placing them in a plastic bag under his seat, he got on his motorbike and sat for a while, discreetly watching as the driver patiently coaxed Faye to her feet, helping her into the back of his car.

As he drove off, Fox started his bike and overtook him, speeding back to town.

Back at his apartment, intending to buy a one-way flight ticket and head for the airport, Fox hastily began packing his belongings.

Thinking about the position that he could take with Mr Somnang, now that Jack was out of the way, Fox stopped what he was doing. Walking over to the drinks cabinet, he poured himself a large whiskey and sat on the balcony.

The driver stopped outside the hospital entrance and went inside to the reception area, returning with two nurses who helped Faye into the ward.

Explaining what had happened, but leaving no details, he got back in his car and drove off.

Faye was taken into a doctor's office and guided onto a chair. Standing on either side, the nurses steadied her while the doctor gave her a quick check over. She appeared to be suffering from concussion, and there was a swelling on the top of her forehead with grazed skin. Her left arm was slightly bruised, and her blouse was torn around the shoulder.

The nurses gave Faye a glass of water and some tablets and then took her into a private room, helping her to lie down.

Chapter 23

Jail

The morning sun shone brightly through the blinds that covered the window, causing Faye to squint as she slowly opened her eyes, staring at the fan as it revolved on the ceiling above her.

Standing next to her bed, the doctor checked her condition and asked how she felt. She mumbled something incoherently and stared at the police officer waiting by the door. After the doctor was satisfied that she was well enough to talk, he asked the nurse to leave and motioned for the policeman to enter the room.

"Good morning. I am Major Wattana. How are you feeling today?" said the police officer as he approached Faye.

"I'm... I'm alright, I think. Thank you," replied Faye as she sat upright on the bed.

"May I ask your name?"

"Faye."

"What hotel are you staying at?"

"I'm staying at The Palms Guest House."

"Miss Faye, there is a lot of blood on your clothes, but I think it is not your blood. Do you remember where you went yesterday?"

"Yes," she said, lowering her face.

"Where did you go?"

"To... a house," she replied, her voice faltering.

"Who was at the house?"

"A man and a boy," she said faintly.

"Do you know the man and the boy?"

She closed her eyes and covered her face, shaking her head as tears ran down her cheeks.

"Do you remember what happened?" he continued.

Faye cried and couldn't say anything.

"I must take you to the police station with me," he said.

The Major spoke to the doctor, telling him to give Faye a new set of clothes to wear, instructing him to put her blouse, jeans, and trainers carefully into a sealed bag and hand them over to a police officer.

Faye was escorted out of the hospital wearing a pair of blue pyjamas and a dressing gown and put into the back of a police van.

En route to the station, they stopped at Faye's guest house. A group of fellow travellers gathered around, murmuring suspicions of drug busts and other allegations as the police searched her room and confiscated her passport. Faye was allowed to change into a different outfit and take with her anything else that she required. They left the room.

Mandy arrived at the guest house just as Faye was being put into the police vehicle, and they didn't get much of a chance to speak to each other.

Starting her motorbike, Mandy followed behind as the van drove down to the police headquarters in the centre of Phnom Penh.

At the station, officers took Mandy into a separate room and questioned her, informing her she could not see Faye until they had completed all of their investigations. They told her to return to the guest house and stay there until they arrived.

They searched Mandy's room and found a bottle of sedatives. She was unable to produce the prescription for the tablets, stating that she had brought them with her from Hong Kong, unaware that they were a controlled substance.

The officers checked her passport. Being absent-minded, Mandy had overlooked the fact that her visa had expired by six weeks.

They fined her for both offences and told her she had twenty-four hours to leave the country. They stated that if she failed to comply, they would charge her, which would lead to a jail sentence.

Faye spent a sleepless night in a jail cell. Early the next day, they moved her to a private room where she waited alone, her mind numb with anxiety.

Major Wattana entered the room, pulling up a chair and sitting down at the wooden desk in front of her. He lit a cigarette and offered her one.

"Miss Faye, a man is dead, and the blood on your clothes is the same as the blood from the dead man. You must give me what information you have."

She stared at him, completely dejected, realising the stupidity of her actions and how she had been so easily and naively set up.

"I don't know what to say," she said quietly.

"Did you kill a man with a hammer?"

"No."

"Your fingerprints are on the hammer, Miss Faye."

"I didn't kill anybody."

"Then you must explain to me how you have that man's blood on your clothes and your fingerprints on the hammer."

"I went to a house to see a boy, and—"

"What boy? What is his name?"

"I think his name is Sov."

"A Spanish boy?"

"A what?" said Faye, unable to hear clearly what he had just said.

"A boy from Spain?" he replied.

"I don't know where he's from. It was too dimly lit. I couldn't see much."

"The man who is dead. Do you know his name?"

"No."

"Who took you to the house?"

"A man. His name is Fox."

"Can you describe this man, this Mr Fox?"

"I think he's from England. He's about fifty, tall, and slim. He drinks whiskey at the mall on Street 51. He has scruffy blond hair down to here," she said, putting her hands just above her shoulders. "That's all I know about him."

"Does Mr Fox have a Cambodian friend, a police officer?" inquired Major Wattana.

"I don't know."

"I think that you are not telling me all of your information," he said, staring at her. "Do you need a glass of water or something?"

"Yes, I'd like some water, please."

He took the top off the glass pitcher on his desk and poured her a drink.

"Miss Faye, I will keep you here until I am satisfied I have all the information I need. Do you understand?"

"Yes," she said quietly, lowering her face.

Faye spent the night in one of the cells by herself, crying endlessly and feeling too distraught to eat the rice soup that was delivered later that evening.

The following day she was put in the back of a small truck, being forced to slide along the wooden bench at the side to make room for some Cambodian men and women, noticing that they were all handcuffed, the men also wearing leg shackles. She had been spared that indignity and wore neither.

She stared wearily through the steel mesh covering the sides, the overhead canopy shading her from the fierce midday sun as the vehicle made its way through the centre of town.

Pulling up outside the local jail, the driver inched forward as the tall wooden gates opened. Faye's heart began to race as they slowly entered.

The prisoners were taken off and ordered down a long corridor into the main cell block.

Walking slowly behind the others, filled with horror and a sense of foreboding, she looked around at the overcrowded cells: men huddled together on the bare concrete floors, others standing, their arms reaching through the bars as she passed. The deafening noise of people shouting alarmed her, and the reek of their body odour churned her stomach.

Faye was separated from the men and taken down another long corridor into the women's section, where she was put inside a cell with four Cambodians, two black Africans, and one white girl.

The sound of the heavy steel door being slammed shut behind her brought home the awful reality of what was happening. She sank to her knees in the corner and cried despairingly.

Knowing that they had plenty of time and that she was best left alone to deal with it by herself, the women ignored her.

The days ground on, sapping her strength and her will to survive. As she was walking down the corridor on her way to the shower block, she saw a guard leading a group of men towards her. As they passed, her attention was drawn to the blond hair on a man close to the end. She stopped and called out his name.

"Hey! Fox!" she shouted. "Fox!"

"Hello, Faye," he said, turning around, grinning at her, his face gaunt, his eyes sunken. "Fancy meeting you here."

"What are you doing here?" she said, looking confused.

"What do you think I'm doing here?" he said sarcastically. "I hit the nail on the head, remember? Hammered Jack. I would've got away with it too but for that little bitch in the shack who remembered my license plate number."

"No, I mean… I mean, why…"

"You! Go!" shouted the guard, walking towards Fox.

Fox was moved along by the guard, leaving Faye in the corridor, trying to make sense of what was going on. The guard approached her, telling her to make her way to the showers. She refused, demanding to see Major Wattana.

After a heated argument and being threatened with a baton, she was taken back to her cell, screaming and shouting.

Later that day she was taken to the administration building and held in a room.

"Do you wish to speak with me, Miss Faye?" said Major Wattana, closing the door behind him.

"Yes. I want to know why I'm still being held in jail," she said angrily.

"Are you asking me why you are here?"

"Yes, of course!" she replied, sounding surprised. "You have the man who killed Jack. I saw him earlier. His name is Fox."

"So you know his name is Jack."

She stared at him awkwardly.

"I saw Fox. He told me he had killed Jack. Why are you keeping me here? You know I didn't do it. You have to let me go."

"Yes, but we are still investigating whether you are involved in the crime. I think maybe you have some information that you are not telling me."

"What are you talking about? Information? What information?"

"I want you to tell me everything that you know about Mr Jack."

Major Wattana listened intently to Faye's encounters with Jack.

"Did Mr Jack have a friend—a police officer?"

"I don't know. Maybe," she said, staring at her feet.

"You must tell me the truth, or you will stay here. Did he have a friend—a police man?" he said, pressing her.

"Yes."

"What was his name?"

"I can't remember."

"What did he look like?"

"I don't know. I only met him once. He came to the hotel, and he only stayed for a short time."

"And what did he look like?"

"I couldn't see his face. He was wearing sunglasses and a cap."

"Miss Faye, I am very busy, so I must return to my station. You will stay here until you can give me the information that I need."

"No!" she shouted as he walked out of the room. "I want to see a lawyer. I want to speak to somebody from my embassy. You can't keep me here. I haven't done anything wrong."

Faye was taken back to the cell. Brooding, she sat alone in the corner, away from the other inmates. The women were friendly, but the Cambodians didn't speak any English, and the Africans spoke mostly French. The other girl was a Russian who communicated mainly by sign language.

Faye lay awake for most of the night thinking about the police officer that she had met at the hotel, hoping that she could give Major Wattana the information that he wanted and be released.

Lying on a thin reed mattress on the concrete floor, she was still awake when dawn broke early the following morning. Ignoring the calls for bathing and breakfast, she began falling asleep until a loud voice caught her attention.

"Miss Faye, please come with me. You have a visitor," said Major Wattana, standing outside.

"What? A visitor? Who is it?"

"A man. From your embassy. Please, stand up and come with me."

"From the embassy?" she said excitedly.

Tired and lacking energy, Faye struggled to her feet and walked slowly towards the door. One of the guards took her arm and helped her out of the cell. They walked slowly down the corridor, halting while the heavy steel door at the end was unlocked and opened, allowing them to pass through and proceed to one of the rooms beyond. The door slamming shut with a clang, the sound of the keys jangling, and the clunk of the lock being turned behind her brought her around.

Entering the room, she was seated at a desk and told to wait. After a few minutes a western man walked in and stood in front of her. He was tall, smartly dressed, and had a stern look on his face that also expressed a sense of melancholy.

"Miss Faye?" he said. "Faye Middleton?"

"Yes."

"My name is Cyril Portishead. I'm from the British Consulate. May I sit down?"

"Yes, of course. Are they going to release me?" she said expectantly.

"I'm afraid that's not why I'm here."

"They have the man who committed the crime! Why am I still here?"

"Miss Middleton, I must ask you to be calm, please."

"What is it then? Why have you come here?"

"I'm afraid I have some very bad news for you. Our consulate was contacted this morning by the police authorities in the United Kingdom, who informed us that both of your parents were involved in a car accident just recently. And that, unfortunately, neither of them survived. I'm so sorry to have to break such bad news to you under your present circumstances, Miss Middleton. You have our sincerest condolences."

She stared at him with a look of incredulity, baring her teeth in a perverse smile, not fully taking in what had just been said to her. He could do nothing but look at her with pity. She tried to speak, but her mind was too dazed, and the words stuck to her mouth, falling silently from her quivering lips. He asked her repeatedly if there was anything that he could do for her, but she wasn't listening. She stared straight through him and began to tremble, her face turning pale. He asked her again if he could help her in any way and then stood up. Apologizing, he excused himself and walked out of the room. Major Wattana closed the door, leaving Faye by herself.

The news about her mother and father had a devastating effect on her, and she passed out, sliding off the chair and onto the floor. Major Wattana, who had been standing outside the door and keeping a close watch on her, quickly sent in two of his staff members. They laid her gently onto a stretcher and took her out of the room.

Faye regained consciousness in the hospital ward feeling nauseous and dizzy. She remained there for two days, heartbroken and shattered. She was on the other side of the world and now felt terribly alone and vulnerable. Her parents had been the only family members that she had, and knowing this, Major Wattana had informed all of the hospital staff and patients to watch over her diligently in case thoughts of suicide began to creep through her mind.

Sitting upright on the bed, she looked around the room, hoping to see someone that she could ask for a drink. But apart from the sick, there was no one. An old woman in the bed opposite smiled at her and pointed to a large water dispenser in the corner.

A single plastic cup hung from the tap. Faye filled it and drank cautiously from the edge closest to the handle, aware that the cup was used by everyone and probably never cleaned.

Major Wattana entered the room and called her name, telling her to collect her belongings and go with him, informing her that she was about to leave the jail. Throwing what was left of the water into a bucket and placing the cup upside down on the tray, she followed him out of the hospital and down the long corridors to his office, excited about the possibility of being released.

Inside his dark office, Major Wattana slid the bolts to unlock the wooden shutters that led onto the terrace, folding the doors open to allow the sunlight in and reveal the nicely manicured gardens outside.

Faye sat at his desk, wanting to know the answers to so many questions but fearful of saying anything that might ruin her chance of freedom. She sat quietly, upright, with her legs closed and her hands clasped together on her knees, conscious even of her facial expressions.

"A very beautiful day, today," he said. "See how the birds fly, Miss Faye. Maybe soon you can join them."

"Why maybe? You have no right to keep me here. You know that I haven't done anything wrong."

"You are a witness."

"A witness?"

"And I think that you also have information related to the murder."

"What information?"

"You have met the police man who was the friend of Mr Jack. I need you to identify this man."

"I have already told you," she said despairingly.

"You have told me?"

"I have…"

She paused, realising the opportunity that she was on the verge of wasting.

"I have told you what he looks like," she continued. "And if I saw him again, then I think that I could point him out to you."

"Excuse me, my English is not so good. Can you explain, please?"

"I am saying," she said slowly, "that if I see the police man again, the one that you are looking for, then I will say to you that he is the man that you are looking for."

"Yes, that is what I want you to do. So I must keep your passport until you can show me who this man is. And then after, you can be free to leave and return to your country. Do you agree with me, Miss Faye?"

"What will you do with me?"

"You must come with me and so I can take care of you."

"Come with you?"

"Yes, you can leave this jail and you can stay at my house until we find this man. Do you agree to help me?"

"Yes, of course," she replied eagerly.

"Good. Do you wish to get anything, or see anybody, before we leave?"

"No," she replied quickly. "I have everything here with me."

Major Wattana locked his office and led Faye to the main entrance where he returned her purse and a few other belongings before signing her out and putting her in the back of his car.

Faye had spent just three weeks in jail, but to her, it felt like three years.

As they drove through the busy streets of Phnom Penh, she stared through the window at freedom, yet her mind was not free. She had been changed, broken, and now felt nothing but a sense of numbness, despair, and confusion.

Pulling into the courtyard of his house, Major Wattana led Faye inside and introduced her to his wife and young daughter. They drank ginger tea and talked for a while before he showed Faye to a private bedroom at the back.

"I think you will be very comfortable while you stay at my house, Miss Faye. This is where you will sleep. Do you enjoy to eat Khmer food?" he said.

"Yes, I'm very fond of it."

"That is good. You can eat with my family. Now please sit down so that I can explain everything for you."

"Yes, alright."

"You know that I want you to find the police officer who Mr Jack introduce to you?"

"Yes."

"Do you know how to drive a motorbike?"

"Yes."

"So you are free to go outside as you please until it is dark. After it is dark you must return to this house. Do you understand?"

"Yes. What do you want me to do?"

"I want you to find the hotel where Mr Jack introduce to you the police man. Do you think you can do this?"

"Yes, I think I can," she said, trying to sound convincing.

"You must take my motorbike around the streets until you find the hotel. But do not go inside the hotel or speak to anybody who is there."

"I understand," she said, nodding agreeably.

"When you find this man, I can return to you your passport and phone, and you will be free to return to your country if you wish."

"Yes, I understand."

"Now it is late in the afternoon, so we will start tomorrow."

"Yes, ok."

"Now I think you should rest. Can I get you something?"

"No, I'm fine, thank you."

"We will have dinner at seven, so my wife will speak with you later when it is ready to eat."

"Ok, thank you," she said, trying to sound enthusiastic, although her voice was flat and emotionless.

After he left the room, she closed the door behind him and lay on the bed, holding the pillow close to her chest, fighting off the tears that were welling in her eyes. She began to feel scared, knowing that the chances of finding the hotel and the policeman were slim, which meant that she could be returned to jail. Burying her face in the pillow, she cried, silently calling her mother's name.

As the hours passed and daylight faded, she heard a knock on the door. It was the Major's wife calling her name. Faye stood up and opened the door, gesturing to her that she felt sick and didn't want to join them for dinner at the table. Mrs Wattana smiled and left.

Faye switched on the bedside lamp and began flicking through the television channels to try and take her mind off things. There was another knock at the door. Faye opened it to see a young girl holding a tray of food. She invited her in.

Placing the tray on the table, the girl smiled and turned to leave. Faye asked her if she would like to stay for a while, and they sat on the bed, talking and sharing the meal. Her name was Pim, and she was twelve, bright and bubbly with a beautiful face and a smile like a little angel. She was Faye's angel, sent as a companion to ease her through the difficult times that she now found herself in. Pim spoke very good English and told Faye how she dreamed of becoming a vet when she was older so that she could take care of animals, especially dogs, which she loved very much.

It was time for Pim to go and finish her homework, and so they embraced each other warmly. Faye felt like a new person, hopeful and confident that she could find the man that Major Wattana was so desperately searching for.

Faye woke early the next morning, and after a light breakfast, she was handed the keys to the motorbike and a detailed map of Phnom Penh. The Major informed her that the fuel tank had been filled already, and that she was to drive carefully at all times, reminding her that she was to return before sunset.

Faye checked her bag to make sure that she had everything she needed and then set off.

As she cruised the streets, the warm breeze blowing against her face made her smile, reminding her once more of how good freedom really tasted.

Driving through the centre of town, she pulled up outside The Green Mango, the restaurant that she and Brent had frequented so many times before. It looked different and was. Her friend, Ary, had sold up and moved out a few weeks earlier, which upset Faye even more, as she was one of the few people around who might have been able to help her find Brent.

Faye parked the bike but didn't go in. Instead, she walked up to the mall, standing outside and looking in at the bars where all of the drama had begun all those weeks before. Feeling apprehensive and fearful that someone was about to approach her, she turned around quickly and made her way back to the bike.

She drove off slowly, confident that she could retrace her steps to the hotel where she had met the policeman, but as she hit the outskirts of town, she realised how all the streets looked the same, and there were no landmarks that she could recognise to pinpoint the way. Fox had made sure to cover his tracks when he took her out there. She carried on regardless, hoping for a miracle and driving around aimlessly until it was late in the afternoon. With the sun sinking and the onset of dusk, she decided to head back, feeling disheartened.

As she pulled into the driveway, she was met by Pim, who ran out of the house, smiling, holding her pet dog. Faye parked the bike and held Pim's hand as she led her inside. Mrs Wattana brought them some tea and cakes, and it wasn't long before Faye started to feel better, looking at Pim's cute little face and listening to her infectious laughter as she told her stories.

Major Wattana arrived home shortly after, telling his wife and daughter to leave the room while he spoke to Faye about the policeman that he was searching for.

She lied to him about finding the area where the hotel was situated, telling him that she hadn't been able to find the actual hotel because daylight had faded, forcing her to return to the house. He was skeptical, but there was nothing he could do except be patient and give her more time. Retiring to her room, she lay on the bed, spending the rest of the evening alone in the dark, thinking about her future.

Nothing changed very much in the days that followed, except that as the gulf between Faye and Major Wattana widened, the bond between Faye and Pim grew ever closer.

She set off early the next day, and after driving around for a while, she decided to head for the mall. It was nine o'clock in the morning, and the place was fairly quiet. A couple of drunken western men from the night before were slumped in their seats, with the odd Cambodian girl still doing the rounds to see if she could score a punter.

Faye took a table and ordered a bottle of beer at the bar where she and Mandy had sat the last time they were there together.

The drink relaxed her mind, and she thought about ordering another, knowing that driving around town in the hope of finding the hotel and the police officer was nothing but a hopeless waste of time anyway. She waved to the girl behind the bar and got her to bring another beer over.

Drinking the beer and listening to the music, Faye started to feel good. She thought about Brent and Mandy, and where they were, and what they would be doing. She smiled, tapping her feet to the rhythm until abruptly the music stopped playing. Turning around, she saw a young western guy standing behind the bar and scrolling through the playlist on the computer. Finding the song that he wanted to listen to, he put it on and turned up the volume.

As the awful sound blasted out of the speakers, Faye scowled at him. He turned the volume up higher. Faye started sulking and was about to complain, but something caught her attention. She listened intently, without knowing why. The song ended and the guy started scrolling again, looking for another tune to play. Faye stood up and walked over to the bar.

"Excuse me," she said.

"Yes? Can I help you?" said the guy behind the bar.

"I was wondering if you could play that last song again for me."

"You want me to play 'Cemetery Gates' again, do you?"

"Is that what it's called? Yes, if that's alright with you."

"One of your favourite tracks too, is it?"

"No. I mean… I just want to listen to it, that's all."

"Sure, no problem. My name's Rob, by the way."

"Yes. Do you work here?"

"I rent the bar. That's my girlfriend," he said, pointing to the Cambodian girl who served the beer.

"I see," she said.

Faye stood at the bar listening to the track being played again.

"Are you feeling alright?"

"What?" said Faye, sounding confused.

"I just asked you three times what your name is," he said, smiling.

"Oh, I'm sorry, I didn't hear you," she replied, listening intently to the song.

"*So*… your name is…"

"What did he just say?"

214

"I said what is your name."

"No, I mean the song. What did he just say?"

"I don't know, but you seem to be fascinated by this track for some strange reason. Would you like me to skip back a bit?"

"Yes! Could you? Please?" she said with urgency.

"Ok, let's try it from about here," said Rob, clicking the cursor halfway along the track.

"That bit, there," said Faye after listening for a moment. "What does he say?"

"He sings 'meet me at the cemetery gates'. Is that what you wanted to know?"

Faye didn't reply. Returning to her table, she sat down and stared into the distance for a while with a blank expression on her face. Leaning forward, she placed her elbows on the table and covered her face with the palms of her hands. Deep in thought, she closed her eyes and began to gently massage the sides of her head.

Rob walked over and stood next to her. She didn't notice him at first, but then he tapped her on the shoulder.

"On your own then, are you?" he said.

"I'm sorry, what did you say?"

"By yourself? No boyfriend?"

"Yes."

"Fancy a bit of company?"

"What happened to your girlfriend? That's her behind the bar, isn't it?"

"Yeah, well, don't worry about her. She's happy counting the money. Mind if I join you?"

"Actually, I'm fine by myself. I was thinking of leaving soon, anyway."

"Hey, let me show you this video that my friend recorded," he said, taking his phone out of his pocket. "That's me singing in the band that I front. We do gigs every Saturday night down at The Pussy Cat Bar, and on Sundays we play at The Last Chance Saloon."

"That's the same song that we were listening to at the bar just now, isn't it?"

"Yes, 'Cemetery Gates'. That's why I play it so much when I'm here. I need to perfect the way it's sung. That and a couple of others. What do you think?"

"Do you want me to be honest?" she said.

"Yeah, sure. Why not?"

"You sound like you're really out of breath when..."

He looked at her, waiting to hear the rest of her opinion.

"When what?" he said, breaking the silence.

Faye didn't say anything more about the song. She just sat there with a disturbed look on her face, realising where she had heard the song before and why she had been so captivated by it. Her thoughts turned to Saigon and the first time she met Jack while she was sitting outside the restaurant, the way he told her about how close Brent was to his grandfather, and the mysterious phone call she had received from Brent's phone.

Rob tried talking to her, but she wasn't listening, so he returned to the bar. Eventually, she relaxed and ordered another beer, her mind now firmly made up about what she intended to do.

Returning to the house later that evening, Faye made sure the fuel tank was filled to capacity and parked the motorbike. The atmosphere inside the house was oppressive, and she went straight to her room and closed the door, feeling very downbeat and solemn.

Pim brought a large tray of food later on and sat on the bed next to Faye, trying to chat with her. But she was too depressed, and they slowly ate together without speaking.

After they had eaten the meal, Faye put the television on and lay on the bed, turning her back to Pim, feeling very downhearted.

As the evening wore on, Faye looked at Pim and pointed to the small clock that hung above her bedroom door, telling her that it was getting late. Pim shook her head, picked up the empty tray, and placed it on the table. Standing up, she walked over to the door and slid the bolt onto the catch, locking it. Turning off the television and then the light, she returned to the bed and lay next to Faye, wrapping her arms around her waist and whispering goodnight.

Chapter 24

Don't Look Back

Waking up early the next morning, Faye packed her belongings and quietly pushed the motorbike outside, while Major Wattana and his family slept.

As she started the engine and got on the bike, Pim came to the door. They stared at each other, without smiling. Pim walked slowly towards Faye and spoke to her.

"Don't look back," said Pim.

"Don't look back?"

"Yes. When you go, you don't look back."

"Is that what you want, Pim?"

"Yes. If you want to be lucky, you don't look back. But you promise me you will return one day."

Faye stared at her for a moment and then smiled.

Putting her hands behind her neck, Pim undid the chain on her jade Buddha amulet and held it towards Faye, who bowed her head as Pim gently fastened it around her, kissing her on the cheek and pointing to the sky. Faye looked up at the birds heading west, as the sun cracked the darkness of the early morning. They smiled at each other and embraced.

Faye removed her cross and placed it over Pim's head, softly pulling her long black hair out from under the beads as she positioned it carefully around her neck.

Pointing the bike towards the road, Faye set off, driving very slowly, wanting to look back. Reminding herself of what Pim had just told her, she dropped back down to second gear, opening up the engine until the rev-counter maxed out, moving up through each gear in the same fashion until she was at high speed. It was game on, and she had until sunset to reach the border with Thailand before Major

217

Wattana raised the alarm and had her posted as a fugitive.

The streets of Phnom Penh were empty, and she was soon on the highway heading out. Having memorised all of the major towns along the way already, all she had to do was follow the signposts.

Having driven all day and stopping just once around midday for some food and rest, she neared the border late in the afternoon.

Faye slowed down as she came through the outskirts of Poipet, the town that bordered Thailand. Dusk was setting, and as she cruised towards the customs and immigration checkpoint, she noticed a dirt lane running off on either side. Knowing that she couldn't cross the border legally because Major Wattana still held her passport, she had to find a safe way to get across undetected.

Being a casino town, she figured there must be people crossing illegally all of the time, coming to gamble and then returning without having to go through the formalities of passing through immigration.

She turned left and followed the path, looking for a way through, but after driving for some time she decided to turn back and try the other side.

It was getting dark as she drove slowly along, but ahead, in the distance, she spotted a line of people walking across the lane and through the trees. Picking up speed, she caught up with them. As the last person in the group disappeared into the bushes, she parked the bike, left the keys in the ignition, and followed them along the trails.

Keeping sight of them but staying far enough back so as not to be seen, she eventually came to a desolate place inside Thailand, alongside a field.

Waiting until it was completely safe, she ventured forth, following the dirt paths until she eventually found herself on the main road heading into town.

Asking for directions, she was informed that the train station was within walking distance and made her way there.

She approached two western travellers who were sitting outside the station and asked them if they had any information about trains to Bangkok.

"Yeah, man," said the guy sitting with his girlfriend. "We missed the earlier one because of my bitch here. She just has to frigging jerk me around all of the freaking time. But hey, whatever, dude. There's a train at midnight, man. That's the one we're waiting for now."

"It leaves at midnight?" said Faye. "Is it the express?"

"The midnight express? Shit, no," he said, laughing. "It would be quicker to walk there, man. It doesn't get into Bangkok until ten in the morning."

Faye bought a ticket and went to the end of the platform, finding a quiet place to sit among the trees, hoping to keep a low profile. She knew that the motorbike would be stolen and probably driven out of town, but she didn't want to show her face anyway.

Resting her head against a tree, she started to doze off, completely exhausted from driving all day. Telling herself that she had to stay awake, she stood up and went outside to talk to the American couple.

The hours passed, and it was time to board the train. Taking her seat, she laid her head against the window and immediately fell asleep.

The sudden jolt of the train as it came to a stop in Bangkok woke her up. She got off and jumped into a tuk-tuk, telling the driver to head for Khao San Road.

She considered going straight to the train station and heading out to Kanchanaburi but decided instead on taking a room for the night and resting for a while.

Faye was quietly drinking coffee in the front garden of her guest house when she was approached by another traveller.

"Hey! You're Faye, aren't you? Do you remember me?"

"Hi," said Faye, looking surprised. "I'm sorry, I can't quite recall where we met, but your face does look very familiar. What's your name?"

"I'm Sarah. We met at the party in Phnom Penh. You're Mandy's friend, aren't you?"

"Yes—oh yes! Sorry, yes, I remember now. How are you?"

"I'm great. I'm off to Bali tomorrow. Can't wait. It's going to be so buzzing."

Faye managed to hide the fact that she was severely depressed and made polite conversation for a while, acting as though everything was fine.

Making an excuse about having to meet somebody, she left, promising to keep in touch.

Crossing the Chao Praya River the following morning, she made her way to the train station and took a train to Kanchanaburi.

After a three hour ride, the train came to a halt. The overhead fans and the lights were shut down as the passengers left the carriage, and Faye sat alone, quietly thinking about how she had come full circle, returning to the place where she had met Brent.

She stepped off the train and walked slowly towards the centre of town, looking for somewhere secluded to stay.

Faye told the landlady that she had given her passport to the immigration department to renew her visa and paid for the room, explaining that she had no baggage because she had just come to see an old friend.

Walking the streets again, she felt lost and confused, questioning why she had gone there. Paranoia set in and she began to avoid people.

Heading back to the station, she bought a ticket and waited for the train to Nam Tok, the small town at the end of the line.

Boarding the train, she looked around at all the empty wooden bench seats and sat alone at the rear of the carriage, turning her back on the handful of local people fanning themselves in the stifling heat.

Leaving the station at Kanchanaburi, the train slowly crossed the bridge on the River Kwai and meandered its way through the jungle, along the Death Railway heading west towards Burma.

As it approached Wang Po Viaduct, the train came to a halt. Faye stood up and opened the door, carefully stepping down onto the track and walking to the side. A couple of Thais jumped off a carriage further ahead, offloading their wares and walking through the trees, down a slope towards a row of shanty huts moored along the bank of the river, way below.

A loud whistle sounded and the carriages jolted noisily as the train set off, slowly crossing the viaduct. Faye waited for a while and then followed it, walking carefully along the single track as it snaked its way along the face of a cliff.

Halfway across the viaduct, she stopped and looked up at a small cave in the rock, above one of the huge concrete stanchions that supported the railway. It was the same cavern that Brent had ventured into after they had visited Hellfire Pass.

Stepping cautiously off the track, she climbed a gentle slope and entered the shallow cavity, which was enclosed on all sides except for the entrance. Inside, incense sticks burned next to offerings of food in front of a Buddhist shrine placed on a large stone.

Sitting at the altar, she closed her eyes. Holding the palms of her hands together, she whispered a prayer for her parents and for Brent. Holding back the emotion that was beginning to choke her, she allowed her mind a brief period of respite and indulged in the total silence and tranquility that surrounded her.

A cool breeze blew across her face, and opening her eyes, she noticed the smoke from the incense sticks being drawn towards the entrance. She stood up and walked outside, stopping briefly to watch the children playing by the riverbank in the distance below.

The faint sound of a train blowing its horn alerted her, and she descended the slope to make her way back, jumping carefully onto the track, mindful of the gaps in between the thick wooden sleepers.

Returning to the place where she had got off, Faye stood next to an old Thai woman waiting at the end of the dirt path that led up from the settlement by the river.

The brakes screeched loudly as the train slowed to a halt, and they climbed on board.

Walking out of the station in Kanchanaburi, Faye made her way to the guest house that she was staying at. Paying what she owed for food and drink, she collected her belongings and left, ambling slowly towards the road that ran parallel to the river. She had heard the story about the police investigation regarding a tourist who had gone missing in the area and walked with her head bowed, feeling completely dejected, fearing the worst.

It was late in the afternoon, and as the sun began to set, she arrived at the guest house where she had met Brent.

Sitting by the side of the road, Faye idled away the time, looking down at the bamboo huts on the river, casting her mind back to that fateful day she had met him.

Walking up to reception, she forced a smile and spoke to the girl behind the desk.

"How much does it cost to rent one of your canoes?" said Faye.

"Kayak? You look," said the girl, pointing to the price list on the wall.

"I'll take one for a full day," she said, handing over the money.

221

"You return same time tomorrow," said the girl.

As Faye was walking down the path towards the river, she heard someone calling her name.

"Faye! Faye!"

She turned around and saw Mandy running towards her.

"Faye! At last, I've managed to catch up with you," said Mandy, feeling very excited. "I've been looking all over town for you!"

"What are you doing here?" said Faye, sullen-faced.

"My friend, Sarah, she sent me an email and told me that she had met you in Bangkok and that you were heading for Kanchanaburi. I flew out of Hong Kong on the first available flight. Faye, it's so fantastic to see you again! How are you?" she said enthusiastically.

"You shouldn't have come here. Why did you come here?"

"Faye! I've been trying to contact you on that phone that I gave you, but there was never any answer."

"I have to go," said Faye, turning to leave.

"Faye! What's wrong? Are you feeling alright?" said Mandy, taking hold of her arm.

"I just told you. I have to go. You shouldn't have come here. Leave me alone," said Faye unemotionally, turning to walk away.

"Faye, what's happened to you? You're acting so strange. Can we go for a drink? I've missed you like crazy, and there's so much that I want to talk to you about," pleaded Mandy. "I had foreigner police men coming to my apartment in Kowloon to ask me questions about you."

"It's over. Everything is over. Done. Finished," she said, sternly. "Turn around and leave, Mandy. Just go. Do you understand?"

"Faye, please... don't say that," said Mandy, her eyes filling with tears, her voice trembling. "We can find Brent or get you back home to England. Whatever you need to do. You can be happy again."

"Home? I don't have a home. Not anymore. I don't have anything."

"Faye, what has happened to you? I don't understand," said Mandy, putting her hands on Faye's arms.

"You just don't get it, do you?" she said callously, pushing her away.

"Get what, Faye?"

"I just used you. I never really liked you. You were just there at a convenient time. Now go away and leave me alone," said Faye, walking off.

"Don't say that, Faye," said Mandy, crying. "That's not true. I know it's not true. I love you, Faye. I love you like a sister."

Faye walked away from her without looking back. After she had turned the corner on the track that she was on, she stopped behind one of the huts. In the fading light, she peered through a gap between the lodgings and looked at Mandy sitting alone on a bench, crying and staring into the night.

Choking with emotion and holding back the tears that were beginning to well in her eyes, Faye whispered to Mandy how much she loved her and then turned to leave.

Chapter 25

Sweet Sixteen

In Saigon, Jay sat in the dark on the balcony of his drab apartment, watching the streets below. It was late in the evening as three Australian men slipped around the back of the noodle shop and climbed the stairs to his room, knocking once before the door opened and they were allowed in.

"Grab a beer from the fridge and sit around the table, fellas. It looks like a job well done," said Jay. "I drank all the Tiger, but there should be a few bottles of Saigon Red in there that are nice and cold."

"Saigon Red it is then," said Cee, walking over to the fridge. "Looks like we caught the dirty barsterds after all, mate!"

"About bloody time too, mate," said another. "Any news about that Pommy bloke, Brent?"

"Yes, thank you for that, Haitch," said Jay, in a very military fashion. "May I just remind everybody to respect the rules of protocol and refrain from using any foul language or derisive terms when addressing others? And may I also point out the fact that we had considerable help from the British authorities in cracking this particular case, which subsequently led to the arrest of a renegade Cambodian police officer as well as one other wanted person. As for Brent Peterson, the British man who went missing, I can inform you that an investigation is underway by the Thai police force, and a search has been conducted around the Chungkai War Cemetery in Kanchanaburi."

"Jeez, mate! You sound all bloody lah-di-dah all of a sudden, don't ya? What's come over ya, cobber?" said the other man, known simply as Em.

"Alright, calm down, now," continued Jay. "While I'm running the show, we'll maintain proper order, and that's that. Which brings me onto the second announcement that I have for you. As of midnight tonight, I will be stepping down. For those of you who will be staying on, you can decide for yourselves which one of you will be taking over as operations controller. That includes Zed, who apparently is still out there in the park, and all of the other operatives in Cambodia, too. So sort it out among yourselves."

"You're leaving, mate? Blimey, you kept that one up your sleeve, didn't you?"

"Yeah, well, like I just said, it's job done," said Jay, lighting a cigarette and taking a swig of beer.

"So what've ya got planned now then? Back to Sydney, is it?"

"Not quite. It's Chup's sixteenth birthday tomorrow, so I've rented a quiet little villa for us on the beach," he said, smiling. "We're heading out there at first light."

The room fell silent, and they all stared at Jay with an incredulous look on their face.

"Wait a minute. We were supposed to be getting the age of consent set at eighteen, weren't we? That's what this operation was all about, wasn't it?"

"I don't know where you got that idea from, mate, but it certainly wasn't from me," said Jay. "I never said anything of the sort, and I just got word yesterday from my contact that Saigon has officially made it sixteen."

"Are you trying to tell me that I've been putting myself in dangerous situations for you so that you could use me to get what you wanted?"

"Dangerous situations? I thought you did three combat missions in Afghanistan with the SA-SR before you joined us?" said Jay.

"Bloody oath I did, mate," said Cee.

"And you're whinging about being put in so-called dangerous situations, are you?"

"Well..."

"Well, listen, mate, it's quarter to midnight, and like I said, I'm done with it. It's game over as far as I'm concerned, and there's something that I want to get stuck into. So if you gentlemen wouldn't mind, I think we'll say goodnight and leave it at that."

"That's it then, is it? We just get up and walk away? Like, *see you later, cunt*?"

"Look, mate," said Jay. "The operation was a success. We got all of the people involved, and—"

"Not all of them, by the looks of it," said Haitch, scowling at him.

"You got a problem there, mate?" said Jay.

Jay was a big, physically imposing figure, and nobody was about to seriously argue with him. There was nothing they could do to change the situation anyway, so they made their way to the door and left as silently as they had arrived.

Chapter 26

The Cemetery Gates

Faye left Mandy and took the track leading down to the river. Crossing the wooden walkway from the riverbank to the pontoon, she passed her room, the same hut that she had taken almost one year before.

The adjoining room, the one that Brent had stayed in, was also vacant. She opened the bamboo door and walked in, moving the mosquito net to one side and sitting down on the edge of the bed. It had just turned midnight. She stared out into the darkness.

The pontoon rocked slowly from side to side on the river. It would come to rest soon.

She lit a small candle and unzipped her bag. Moving aside the bottle of tablets, she took out a package and carefully unwrapped a flower, holding it gently for a while, cradling it thoughtfully in her arms.

The candlelight flickered and dimmed. It was time to go. Faye readied herself and left the hut, gently closing the door behind her.

She untied the canoe from its mooring and cautiously stepped inside. Taking hold of the paddle and placing her feet on the rudder controls, she set off.

The monsoon season had already begun, and the wide, flat, swollen river was now flowing faster than normal.

The moon was full and lit her way, but a storm was gathering and grey wispy clouds began to blot out the moonlight.

Going downstream with the flow meant that all she had to do was steer the craft into position.

Eventually, she found herself at the widest part of the river, the confluence of the rivers Khwae Noi and Khwae Yai, and she could see on either side, in the distance, the tiny dwellings in the villages, dimly lit in the night.

In the darkness, she had overshot her intended destination and maneuvered hard right to reach the shore. The canoe started to lean as it was now broadside to the current, and she had to dig the paddle hard over the side to correct her balance.

The sky quickly darkened, and rain lashed down fiercely, forcing her to lower her face. The downpour was heavy, and water soon began to collect around her feet. Turning ninety degrees, she fought harder and harder, digging the paddle into the river at a faster rate to stop herself from being carried away by the current. Paddling upstream, completely exhausted, she inched closer and closer to where a small jetty protruded from the bank. Passing the jetty, she turned hard left and allowed the current to wedge the side of her canoe against its wooden frame. Grabbing hold of the structure, she secured the canoe, put her sodden bag around her neck, and climbed out, slipping on the wet timber and almost falling backwards into the river.

A short dash along a tree-lined path led to the cemetery gate where she took shelter beneath the arch at the entrance.

The rain stopped almost as abruptly as it had begun. The night was still, the air was warm.

Faye opened her bag and took out the red rose and the bottle of tablets, placing them on the ground in front of her.

Tears welled in her eyes as she softly whispered Brent's name. The air suddenly turned cool, and a faint rumble of thunder sounded in the distance. She called his name again, and a sudden rush of wind passed quickly through the trees that she was sitting under, causing her to shiver. The air turned cold. The thunder grew louder.

Printed in Great Britain
by Amazon